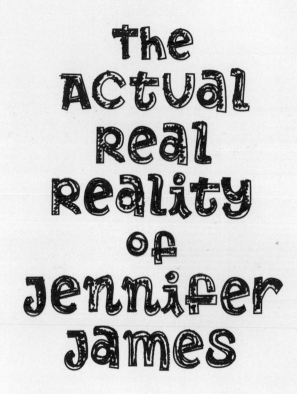

the ACtual real reality op jennifer james

GILLIAN SHIELDS

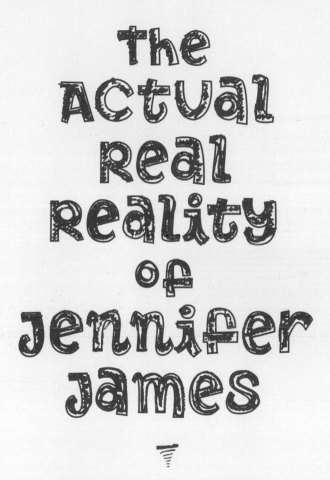

The Actual Real Reality of Jennifer James

KATHERINE TEGEN BOOKS
An Imprint of HarperCollins*Publishers*

HarperTempest is an imprint of HarperCollins Publishers.

The Actual Real Reality of Jennifer James

Copyright © 2006 by Gillian Shields

Library of Congress Cataloging-in-Publication Data

Shields, Gillian.

    The actual real reality of Jennifer James / Gillian Shields.— 1st ed.

      p. cm.

    "Katherine Tegen books."

    Summary: While competing on a reality television show being filmed at her English high school, shy and bookish Jennifer James records her experiences in her diary.

    ISBN-10: 0-06-082240-6 (trade bdg.) — ISBN-13: 978-0-06-082240-8 (trade bdg.)

    ISBN-10: 0-06-082241-4 (lib. bdg.) — ISBN-13: 978-0-06-082241-5 (lib. bdg.)

    [1. Self-confidence—Fiction. 2. Interpersonal relations—Fiction. 3. Reality television programs—Fiction. 4. England—Fiction. 5. Diaries—Fiction.] I. Title.

PZ7.S55478Act 2006   2005017755

[Fic]—dc22   CIP

                                                   AC

Typography by Karin Paprocki

1 2 3 4 5 6 7 8 9 10

❖

First Edition

For Brian

contents

cast List

THE HEROINE:

Jennifer James: Most Unpopular Person in her class, burdened by Brains and Her Mother. Deep inside Jennifer is a Total Babe struggling to get out. Is in love with Mr. Webster. Should be in love with Marcus Wright.

THE HERO:
Marcus Wright: Most gorgeous boy on the planet, irresistible to everyone except Jennifer.

THE RIVAL:
Tallulah Perkins: Bosom on legs, has her claws into Marcus, hobby is tormenting Jennifer.

THE HEROINE'S BEST (ONLY) FRIEND:
Vicki Rivera: A Mega-Babe, loyal, truthful, cool.

THE LOCATION:
London Road Comprehensive, Midcaster. Rubbish school in rubbish town.

THE VILLAINS:

Storm Young: TV producer with naff ponytail and supersize ego.

Miss Maybelline Moodie: Power-crazed deputy head at London Road.

THE TV PRESENTER:

Abi Sparkes: Ultra-gorgeous, ultra-brainy, ultra-nice.

THE PARENTS:

Mr. Eric James: Absentminded Scientist Dad with Heart of Gold.

Mrs. Sheila James: aka *Jocasta*, Serious Feminist, Serious Mother, Serious Problem to Jennifer.

THE TEACHERS:

Mr. Orlando Webster: English. Groovy poet, thinks he's the Johnny Depp of the classroom. Jennifer's Hero.

Mrs. Mandy Schuman: Drama. Drop-dead cool, totally wasted in Midcaster.

Mr. Potter: History. Disillusioned teacher with secret passion for camping.

Mr. Rock: Physical Education. Vile.

Mrs. Woolacott: Math. Seriously glams up for the cameras.

Mr. Barker: Art. Has a thing about punctuality.

Mrs. Stringer: Biology. Withered-up old stick.

Mrs. Clegg: Geography. Ditzy blond type.

Mr. Bill Smedley: Head of London Road Comprehensive, never turns up for school.

AND INTRODUCING . . .
THE CELEBRITIES!!!

Celia Bunch: TV cook, the nation's darling, never lets her puddings flop.

Professor Barbara Beer: One of those sneery intellecttual types.

Carrie Chaplin: Lifestyle guru to the rich and famous—you know, crystals and horoscopes and stuff.

Seth Dale: TV soap star, wannabe pop star, world's worst singer.

Sir Harvey Harvey: Olympic hero, possibly the last old-style "British Gent" left.

Lady Amelia Itchpole: No useful occupation, apart from being mega-rich.

Amanda Knox: Glamor model, big on Page 3 (tacky

lingerie shots in tacky newspapers), short on brain cells.

Julian Lambrusco-Llewellyn: Makeover maestro, all style and no substance.

Jeremy Lurcher: A member of Her Majesty's Government before being detained at Her Majesty's Pleasure (chucked into prison) for dodgy dealings.

Freddie McCrum: Please refer to Lady Amelia Itchpole, only mega-stupid as well as mega-rich.

Nazzer McNally: Verbally challenged ex-footballer.

Oggy Ogden: A living legend, the Granddaddy of Rock.

AND . . .

THE STUDENT CONTESTANTS!!!

Alice Redknapp: Gets angry and cries a lot. Chances Of Winning (COW): Not all that good somehow.

Dwight Thingummybob: Gangsta rap dude. COW rating: He's cool; innit?

Jennifer James: Our Heroine. COW rating: Less than mega-zero.

Julie Postlethwaite: Role model for plump girls. COW rating: Slender.

Little Ollie Cotton: Nice kid-brother type. COW rating: Aah, wouldn't it be sweet if he won?

Mattie and Maddie: Mega-identical twin sisters. COW rating: Double or nothing.

Rabbit-Teeth Boy: Dentally challenged weirdo kid. COW rating: Not a hope in hell, unless his mother votes for him like a million times.

Serena Dickinson: The Perfect Girl. COW rating: Super-hot favorite.

Sophie Simpson: Who?

Tallulah Perkins: You know who. COW rating: What a cow.

Will-with-the-Mohawk: Guy with guitar. COW rating: In with a chance.

. . . AND FINALLY!!!

The Goat: Um, well, kind of a goat actually . . .

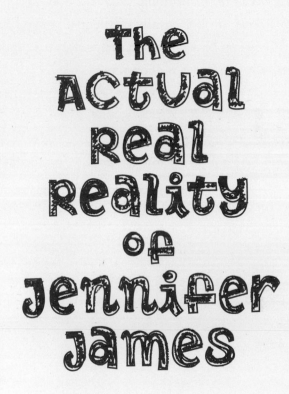

The Actual Real Reality of Jennifer James

August 31–September 5: "You Are Ruining My Life!"

TUESDAY, AUGUST 31
11:10 A.M.

Totally incredible morning! Jocasta,[*] my darling mother, is going round looking as though she has I DO NOT APPROVE tattooed on her angry little forehead, but I think it's mega-fab! The thing is, after Dad had gone to work the post came, and it was a letter from Miss Moodie, saying that London Road Comprehensive is going to be in a television documentary next term!

Can't believe that our school has really been chosen by the TV company, Haydeeze Productions. It's so, so amazing. I mean, I would probably die of embarrassment if they actually interviewed me or anything for this documentary, but I'd like to be in the background. AT LAST—people will finally see what we have to put up with in Midcaster's most mediocre school! It's like getting a real wish out of a Christmas

---

[*]*Ancient Greek queen who married her own son and stabbed herself in her private parts when she realized her little mistake.*

cracker instead of a pink plastic ring.

I know Miss Moodie does her best to bring Order, Purpose, and Discipline (her three favorite words) to London Road, but it's really difficult when the headmaster, Mr. Smedley, is hardly ever there, and she's only the deputy, and we have teachers who turn a blind eye to what goes on. Like in our history class, if you don't want to work, you can sit in the back row and file your nails or pick your nose, or whatever, and Mr. Potter says he doesn't care, he's not going to waste his breath trying to teach morons who are destined to stock supermarket shelves. And Dean Wiggins listens to his Walkman in all Mrs. Woolacott's math classes and she doesn't even seem to notice. So I think this documentary is a Good Thing.

But Jocasta doesn't see it like that.

I do really, really wish that she wouldn't insist on being called Jocasta. It's not even her real name. I mean, what's wrong with Sheila? I'm sure there are lots of nice, cozy, normal mums called Sheila. Like Mum used to be, in fact, before she started doing all these weird "Wimmin's Studies" workshops. It was when we moved here last year to Mega-Dump Doomsville (aka Midcaster) and Dad got so busy with his job at the nuclear power station, that she got into this Jocasta stuff and started being all Angry and Radical.

Anyway, she just swept a scalding eye over Miss Moodie's letter and said, "I've told you before, Jennifer, that Television is the Opiate of the Masses and we are NOT going to have anything to do with it." Then she threw the letter and, even worse, the permission slip you MUST have signed by a parent into the bin for the compost, on top of some old bits of porridge.

I totally lost it. I yelled at her about everything, about her banning television from our house, the awful clothes she buys me, and the whole Serious Woman feminist psychobabble rubbish that she's shoveling down my throat every five minutes. I can't remember exactly what I said, but it did end with me screaming, "YOU ARE RUINING MY LIFE!"

It didn't go down very well, somehow. In fact, I don't think we will ever speak to each other again.

...

5:15 P.M

Went to Vicki's this afternoon to get away from Troll*
Mother.

Her dad had signed her form before he went off to
work at his *Reggae 'n' Rasta* record shop. Amazing
that people must spend enough money there to feed
them both. Anyway, she was so Vicki-ish and support-
ive and said that this documentary will probably be
dead boring anyway, just teachers and sixth formers
yakking on about themselves, and that if I can't be in
it, she won't hand her permission form in either.

Vicki really is my dearest (only) friend. She's such a
babe, as no doubt the evil Tallulah Perkins would say
about her creepy sidekick, Chelsea.

Midnight

Have done something that will drive Jocasta to the
Outer Limits of Maternal Wrath! Just got to get to
school tomorrow morning before she finds out.

12:20 A.M

Lying awake worrying. Can't stop thinking about What

Drop-dead stupid mythological creature with very thick skin.

I've Done and what my mother is Going To Say.

After I got back from Vicki's, I really did try to make things up with Jocasta, as I felt kind of bad about what I'd said. She probably gets stressy and uptight because Dad is so wrapped up in his work and the Joy of Science and all that. In fact, I think she's lonely. So I said I was sorry about all the ruining-my-life stuff, but THEN she acted so martyred and noble and forgiving about it, like the mother superior in *The Sound of Music*[*] that she annoyed me again, especially as SHE started the whole thing with her bonkers ideas! Doesn't she know that not being allowed to have a shot of the back of my head in this dumb documentary will make me look a bigger saddo at school than I do already?

So by the time she went off to her Midcaster Militant Book Discussion group, or whatever it is (leaving me to babysit Jonathan because Dad was working late), I was feeling totally hacked off again. But then, when I was putting Jonathan to bed (my baby brother is so lovely when he's just had a bath), I heard Dad's car pull up at the front and I had a Fantastic Idea.

[*]*Film about unnaturally musical family dressed in curtains escaping from Nazis.*

I ran downstairs, flew out of the back door down to the compost heap, and scrabbled about until I found Miss Moodie's permission form. It was covered in quite a bit of porridge and tea leaves and disgusting yucky stuff, but I ran back to the kitchen, wiped it all off with the dishcloth, and had it smoothed out on the kitchen table before Dad had his key in the lock.

I said, mega-casually, "Oh, could you sign this for school, Dad?" He looked vague and said "Ah," then "Oh," like he does, then he signed it and said he didn't want any supper, he was going to write up some notes in his study. Couldn't have been easier. After all, it doesn't say BOTH parents have to sign it, just A PARENT. No reason why Absentminded Father's signature shouldn't be just as good as Rampaging Mother's little scribble.

She will be rampaging when she finds out what I've done. Only hope it's after I've handed it in.

1:15 A.M.

Have just remembered it is Jonathan's first day at

school tomorrow and I haven't got him a present. Will go and make him a card.

1:35 A.M.
Buzz Lightyear much harder to draw than he looks.

WEDNESDAY, SEPTEMBER 1
5:15 P.M.
Handed form in. Jocasta still doesn't know. Hope Dad will forget all about it and not mention it to her. I mean, he's usually pretty vague, so there's a good chance that he has sent our entire conversation to his mental recycling bin.

EVERYBODY at school talking about the documentary. Mr. Smedley is still away with his nervous breakdown and Miss Moodie is in charge as usual. Can't wait for Mr. Webster's class tomorrow.

10:35 P.M.
Wonder why London Road has been chosen for this TV program? I mean, it's nothing special. Unless being specially awful counts.

Can't help wishing I went to a different kind of school. One with a proper uniform and "Houses" named after obscure dead people and Latin and prizes and exams and definitely no Tarty Tallulah. I'm sure I could get a prize for English. Or French. *Parce que mon français est absolument parfait.*[*]

In actual real reality, the only prize I would get at London Road is for being the prize nerd.

Swot. Boffin. Book Brains. Computer Head. As in, "Hey Jennifer, what's it like being a sad ugly nerd brain?"

IT'S NOT FAIR. I mean, I can't help liking school-work and books and reading. And I do. I just LOVE books, and "Words, Words, Words".[**] But that seems to make the rest of London Road hate me even more.

Why is it so uncool to try hard at school? Or perhaps it's just my school? There was some government person who got into trouble for calling schools like London Road "bog-standard",[***] and okay, that's kind of offensive, but honestly, what else can you say? I mean, you can see someone made an effort once in a fit of enthusiasm (obviously not Mr. Smedley), but it

---

Translation: Because I speak French like a real Euro-babe.

**Quotation: Shakespeare's Prince Hamlet, a bit bonkers but clever.*

***Translation: I'm a government minister and I wouldn't send my kid to a rubbish school like that.*

8

never came to anything. There's that boat a Year 9 class once made in Design and Technology. But it never got near any water (and the nearest boating lake to Doomsville is where?) and it just sits slowly rotting in the yard behind the art block, like the ghost of a boat. Oh, and there was the brilliant idea of having a miniature farm on the school campus. Only somebody pinched all the rabbits, and the sheep were smuggled out and left wandering around on the main road, with some very nasty consequences. The only animal that's left is a single moth-eaten, mad-looking goat, tied up on that little patch of grass by the school gates. "Welcome to London Road Comprehensive—the Gold Standard of Bog-Standard!"

But Jocasta says that grammar schools and EVEN WORSE, private schools, are Tools of Oppression, used by the Minority to suppress the Majority. Though she didn't say that when I passed my exam to get into the girls' grammar in Kent. No, it was joyful celebration and "Well done, darling Jennifer" back then. Oh well.

GOT to go to sleep, I'm SO tired!

Mega-wonderful to see Mr. Webster again. He has grown his hair and looks even more like Johnny Depp.[*] He kept running his fingers through his hair as he outlined the term's work, looking all brooding and intense.

We're doing *Romeo and Juliet*[**] this term. Mr. Webster gave out some books and his hand touched mine and it was so, so . . . oh, he is gorgeous. And deeply sensitive, you can tell. Wouldn't it be great to have your first kiss with someone like him? In fact, with precisely him, Mr. Orlando Webster.

I know that wouldn't be right in actual real reality because he's quite old and I'm too young for him and all that, but the general idea of it is so much nicer than fumbling around with one of the Spotty Youths behind the art block, or at the bus stop, like Tallulah Perkins and her crew.

And I know it's pathetic not to have been kissed yet. But it just never happened, what with going to a girls' school when we lived in Kent, and then coming here

[*] *World's most beautiful man.*
[**] *Better known as Leonardo DiCaprio's Romeo + Juliet, teenage suicide-pact weepie.*

and Jocasta making sure that I am the most unattractive girl in Doomsville. I mean, I've been along with Vicki to a school dance and some parties and stuff, but everyone thinks I am weird and doesn't come near me. Anyway, the idea of grabbing a random male and "pulling" or "snogging" in the corner of someone's kitchen after a couple of alco-pops is SO unromantic and meaningless.

Oh Lord, perhaps I am weird. Every other girl at London Road seems to think that snogging the face off some gangly yob is the height of cool. Even Vicki has had close encounters with a few of the boys in our year.

I just know that I want my first kiss to be with someone special. I want it to mean something. Like that poem by Elizabeth Barrett Browning,* "How do I love thee? Let me count the ways . . ."

Oh, how do I love thee, Mr. Webster?

FRIDAY, SEPTEMBER 3
5:10 P.M.

Everyone getting excited about the telly thing. Apparently filming is due to begin in two weeks. There

---

*Victorian poetess who lay crippled on a sofa for five years guarded by her horrible dad, then jumped up and ran off with her poet boyfriend to sunny Italy.

were men all over the school today, starting to fix up cables and lights and bringing beds into the science block. The classrooms on the top floor of that block have been shut off and are going to be used in some way for the filming.

Wonder what they want beds for?

It's really annoying that I'll never actually be able to see the program, as I'm the only girl at London Road without a television. Or highlights. Or at least one body piercing.

Gym this afternoon. Tried to keep going back to the end of the line for jumping over the stupid horse or vault or whatever it is, but Tallulah and Chelsea spotted me and pushed me to the front (Chelsea actually kicked me). Was the only girl in the class not to be able to jump onto it, never mind over it. Mr. Rock horrible as usual. I do NOT run like a dying kangaroo. Still, glad it gave everyone else a good laugh.

Afterward, when we were coming out of the gym, Paul Johnson's friend Marcus kind of went to go through the door at the same time as me, but then he stopped and let me go through first. He smiled at me and said "Nice jumping, Jennifer."

So pleased that it amused him. Now of course, Tallulah, who was just behind, has decided to call me Jumping Jennifer, along with everyone else in my class (except dearest Vicki). Will have to accept that I am the Most Unpopular Girl in my school, but oh Lord, I would do anything to get away from the Valley of Humiliation that is London Road Comprehensive. Please, PLEASE help me.

SATURDAY, SEPTEMBER 4
8:35 P.M.

Spent the day reading *Romeo and Juliet*. It is fantastic, even the long bits. Jocasta came up to my room with a plate of pumpkin-seed cookies (vile) and went on about how marvelous the film was. I said I didn't think she liked Leonardo DiCaprio[*] and she looked totally blank. Turned out she was talking about some ancient version that was made in the 1960s or whenever. Still, it was good to see her excited about something that didn't involve banning stuff, and she even promised to dig out a video of her old film so we could watch it

[*]*The Peter Pan of Hollywood.*

together. Then she remembered that she has chucked out the VCR, TV, and DVD player. Nice one, Mum.

That Marcus person has got green eyes, in actual real reality.

THE DAILY RUMOR

TV ROUNDUP

MONDAY, SEPTEMBER 6

London Road Comprehensive is the unlikely setting for the latest reality TV show, Down The Bog. Top Celebs will battle it out to become the King or Queen of the Playground, by proving that they can teach at the school and win the hearts of the public. An insider at Haydeeze Productions revealed that London Road was chosen because it is "a typical, 'bog-standard' comprehensive. . . . We want our Celebs to face the reality of a teacher's life, with discipline problems and the lot. They'll also be sleeping at the school in specially adapted classrooms. It's going to be tough, with some real surprises. It's a blackboard jungle Down The Bog!"*

Haydeeze Productions have already scored hits with Nosy Neighbor and I'm a Weather Girl, Get Me

Out of Here! The names of the Celebs on this new show are a closely guarded secret, but the RUMOR's hot tip is that busty blond model Amanda Knox and former football star Nazzer McNally will be reporting for class. "It's a great way to kick a flagging career in the butt," said top publicist Zak Clifford. "Going down well on Down The Bog could be worth millions."

Every week, the viewers will get the chance to vote for their favorite Celeb, and the one with the fewest votes will be booted off the show. The money raised by the telephone voting lines will be donated to charity. In another twist, the public will vote not only for their favorite Celebs, but for their favorite teacher and pupil, and big prizes are promised.

MONDAY, SEPTEMBER 6
4:35 P.M.

Tallulah burst into Assembly this morning with a copy of *The Daily Rumor*. So THAT'S why they brought in the beds.

The only ray of light is that Jocasta despises the *Rumor* and never reads it. Thank you for that, Lord. Now can you please arrange for her to be temporarily blind and deaf, from now until the Christmas holidays? Mega-please?

Was having a bath after supper when Jocasta actually started banging on the door, and ranting, "What are you doing in there, Jennifer? I hope you aren't becoming obsessed with Artificial Standards of Hygiene and Body Image?"

No, Mum, I'm just having a bath.

When I got out, she gave me a lecture on the evils of too much washing. Apparently it is Womanly to have Natural Body Odor. Okay, but I'd rather be unnatural and not actually smell. It's bad enough her banning TV, pop music, magazines, and all traces of fashion from the James household, but if washing is going to be on Jocasta's list of things a Serious Woman should despise, then I will just turn myself in to social services and ask to be adopted.

I can just see Tallulah Perkins telling the whole school: "Not only is Jennifer James the biggest nerd, geek-brain and fashion-free zone, she actually, like, totally stinks."

Except she couldn't manage a sentence as long as that.

17

Ever since I arrived at London Road Comprehensive, Tallulah has done her best to make my life a misery. Okay, stepping on her brand-new portable CD player (how was I to know she had left it on the locker room floor?) and then laughing in English because she said that Henry the Fifth* was a new boy band (I thought she was joking!) was probably not the smartest way to behave around her on my very first day. But how was I to know that she is London Road's official Queen of Mean and that upsetting her would doom me to her Perpetual Displeasure?

In other words, she hates me.

Just don't know how Tallulah gets away with it at school. She never does any homework, doesn't wear the proper uniform, and talks back to all the teachers. Vicki said she heard that Miss Moodie is actually frightened of Tallulah's mum. Apparently Mrs. Perkins is really, really scary, and anytime Miss Moodie tries to tell Tallulah off, her mum turns up at school ready to bash Miss Moodie's face in with a bag of Perkins Frozen Cabbages. (Tallulah's dad started with a market stall and is now the frozen-veg king of

*All-action hero from W. Shakespeare.

Midcaster, and Tallulah is his darling princess who can do no wrong.) Whenever Miss Moodie speaks to Tallulah, it's as though she's being forced to swallow poison. And it's not just the little things that Tallulah does, like chewing gum and being late for all her classes. I mean, she actually beat up some kids in year 7 last year, and made Chelsea pour superglue into the car door locks of the school inspectors last time they came, just for a laugh. Yeah, really funny.

Actually, I find Tallulah pretty scary, so I wouldn't like to see her mum in action. Perhaps there are worse things than Jocasta.

10:35 P.M.

Can't believe there is really going to be a TV show about London Road Comprehensive. What a world.[*]

...

[*]*Famous last words of the Wicked Witch of the West.*

THE TRIBUNE

"It's an insult," *says Hatter*

TUESDAY, SEPTEMBER 7

Teachers' unions have reacted angrily to the newest reality TV offering, *Down The Bog*. The show claims to be "an amusing and challenging look at the world of teaching," but Barry Hatter, leader of the radical Utopian Teachers' Cooperative, said yesterday, "It's disgusting. This show denigrates the excellent work of teachers in this country and reinforces the stereotype of the 'bog-standard comprehensive.' Even worse, the prize for the most popular student is a scholarship to an overprivileged boarding school. What kind of message does this give to the pupils of London Road? It's an insult to the comprehensive ideal of opportunity for everyone. That Luciani Mephistopholousos [*the enigmatic media tycoon and chairman of Haydeeze plc*] wants his head kicking in."

However, other leading educationalists have given the idea a cautious welcome. Mr. Hugo Harbottle,

Chairman of the Boarding Schools' League, said that "Whilst the excesses of reality TV are to be deplored, anything that gives a young person the chance to go to a fine school like St. Willibald's College has to be viewed positively. And I wouldn't mind trying out for that teacher's prize myself!"

Mr. Harbottle was referring to the fact that the public will vote not only for their favorite celebrity and pupil, but for their favorite teacher. The member of staff at London Road Comprehensive who attracts the most votes will be offered a job as a presenter on the new digital educational channel, Love 2 Teach!, which is to be launched next year as a joint venture by the government and Haydeeze Productions.

The Utopian Teachers' Cooperative later issued a statement saying that they did not endorse any form of physical violence and that Mr. Hatter's remarks about Mr. Mephistopholousos had been taken out of context.

TUESDAY, SEPTEMBER 7
6:30 P.M.

Jocasta showed me her copy of *The Tribune* when I got home from school. So the cat has well and truly bolted from the stable, or whatever. She is Disgusted,

Horrified, Sickened, you name it, at the scummy depths of *Down The Bog* and is demanding Miss Moodie's resignation. But all I can think about is That Prize.

I sneaked into Dad's study (desk in corner of garage) after supper, whilst he was still at work, and looked it up on the Internet. "St. Willibald's College is one of the most successful and respected independent schools in the country. Located in a Grade 1 Listed Building[*] and set in beautiful grounds, St. Willibald's academic standards are extremely high, yet a friendly school spirit of mutual support is maintained. . . ."

I can remember every word. You don't even have to do horse vaulting or netball or get bashed with hockey sticks or any horror like that. "A variety of physical activities is provided for our students, including Yoga, Deep Relaxation, and Indian Dance for those who are not attracted to traditional sports. . . ."

St. Willibald's is Paradise. I must win, I must win, I must win.

6:35 P.M.

I am never going to win.

*Posh Pile.

First of all, Jocasta doesn't know yet that Dad signed that permission form for me. If she was going *to go mad* when she found out about me being in a boring old documentary, what on earth will she say about her daughter betraying her Serious Womanhood by appearing on a Disgusting, Horrifying, and Sickening reality TV show?

Second, let's just have a moment of real reality here. I couldn't get voted on to a working party for cleaning the toilets, never mind win a fantastic prize like that. Jumping Jennifer, sad, boring, nerd-brain Jennifer, will not rake in the votes. So good-bye, little dreams of St. Willibald's College and the rolling acres of gardens, good-bye to studying Latin and Greek and Shakespeare and gentle little Indian dance movements, surrounded by like-minded people dressed in impeccable uniforms. . . . IT IS NEVER GOING TO HAPPEN.

7:35 P.M.

Anyway, Vicki said the whole thing might even be called off if all the parents object, although most people at school seem to think it's a fantastic idea. No one did any work today, and even the teachers were excited, which is a miracle at London Road. Dean Wiggins has started taking bets on who the celebrities are going to be, and topless photos of Amanda Knox in her Page 3[*] days are going round the school quicker than a dose of mono.

Oh well, I'm not going to think about it anymore.

7:45 P.M.

Can't stop thinking about it.

London Road Comprehensive
London Road
Midcaster
Wednesday, September 8

Dear Parents/Carers and Pupils,
I am writing to apologize for the confusion surrounding the school's proposed television appearance. I can assure you that I was seriously misled by Haydeeze Productions about

*Essential news coverage of glamor models.

*the nature of the program in which we had
been asked to participate. However, having dis-
cussed the situation with the School
Governors and a representative sample of parents, it has been decided to continue with the
project.*

*Whilst a tiny minority of parents have
expressed concern about* Down The Bog, *the
overwhelming response is one of enthusiasm.
This is London Road's chance to demonstrate
to the nation that this school is, despite some
difficulties, a vibrant and individualistic com-
munity.*

*In addition, Haydeeze Productions have
promised to make a substantial donation to
enable the school to replace the Portaloos
(which were installed next to the auditorium in
1973) with a modern backstage facility. This
will be invaluable for future theatrical productions.*

*And finally, all the profits from the show's
telephone voting lines will be donated to the*

popular charity, How Much Is That Doggie?,
*which auctions off celebrities' discarded pets
and other memorabilia to raise money for children with terminal illnesses. I know from our
very successful "Throw a Brick at a Teacher"
stall, which raised over five hundred pounds
for HMITD?* at the Summer Fayre *last term,
that this worthy cause is very dear to your
hearts.*

Overall, our participation in Down The
Bog *should be seen as a positive contribution to
educational standards. Pupils taking Advanced
level Media Studies Unit 4, Reality
Television and Its Cultural Impact, will also
find themselves distinctly advantaged when
it comes to preparing coursework for this
module.*

*Further details of the filming schedule will
be announced shortly.*

Yours faithfully,
Miss M. Moodie B.Ed. (Univ. Bognor)

7:45 P.M.

We were all given copies of Miss Moodie's letter to take

home after school today. Jocasta just looked at it coldly and said, "At least you won't be wasting your time with such rubbish," then threw it into the compost bin. Is everything she doesn't approve of destined for the compost? If I come downstairs with purple hair one morning, will she simply chop it off and feed it to the roses?

Have permanently churning feeling in my stomach. Even *Romeo and Juliet* doesn't help. I need some Yoga and Deep Relaxation.

There's a rumor going round school that Seth Dale is going to be one of the "Celebs" and Tallulah is practically wetting her knickers with excitement. She has been in love with him since she was about eight and he played the bad boy in that kids' TV show *Grunge Mill*. Then he graduated to *The Cop*. I remember seeing him before Mum turned into Jocasta and the TV ban came into force. He played a gay policeman called Darrel Barrel, but apparently his character was killed off by a crazed gunman in last year's Christmas special (missed that one, funnily enough), and he wants to launch a new career as a pop singer.

Tallulah actually brought in a scrapbook she had

made of him and was poring over it with Chelsea in the back row of Mr. Potter's history class. (Chelsea had a distinct zit on the side of her nose today. Thank you, Lord.) Tallulah has literally millions of pictures of Seth Dale. I think he looks like a bad photocopy of Justin Timberlake,[*] but she can't get enough of him.

Actually, it was really almost sweet; I have never seen her so enthusiastic about anything. Not her usual "let's be cool and cynical" mode at all. I could imagine her with her little blond pigtails (or perhaps she was mousy in those days?) glued in front of *Grunge Mill*, her little heart palpitating with joy. . . .

Get a grip, Jennifer.

THURSDAY, SEPTEMBER 9
5:10 P.M.

That Marcus guy blatantly thinks he is so cool and funny. Why do some people have this incredibly high opinion of themselves? He was trying to wind up Tallulah before English today by singing Seth Dale's latest lame song to her, as if he were Romeo serenading Juliet. Ha-ha. She loved it

Better-looking version of Seth Dale.

really, of course. Anything for attention. Correction, anything for MALE attention. Then he pretended that I was the Nurse[*] and that he was Juliet and he warbled in my face and sobbed on my knees. Ha-double-ha.

Vicki said that Paul Johnson told her that the Marcus creature is in a band called The Electric Fish and that Paul is the band's "roadie." Give a boy a cheap electric guitar and he thinks he's a god.

Mr. Webster's lesson was brilliant. But I had a horrible thought: what if he wins the teacher vote on the show and leaves London Road? He could win easily, because he's really fit (even if he is quite old), and I bet loads of people will find his lessons inspiring when they see him on TV. Oh no! Just thought of something even worse! What if Mr. Webster wins the teacher's prize and Vicki wins the student prize and they both leave? I mean, I think they should because they are both the best, but what about me? My life without them here would be the Abyss of Awfulness, left to the mercy of Tallulah and Chelsea and now this singing Marcus ego-head.

*Juliet's mad old nanny.

He can sing quite well actually.

Feel very Low.

HAYDEEZE PRODUCTIONS

FRIDAY, SEPTEMBER 10

TO: ALL PUPILS AT LONDON ROAD

COMPREHENSIVE

Hi Kids!

Time to meet your producer—the guy one of you will be thanking for your lucky break when you hit that top spot on DOWN THE BOG!

Storm Young here, and I'm going to explain THE RULES. You all know that the winner of the student competition will be delivered from bog-dweller existence in small-town hell (just kidding!) and catapulted, free and gratis, to the green and pleasant lands of St. Willibald's College.

Now, there isn't enough time, in a show that starts midautumn and ends before the Christmas schedule really heats up, for Joe Public to get to know all of you sweet young things. So the bottom line is this. Before the show starts properly, each one of you will be allowed to vote for TWO of the pupils in your own year group. Except for poor old year 13, because it is blatantly too late for them to go gallivanting off to a new school, isn't it? The top twelve little starlets from years 7 to 12 who get the most votes from their classmates will be on the show, competing for that place at St. Willi's.

These twelve lucky kiddies will be followed around by the cameras whilst at school—in class, on the playing fields, in the lav, snogging behind the bike sheds, you name it. Yes, that's the WHOLE SCHOOL DAY filmed for the live digital streaming (available exclusively on Haydeeze Digital—channel 666). And there'll be a special "Challenge" every week for both Students and Celebs, to liven up the action!

The highlights—or best Bog Bitz—of all this frolicsome fun will be shown by the BBC on Tuesday and Friday nights to an audience of millions! The Friday-night show will also include the LIVE broadcast of the voting results! This will decide who will stay on for another week, and which sad little nerd with the fewest votes will be "expelled," i.e., booted off the show in an orgy of public humiliation that will rack up the ratings. Just kidding!—we'll be sincerely sorry to let them go. Sincerely.

This elimination process will happen every Friday until the twelve Chosen Ones are whittled down to the last three for the Grand Finale.

IS THAT CLEAR?

So—you'll get your chance to vote your favorite schoolmates on to the show on Monday, with the results being announced on Tuesday, when our gorgeous presenter Abi Sparkes will be here to meet the twelve lucky contestants. The question is: will YOU be one of them?

Okay, gotta go. See you DOWN THE BOG on Monday!

Storm

SATURDAY, SEPTEMBER 11
10:10 A.M.

Just read Storm's letter again. Feel Lower than Low. I can confidently say that I would get one vote. Vicki would not let me down.

10:15 A.M.

Wonder if Storm's parents actually called him that in real reality?

...

Decided to go to church this morning. Haven't been for ages. There were prayers remembering the anniversary of 9/11 yesterday. Felt really bad afterward that I have been obsessing about this TV thing and have neglected important stuff, like Jonathan starting school and Dad working himself to death and hardly talking to anyone, and Mum being all strung-up and stressy.

What's happening to our family? When we lived in Kent it all seemed so normal and easy. Dad commuted to that science research center in London, I was at the girls' grammar school, and Mum seemed happy to stay at home and make things nice for everyone, instead of doing all these Wimmin's Workshops and going out to slave in that horrible wholefood-organic-save-the-rainforest café, where everything tastes of mud. And I remember we were all so excited about Jonathan being born. But we don't seem like a real family anymore.

Decided to launch Operation Family Fun.

Started by taking Jonathan to the park this afternoon. Did the swing, slide, sandbox, and jungle gym. We were running around with our arms stuck out, making airplane noises, when I noticed some Spotty

Youths hanging round the basketball hoop. Marcus and Paul Johnson and a couple boys from the year above, to be exact.

Even worse, they started to come over to us. Oh help, I thought, do they have to do this to me? Will it be Easy-Jet Jennifer next? Or do they beat up little boys for fun in between shooting baskets?

"Hi," Marcus said, his green eyes smiling slightly.

"Oh . . . er . . . hey . . . hi," I mumbled, like an alien with a stutter.

"Do you know Will and Gonzo? From the band?"

"Oh . . . er . . . hi . . . hey," I managed brilliantly.

Then my poor innocent brother went up to the one with the red Mohawk and said, "Will you play with me?"

I could have died, but Mohawk Man (I think that one is Will) actually picked him up, and showed him how to throw the ball through the hoop. Then he and Marcus and Gonzo, or whatever his name is, started to fool around, pretending to drop the ball to make Jonathan laugh. I just stood in a daze next to Paul whilst these Dude Rock Band types played with my baby brother. Finally, Marcus said they had to go and start rehearsing, but Jonathan was shouting, "More!

More!" so Marcus laughed and said, "Maybe next time." Then he kind of smiled at me again, and they went off.

At least they hadn't seen me when Jonathan was pretending to be Buzz Lightyear as I was being Zurg.

6:20 P.M.

Marcus hasn't any zits. His quota of them seems to have transmigrated to Paul.

september 13–19:
vote for your mates....

1:35 P.M.

The Worst Day Of My Life. Can hardly bear to write about it.

When I got to school everyone was milling around noisily and the camera crew was there, setting up a whole lot of lights and cables and stuff in the auditorium. I think the guy with the ponytail and leather trousers was Storm. In Assembly, Miss Moodie was clutching a little clipboard and looking excited, like a slightly demented bird, in a tartan skirt and hideously clashing blouse. She announced that each year group would get a turn to go into the auditorium and that anybody who wanted to be voted on to the show could make a little speech saying why they deserved to win the prize, etc., etc.

She made it all sound so simple. "Hi, I'm Jumping Jennifer—vote for me!"

Just thinking about it makes me feel slightly sick,

even now. Anyway, in our year, Kelly Trundle had a gang of friends wearing VOTE FOR KELLY badges and Dean Wiggins had a placard saying WIGGINS ROOLS. Wiggins drools would be more like it.

But all that was totally upstaged by Marcus and Tallulah. They had put up posters literally everywhere, saying things like MARCUS AND TALLULAH EQUAL SUCCESS and MARCUS AND TALLULAH ENTER STARDOM, all cleverly designed to read "M.A.T.E.S." And they had leaflets and badges with VOTE FOR YOUR MATES and stuff like that. Vicki said that she'd heard in the girls' toilets that Tallulah's parents had spent a fortune having it all printed up over the weekend. "They should have put 'Marcus And Tallulah Eat Slugs,'" she said.

Tallulah, of course, was hanging round Marcus like a wasp on a squashed jam tart. But Marcus looked up and saw me, and he actually had the cheek, the nerve, the audacity, to slide over to me with his lazy green-eyed smile and his zit-free complexion, and say, "Hi, Jennifer," and push one of his Tallulah-tainted leaflets into my hand. I was just about to turn away In Silence and With Total Dignity, when he said, "Hang on, I want you to have one of these." Then he pulled out a badge saying MATES 4 EVER and ACTUALLY PINNED IT ON MY BLOUSE!

"You can give that to Jonathan from me," he said.

"Okay," I said, like a hypnotized rabbit.

"Okay then," he said, and did the little secret smile thing and walked off, back to Tallulah.

Okay? Okay? How can it be okay to plaster yourself all over the school inextricably linked to T. Perkins???!!!

3:10 P.M.

Had to go and get something to eat. Could only find some rock-hard whole-wheat fig bars. Better than nothing. If I don't write all this down now, I shall dream about it, and I never want to think about this next bit again, so here goes.

Eventually a woman from the TV people, with purple hair and a little clipboard like Miss Moodie's, came in and said it was time for our year to go to the auditorium. She said that anyone who wanted to get voted on had to make a speech, and that all the speeches would be filmed.

When we got there, it was so weird to have all these

cameras in our dreary school hall, and to think that people watching TV at home could actually see us. Why they would want to watch some crummy school at ten o'clock in the morning I couldn't imagine, but it was still kind of spooky. People seemed to react in different ways, either going all quiet and self-conscious, or rocketing into super-show-off mode, like Tallulah.

Kelly seemed pretty perked-up by the idea of Being On Telly, and was the first one to go on the stage. Oh Lord, she is powerfully built. She droned on about how she had been a lunch monitor and on the hockey team and how she would love to represent London Road Comprehensive to the wider world, and then Dean Wiggins managed to say "Hasta la vista, Baby."*

Lauren Pike said she wanted to be on the show because she'd once been an extra in an advert for Clearasil** and it was the most exciting thing that had ever happened to her, then loads of other people were getting up to have a turn, when a really weird thing happened. Someone tapped me on the shoulder, and it was Miss Moodie, beckoning me out of the auditorium

*Translation: I am a plonker.
**Zit Zapper.

into the corridor, away from the cameras. She said, "Now Jennifer, I do hope you are going to put yourself forward for this interesting venture."

I sort of mumbled that I didn't think there was much point.

"Nonsense! Lots of people must admire your diligence in pursuit of academic excellence."

She really does talk like that.

"Besides," she added softly, "we do need one intelligent person to represent London Road to the public at large, don't we?" She sounded spookily like a Kelly clone. "So go back in, Jennifer, get up and make your little speech, and we'll look after the rest."

Then she trotted off. Over my dead body was I going to get up and make a complete dingbat of myself, in front of the entire year, never mind the entire daytime-TV-watching nation.

When I got back to my seat, Vicki grabbed me and jabbed her finger at the stage, where Paul was lugging a whole lot of equipment around, amps and a mike and stuff, as Marcus and Tallulah went up onstage together. Let's just say her outfit wasn't Standard School Uniform. Then Marcus plugged his guitar in and sang a song about "I Rate Great Mates" or some such drivel, whilst Tallulah wiggled her gazzongers and shook her maracas, or whatever, and looked fantastic. The whole place was dancing and clapping, and I have to say that Marcus was in actual real reality very, very good.

That's it, I thought, they will be voted in, no contest. But when all the noise had finally died down, the TV woman with the purple hair said, "Is there anyone else who'd like to be considered?" Vicki was digging me in the back and I was muttering, "No way," when Miss Moodie jumped out of nowhere with her little clipboard and said brightly, "Yes, we have one more candidate, Jennifer James!"

A million heads swiveled round to me In Silence. I didn't move until Vicki pushed me down toward the front of the auditorium. A cameraman suddenly appeared, like a sort of manic hunchback, practically touching my cheek with this huge camera that he was lugging around. I didn't dare look at it, so I stared at the ground and I shuffled forward in a daze, like a prisoner taking the last walk to the gallows. Everyone was whispering and sniggering and my insides turned to water, but I got up onto the stage somehow, and it was truly the Abyss of Awfulness, all those faces staring up at me, willing me to make a fool of myself. I thought I wouldn't be able to say anything, but I sort of stuttered, "I'd like to learn Latin."

The whole place exploded with laughter. I could see Tallulah and Chelsea nearly crying, they were laughing so much. Suddenly, I felt really, really angry. Without thinking, I marched over to the microphone that Marcus had left onstage, grabbed it, and said, "Yes, I do want to learn Latin, and Greek and history and politics, and anything that really teaches me something about the world we live in. I don't just want to know stupid gossip about fashions and pop music and what's on television. And I want to go to St. Willibald's College, not because it's posh or anything like that, but because I want to go to a school where they don't throw things at the teachers, or despise you if you want to read a book, and I think if I went there I could be myself and not be tormented or laughed at or treated like a leper. So yes, I do want to win, and I know I've no chance, but at least I've tried."

Then I couldn't say any more. I was shaking and nearly in tears and I practically fell down the steps from the stage, but someone caught me in time, and it was Marcus. And he wasn't smiling now, but he just looked at me in that green-eyed way and said quietly, "Nice one, Jenny," and I felt his hand on my arm, and I think some people were clapping, but I didn't care. I just grabbed my things and ran home and I don't think I'll ever go back there again.

TUESDAY, SEPTEMBER 14
9:30 A.M.

In bed. Persuaded Jocasta that I felt too ill to go to school. She's not going to work until ten this morning, and is doing some last-minute reading for her book group tonight. They have moved on to *The Female Eunuch.*[*] Just to make them feel happier about being Serious Women.

Suppose I'd better make some notes for Mr. Webster or something.

Text messages 9/14
10:15: Jen u r in! Viki
10:18: wot u mean? J
10:20: in the bog
10:21: ??

[*]*The Feminist Bible.*

10:24: in tv show!

10:27: u r jokin

10:29: no itz tru they want u here asap

Vx

11:05 P.M.

!!!!!!!!

Exhausted. Abi Sparkes is the most beautiful person I have ever seen. She makes Naomi Campbell look ordinary. She has long dark hair, long dark limbs, gorgeous eyes. And she was so nice! Think when I wake up tomorrow all this will be a dream, like it was for Dorothy in *The Wizard of Oz*.*

12:10 A.M.

Can't sleep. Just can't think how this has happened. Can't believe that so many people must have voted for me. It's weird. *Totalement Incroyable*.**

So it's me and Tallulah—and ten others.

12:20 A.M.

Can't understand why Marcus didn't get in.

Brightly colored film in which wearing red shoes is punishable by death.

**Translation: Utterly Unbelievable.*

12:40 A.M.

Jocasta is bound to find out now.

12:55 A.M *TOP SECRET DIARY ENTRY*

I think I might, just might, have voted for Marcus.

THE DAILY RUMOR

TV ROUNDUP

WEDNESDAY, SEPTEMBER 15

*Twelve lucky youngsters from London Road Compre-
hensive have been chosen to fight for a place at
upper-crust St. Willibald's College, on the new
reality TV show* Down The Bog. *A sneak pre-
view of their excited reaction was shown last night
in a trailer for the series. Tallulah Perkins, a
young Pamela Anderson[*] look-alike, said she was
"thrilled" to be appearing on the program.*

*"It's a dream come true that Seth Dale is on the
show. He's my hero. And I'm hoping that being on
TV will help to start my own career as a pop singer.*

[*]*Blonde, Bosoms, Boy magnet.*

Anyone who is interested can get in touch my man-
ager, Shandy P."

But others weren't quite so outspoken. Young
Jennifer James seemed reluctant to be filmed, saying,
"My mum doesn't actually know yet that I'm in the show,
because my dad signed the permission form. She is going
to go mad because she doesn't approve of television."

Apparently all TV and radio has been banned in
the home of straight-A student Jennifer. The show's
presenter, Abi Sparkes, famously a member of
Mensa,[*] as well as being voted one of the "World's
Most Beautiful Women," has taken up Jennifer's cause.
"She seems to want to be on the show to have the
opportunity of going to a good school. For some of the
other kids it's just a bit of a laugh," said Abi. "Jennifer
seems stunned that she's been voted on by the rest of her
year. I think her mum should let her have a go."

So the RUMOR's message to Mrs. James is
Let her do it, Mum!

Meanwhile, the teachers at London Road are
brushing up their technique to get ready for the cameras, and on the celebrity front, ex-footballer Nazzer

*Club for mega-brainy types.

McNally and lifestyle guru Carrie Chaplin are lined up to appear. Controversially, the disgraced former MP Jeremy Lurcher has approached Haydeeze Productions and actually asked to be sent "Down The Bog." Speaking from his luxury Docklands penthouse, Lurcher said, "It's just what I need to show the public that I am a reformed character after my time inside—honest hard graft with some yob kids from a sink school in a grotty town. What more can I do to get reselected as an MP?"

But Barry Hatter, firebrand teachers' union boss, commented, "That right-wing, cheating, lying, scumbag snob wants taking out and shooting."

WEDNESDAY, SEPTEMBER 15
9:50 P.M.

Dad came home early tonight as we were having tea with Jonathan in the kitchen. He literally burst in, waving a newspaper around. My heart plummeted to my feet faster than a ride on a broken roller coaster when I saw it was the *Daily Rumor*.

"Have you seen this?" He gabbed, brandishing it

under Jocasta's nose. "It's today's paper! Dave Johnson, one of the workers on the afternoon shift, brought it in to show me. Said his boy is in Jennifer's class and weren't we proud of her—I mean, Sheila, do you know anything about it?"

"It's Jocasta, I'll thank you to remember," Mum snapped at him, as she snatched the paper and scanned it in a micro-milli-second.

"I refused to sign that form! What's going on?" she hissed.

"Form?" said Dad. "I don't remember any form."

Then they both looked at me and waited. It was like that moment in the auditorium all over again.

"Um, for the TV documentary at school," I started. "You didn't want to sign it, so I asked Dad to . . ."

"Doc-u-men-tary? DOC-U-MEN-TARY?" she repeated, as if I was deaf and mentally disadvantaged as well as in big, big trouble. "You call this *Down The Toilet* reality rubbish a documentary?"

"Bog," I muttered, "it's called *Down The Bog*."

"Oh, that makes all the difference then, doesn't it? *Down The Bog*. How delightful. Well, young lady,"—I absolutely HATE it when she calls me that—"you can jolly well go into school tomorrow morning and tell them you won't be appearing in such trash."

At this point Jonathan burst into tears over his lentil bolognese, encouraged no doubt by the happy family atmosphere.

"Now Jonathan, don't get upset," Dad said soothingly. "Mummy's only—"

"It's not Mummy, it's Jocasta!" she bellowed.

Then Dad did an amazing thing. He went over to Mum, trying to look dignified (difficult when you're clutching a weeping four-year-old) and said, "Now look here, Sheila, I've had enough of this Jocasta larkery. I don't quite know how all this has happened, but if Jennifer wants to go on this show for the sake of her education, then good luck to her. And I don't want you stopping her or giving her a hard time about it, Sheila. I mean, you're in charge of the house and all that, and I know I'm busy at work, but I do notice some things and I've seen the clothes you get her and I've seen the other young kids out in town, and, well . . ."

He stopped for a bit and looked faintly surprised.

"Well, Jonathan and I are going out to get some fish and chips, that's all."

And off they went. First time I've ever seen Jocasta speechless.

I do love Dad. I don't always remember that, but I really do.

6:55 P.M.

Mr. Webster assigned us an essay on the character of Juliet. Someone asked him if he thought he had a chance in the teachers' competition on *Down The Bog,* and he ruffled his fingers through his hair, looking a bit self-conscious. So I suppose that means yes. Apparently the teachers don't actually get chucked off the show every week. Instead, all the votes they get through the whole series are added up at the end, and the one with the most wins the prize. Vicki said it's to keep them all keen so that they do interesting lessons for the cameras. Not sure that some of them are actually capable of that.

Dear Lord, please let me win and please let Mr. Webster be appointed head of English at St. Willibald's.

...

10:30 P.M.

Tallulah cornered me in the showers after gym, wearing only a very inadequate towel (I wonder if she's had a Breast Augmentation Operation?*), and said in her usual charming way, "Look, Ugly-Head, I don't know how you bribed your way onto the show, but you must have done, as you couldn't get enough votes to cover a false nail. Let's get this straight, shall we? Whatever old Moodie-Cow was whispering to you outside the auditorium on Monday, there's only going to be one winner, and it isn't going to be little miss Jennifer "oh please give me a chance to study" James. And I saw you throwing yourself at Marcus after your dying duck speech, so let me spell it out: I want to win and I want Marcus, at least until something better comes along. And I like getting what I want, know what I mean? So when those cameras start rolling on Monday, you go back to being one of life's losers. Like, just be yourself. Nobody. And keep out of the way, okay?"

"Okay, okay," I muttered.

"And by the way, Jenn-ee, if you think Marcus is at

Boob job.

all interested, think again. He said he's never seen anything like you and your kid brother playing Teletubbies
together down at the park. So back off, James, or
you're dead meat."

So sweet. You have a nice day too, Tallulah.

Couldn't help noticing, as she flounced away and
hitched up her miniscule little towel, that she has a
tattoo on what my gran would call her sit-upon. It's
a horrible thing with a heart and flames and a snake
wrapped round it all. Makes her look as though her
butt is on fire.

Wish it was.

11:10 P.M.

Wonder if Marcus really said that to her?

11:15 P.M.

Wonder what Miss Moodie meant when she said, "You
do your speech, and we'll take care of the rest"?

SATURDAY, SEPTEMBER 18
10:05 A.M.

Wonder what kissing Marcus would be like?

...

THE SUNDAY RUMOR

TITTLE-TATTLE TIDBITS

SEPTEMBER 19

Well-endowed model Amanda Knox looks set to be a very popular feature on the new show, Down The Bog. *She was spotted yesterday at trendy night spot The Chicken Fillet with teen heartthrob Seth Dale. Could this be a glimpse of things to come when they are both enrolled in school?*

"She's an outstanding personality," said her publicist, Zak Clifford. "She's just got something about her that sticks out."

SUNDAY, SEPTEMBER 19
11:10 P.M.

Getting late. Must get a good night's sleep before tomorrow. The first day of proper filming for the show. Really nervous about the cameras, the TV people, Tallulah, everything.

11:45 P.M.

Nearly tomorrow.

Have decided that I'm going to stop bothering about what Tallulah said. Surely I have as much right as she has to try and win the prize? And I really, really do desperately want to go to St. Willibald's.

11:50 P.M.

It's not very probable that either of us will win anyway. Much more likely to be someone incredibly cool from year 12. But even if I've no hope of winning the competition, don't I have as much right as Tallulah has to try and win Marcus. I mean, if I really wanted to. Which I don't.

11:55 P.M.

At least, I don't think I do.

Midnight

Have a feeling that whatever happens, the actual real reality of Jennifer James is never going to be quite the same again.

Can't wait.

september 20-26:
"The Most Unpopular Girl
in our Year ..."

MONDAY, SEPTEMBER 20

5:30 P.M.

Woke up feeling absolutely sick this morning, and couldn't eat any breakfast. Jocasta very frosty, but when I was leaving, she suddenly said, "Oh, Jenny-love . . ." in her old Sheila-Mum way, and gave me some of her special tofu-on-pumpernickel sandwiches.*

I nearly collapsed in a sniveling heap. I wanted to say, "Please don't make me go to school," like when I was about ten and pretending to have a stomachache. It was at that moment that I suddenly realized what I had actually landed myself in, and couldn't help feeling that it would all end in more Humiliation and Awfulness, probably this Friday night in front of an audience of millions. But it was too late, so I just swallowed tears, pride, snotty stuff, you name it, and said, "Thanks Mum," and she actually smiled.

Form of food torture.

When I got to school there was a big commotion outside the gates, with TV cameras, vans, and crowds of people hanging about. A massive sign had been put up, saying DOWN THE BOG — SPONSORED BY WAZZLE TOILET TISSUE!

There was a kind of scuffling heap in front of the gates, which turned out to be Kelly and her gang, holding up banners and placards, which said things like NO ELITES AT OUR COMP and NO TO THE LONDON ROAD TWELVE! And in the middle of it all, a weird-looking man with a shaved head, glasses, and a megaphone was yelling, "No elites! Haydeeze out!" Then Kelly and the others started screaming, "Haydeeze out! Haydeeze out!"

I'd just managed to find Vicki in the scrum, when one of the TV guys shoved a microphone into my face and shouted, "Do you support this protest about *Down The Bog* only being open to twelve preselected pupils?" I opened and shut my mouth like a demented goldfish, but Vicki grabbed the mike and said, "This is my friend Jennifer James and she's one of the twelve! It was all totally fair and if people don't like it that's their problem. Vote for Jenny!"

I tried to drag her away and slink into school, but she said, "Hang on, something's happening." A whole lot of big cars drew up at the gates, and everyone started whistling and cheering as Amanda Knox got out of a silver sports car. Celia Bunch, the TV cook, got out of another car with some people I didn't recognize, then I heard a kind of wailing banshee noise, and it was Tallulah and Chelsea screaming "Seth! Seth!" and Seth Dale's car was actually mobbed by hordes of frantic girls, but Tallulah was the most hysterical. How she managed A) to climb on top of the car and B) get her school blouse as low-cut as that, I can't imagine.

At this precise moment, someone had the great idea of letting the goat off its rope. It took a great charge up to Amanda Knox's pert behind and sent her flying, whilst the shaved-head maniac and Kelly's gang were screaming, "NO ELITES AT LONDON ROAD!" and chucking eggs, and one hit Miss Moodie right in the face, and I thought, This is my school, and I'm going to die of shame.

But apparently Storm was dead chuffed with the welcome party. Apparently it was Great Television.

Perhaps Jocasta has a point.

THE TRIBUNE

Hatter in Tree as Professor Plunges into Bog

TUESDAY, SEPTEMBER 21

Filming for *Down The Bog* got off to a stormy start yesterday at London Road Comprehensive. Teachers' leader Barry Hatter is fanning the anger that some students feel over the selection of only twelve pupils as possible winners of the prize place at St. Willibald's College.

"This is elitism at its height," he declared. "There's no place for a toff school like St. Willibald's in today's society, but if there is going to be a stupid prize, then everyone should have a chance to win it." Hatter later climbed up a tree outside the school gates and chained himself to it, saying, "I'll stay here until the government brings forward legislation to transfer the whole of London Road Comprehensive to St. Willibald's College."

But Seth Dale, the former *Cop* actor and would-be pop star, was greeted ecstatically by a crowd of screaming adolescent girls. Other celebrity participants include Freddie McCrum, a school contemporary of Prince William, who has previously failed to be selected as a contestant on *Thick Rich Kids*. Also appearing is Sir Harvey Harvey, who represented Great Britain in the 1958 Olympics, winning a bronze medal in the walking race. In recent years, Sir Harvey has devoted himself to charitable work with young offenders in Tunbridge Wells.

A more surprising contestant is Professor Barbara Beer, whose postfeminist critiques of contemporary culture have often included scathing attacks on broadcasting standards.

Down The Bog is being shown on Tuesdays and Fridays, the latter being when the "expulsions" will be announced. A continuous "stream" is available to digital viewers. Whether the show will attract the enormous numbers who tune in to *Nosy Neighbor* and *Child Swap* remains to be seen.

HAYDEEZE PRODUCTIONS

TUESDAY, SEPTEMBER 21, 9:00 A.M.
TO: THE STUDENT CONTESTANTS
FROM: STORM YOUNG

Hi there, my darling dozen!

So this is it, the beginning of your fifteen minutes of fame, you lucky little mini-trogs! Now seriously, down to business. You need to check this bulletin board EVERY DAY for essential info.

This week's highlights are as follows. There will be a meeting with yours truly TODAY at 10:00 A.M., then you will all be interviewed by Abi for tonight's opening show.

On Friday you have to be here after school for the first LIVE EXPULSION! One of our celebrities will also be expelled every Friday, so you're in good company. This will be filmed in the school auditorium, details to follow.

Well gotta go, see you at ten, and there'll be a schedule pinned up later for your interview times. DON'T BE LATE ON PAIN OF DEATH.

Wotcha!

Storm

TUESDAY, SEPTEMBER 21
4:55 P.M.

Another amazing day. Still so odd seeing cameras and lights and strange technical-type people all over the school. There are some big trailers parked in the school grounds and huge generator vans and catering vans for the crew. A crowd of people was outside the gates this morning hoping to catch sight of Seth and Amanda and the rest of the "Celebs," but they are all hidden away in school doing a crash course in Teaching Skills. Hope it's not dreary old Mrs. Stringer teaching the teaching skills. She's due to retire next year, but I think her skills retired years ago.

Vicki, who seems to know these things, said that most of the filming will be done by the little fixed cameras that have appeared everywhere. They swivel around when you walk past them, and Tallulah already seems to have discovered their locations like a heat-seeking missile. She spends every break time conveniently hovering around them with her blouse practically open to her navel. But there are some real-live camera and sound people in the school too, whose mission is apparently to dash around the school to film Assembly, or football practice, or any fights breaking out. In fact, anything that looks remotely interesting. Which is usually precisely nothing at London Road.

Until now.

Storm had a meeting with the twelve of us who are

on the show. So amazing that I am one of them! Will from The Electric Fish was there, with another guy from his year; I think he's called Dwight. Tallulah clamped herself on to them like a giant slug, and whispered loudly, "What a shame about poor Marcus not getting in," whilst giving me the Evil Eye. She really is Cruella De Vil[*] reborn in the body of Britney Spears.[**]

Can't help wondering if Marcus does mind. Have hardly been in class properly the last couple of days, what with these meetings and stuff going on, so I haven't really seen him. Wonder if I should say something to him? I kind of feel that I've taken his place. Oh, I don't know, if I did see him I probably wouldn't know what to say. I just hope he doesn't feel bad about it.

Anyway, there were the twins from year 9, and Serena Dickinson from year 12. I would bet a million pounds that she will win. She's got everything except brains, and perhaps they aren't necessary when you're dripping with Natural Talent. Don't know why the other year 12 girls don't just lie down and die whilst she's around. Alice Redknapp, who's also been voted on, looks as though she already has. AND there were

[*]*Puppy murderer.*
[**]*Singing Barbie.*

two tiny new kids from year 7 who just can't believe what has happened to them, Big School and Being On Telly, all in the space of three weeks. One of them has the most stunningly sticking-out teeth I ever saw, like a rabbit needing braces. Poor little things looked terrified when Storm came in, wearing red leather trousers and a shaggy poncho that made him look like an extra from a spider horror movie. I do think he is awful.

I was just beginning to think that doing this whole TV stunt had definitely been a Horrendous Mistake, when Abi Sparkes walked in. It was like the sun coming out, because she's so incredibly nice and shiny and happy. She made those little year 7 sprogs grow six inches just by smiling at them. And it was so easy being interviewed by her for the opening show tonight, because she makes you feel you are her most favorite person, without being in the least bit creepy.

Shame Miss Moodie hasn't quite got that technique nailed.

5:25 P.M.

Funny to think this could all be over for me on

Friday, as the first person will be "expelled" then. I have to say it would be the Abyss of Awfulness to be the first person chucked off. Jennifer James: Number One Reject! Though it has to happen to someone. Hope it's not little Rabbit Teeth. On the other hand, it would be mega-glorious if Tallulah was the first one of us to take a nosedive. Please Lord, can you fix this for me?

Can't help wondering what the show will be like tonight. Wish I could watch it. Oh well, better start my history homework.

That weird guy is still in the tree.

9:15 P.M.

I worry about my family, I really do. Jocasta put Jonathan to bed and then came downstairs just before eight o'clock, saying she was going out with her Serious Wimmin Study Group pals. So then Dad jumped up from behind the newspaper like Pinocchio* and said, "Good idea, Sheila dear; I've got some work to do in the study," and rushed out to the garage.

Then, even stranger, about an hour later, he came up to my room, which he never usually does, and knocked

*Well-meaning woodenhead.

on the door. I was making some notes about the causes of the Second World War for Mr. Potter, when Dad came in and stood about awkwardly, saying, "Ah," and "Oh," like he does. Then he suddenly muttered, "I'm very proud of you Jennifer, whatever happens," and disappeared again!

Parents are Very Strange.

THE DAILY RUMOR

TV ROUNDUP

WEDNESDAY, SEPTEMBER 22

Hot new show **Down The Bog** *got off to a sizzling start last night, as celebrity contestants Seth Dale and Amanda Knox shot to the top of the class in the cheeky stakes. Ex-Cop star Dale was filmed helping the blond beauty massage cream into her famous curves, after she complained of a "bruised bottom" as a result of encountering the school's goat. The more mature contestants were also settling in, with highbrow feminist Barbara "Barabbas"* Beer*

**Nasty type voted for by biblical crowd instead of Jesus. Big mistake.*

accusing Celia Bunch, one of TV's most popular cooks, of "promoting an outdated image of women as domestic slaves." The two nearly came to blows and had to be separated by old-timer athlete Sir Harvey Harvey.

Prince William's former classmate, toff Freddie McCrum, was shown puzzling over how to use a can opener when the Celebs had to cook their own supper in their "Private Parts" living quarters. He later managed to get locked in a store cupboard, saying, "I thought it was the en-suite." Tomorrow all the contestants will face taking their first class with pupils at London Road Comprehensive.

Some of those pupils were also on the show last night, being interviewed by Abi Sparkes, and two of them immediately caught the public's eye. Tallulah Perkins and Serena Dickinson have already become the bookies' favorites to reach the Grand Finale.

One celebrity and one pupil will be "expelled" on this Friday's show. A spokesperson from Haydeeze Productions said, "It's early days, but we are really pleased with the numbers who watched the first show. This can only get bigger and better. Our

sponsors are delighted too—so don't forget your
Wazzle when you're Down The Bog!"

The WHOLE SCHOOL talking about last night's show, and I'm the only one who didn't see it. Kelly still waving her banners at anyone who will take any notice.

Vicki said there was a great shot of Tallulah's knickers when she climbed up onto Seth's car, and that my interview with Abi was "cool"—but she would say that, even if I really came across as a banana head.

The awful news is that Abi is, in actual real reality, Storm's girlfriend. Vicki read it in *HEY!* magazine. It's so sad.

Trying to get used to the little cameras all over the school swiveling around and filming in the classrooms, auditorium, cafeteria, in the loos (only in the hand-washing part, thank goodness), and even all over the playgrounds and sports fields. Apparently we are being filmed all the time for the live streaming, which is shown practically all day long on some obscure digital TV channel, then the best bits are highlighted on the main Tuesday and Friday shows. The live streaming starts at 6:00 A.M. when the Celebs get up. Who on earth would want to get up at six o'clock, just to watch someone else getting up?

Although Vicki's dad didn't open his shop yesterday so that he could stay at home and watch the whole thing from the very beginning, to see what was going on. He told her the Celebs have to discuss their lesson plans with "educational experts" over breakfast before being allowed into school. Then cameras film the whole school day! The live streaming keeps switching from shots of the Celebs, to the teachers, to us, to the dinner ladies (sorry, Lunchtime Assistants), whatever, and after school it switches back to the Celebs' "Private Parts" on top of the science block. (It really is called that—there's a big sign at the top of the stairs, blocking the way to what used to be classrooms H11, H12, and H13).

Up there they get feedback on what they have "achieved" and have more "experts" telling them what to do, then they play daft bonding games, make dinner over the Bunsen burners, and apparently drink vast amounts. I suppose Haydeeze are hoping that they will get horribly drunk and rampage around their Private Parts, either screaming at each other, or snogging each other, or very possibly throwing each other out of the science-block windows.

Yeah, great television, Mr. Have-I-got-a-ponytail-for-you Storm. I just cannot imagine who on earth would want to watch it.

Apart from Vicki's dad, obviously.

10:05 P.M.

Year 7 had a class with Jeremy Lurcher. He was an MP[*] who went to prison for lying about some cover-up thing, can't exactly remember what. Apparently he just read them loads of boring stuff from his autobiography, which he wrote in prison, and he kept looking into the camera in the corner of the classroom and saying what a great TV series his book would make. They were supposed to be doing geography. And Freddie McCrum took year 11 for a "cross country" run (down past the disused mine and through the old slag heaps) and lost half of them. They turned up later in a pub.

It was kind of weird today, knowing that you were

---

[*]*Self-promoting member of exclusive boys' club.*

being filmed in biology or whatever. The quiet people have gone quieter, and the noisy people are noisier, and the teachers are trying a bit harder. Mr. Potter even had a new tie on. It's like having school inspectors around all the time. I suppose we will get used to it.

Just thought—will die if I am filmed playing hockey.*

11:35 P.M.

Feeling deadly sick about appearing on Friday's live show. Having a camera stuck in the corner of your classroom is one thing, but actually being broadcast to the nation as the first person to be Kicked Off and Utterly Humiliated is quite another.

THURSDAY, SEPTEMBER 23
8:35 P.M.

Only one more day to go to the Moment of Doom.

Chelsea told Marcus, who told Paul Johnson, who told Vicki, who told me that Tallulah's mother has arranged to have EVERY SINGLE MOMENT of the live streaming recorded, then she's going to have it professionally edited into a "program" all about

---

Barbaric ritual disguised as game suitable for girls.

Tallulah, and send it round to agents to try and get her work as an actress/singer/airhead. And I thought my mother was bad enough. Vicki is so lucky that her mother ran off with that panpipes player to South America when she was two.

Kelly is still not speaking to me, but I can't say her conversation is something I really miss.

We had our first proper class with a Celeb today and it was brilliant. Sir Harvey Harvey took hockey practice instead of the Rock and he was so, so sweet and old-fashioned and gentlemanly, but as soon as anyone (Tallulah) tried to show off, or muck about, he was on top of it like a little terrier. I actually started to see that there is a vague point to the game. Sir H. showed me how to line up the stick thingy with the ball to make a really good thwack.

He was fab. Glad that the camera crew was there so that the viewers will see that Sir H. was so cool.

Would like to make a good thwack with a large stick on Tallulah's flaming butt.

...

TOP SECRET

Saw Marcus today. It was in that little back corridor that leads to the art block. I was rushing down there as a shortcut because I was late and I slammed into him coming the other way (he does drama instead of art). He looked a bit startled, to say the least. Then we did that AWFUL thing when one of you tries to let the other pass, but they step the wrong way, and then you step the wrong way, until you are jumping from side to side like some sort of hoedown in a barn dance. Eventually he stopped and laughed, and said, "We seem to have a problem."

"Yeah," I said intelligently. Then I saw that one of his MATES posters with Tallulah was still on the wall in that bit of corridor. I found that I couldn't stop staring at it, as though I was hypnotized, and I actually started going red. So then he looked at it, and laughed again, and said, "Well, I won't need those anymore." And even though he was smiling, his green eyes looked sort of sad, so I blurted out, "Honestly, Marcus, I'm really sorry, I don't know how it happened, I never even meant to enter, it was . . ."

I was going to say, "It was Miss Moodie's idea," but

something stopped me.

"It was good," he said. "I mean, your speech, that day." And then he touched my arm again, ever so gently, exactly where he had caught me when I had fallen down the stage steps. I was just beginning to notice that his eyes are actually flecked with tiny threads of amber, when a whole crowd of boys came up behind him and he dropped his hand and just walked away. When they had all gone, I stood there and held my arm where he had been touching me, and it was still warm.

Was late for art. Mr. Barker went ballistic.

EDUCATION REVIEW WEEKLY

"UNPOPULAR GIRL IN *BOG*," GRUMBLES TRUNDLE

FRIDAY, SEPTEMBER 24

A new television program, *Down The Bog*, has so incensed the leader of one of the more radical teachers' unions that he has tied himself up a tree in protest. Barry Hatter (Secretary of the UTC) has refused to come down from the tree since

Monday of this week. Supplies of food, drinks, and blankets are being delivered by a rebel group of pupils at the school involved, London Road Comprehensive. They are also opposing the show because of its "exclusive" nature, as only twelve pupils have been invited to participate.

Kelly Trundle, spokesperson for the disgruntled students said, "I can't believe Jennifer James was voted on. She's the most unpopular girl in our year. It must be a fix."

FRIDAY, SEPTEMBER 24
11:35 P.M.

What an awesome day! Can't believe it all actually happened. Am too exhausted to write diary. Must, must, must go to sleep.

I had no idea Kelly disliked me so much. BUT . . . I am still on the show.

. . .

THE DAILY RUMOR

TV ROUNDUP

Hapless dog-food heir Freddie McCrum, whose father owns the multimillion-pound Crummy Yummy Corporation, was the first Celeb to be expelled from reality TV romp Down The Bog *last night. He had earlier been shown setting fire to his eyebrows whilst attempting to make a bacon sandwich in a food technology lesson, and bursting into tears during a math class. He claimed that he was suffering from post-traumatic stress disorder after failing all his A levels at the third attempt last year. Any sympathy vote he may have attracted wasn't enough to save him on last night's show, and he wept again as the results were announced.*

Fellow socialite Lady Amelia Itchpole, who is also a contestant, said, "Everyone knows Freddie is an acre short of a grouse moor. * *He can't help it. Nice bum, though."*

**Outdoor playground for mega-rich types.*

After leaving the show's London Road venue, Freddie was supposed to appear on the Man Friday *late-night chat show. However, he failed to turn up, apparently getting lost on the way. The* Rumor's *sources report that he may now have gone into hiding on his father's estate, Crummy Towers.*

SATURDAY, SEPTEMBER 25
6:15 A.M.

Last night seems so weird. It's all going round in my head again and again, like an endless replay of a really bad song.

Wonder how everyone else is this morning? When I left after the show, the twins from year 9 were not speaking to each other, as Maddie had been voted off. Vicki rang late last night and said that in Maddie's "postexpulsion" interview on telly, she went on and on about it not being fair, because people blatantly couldn't tell whether they were voting for her or Mattie, with them being so eye-bogglingly identical. Vicki said Maddie was in total hysterics, yelling that she hopes Mattie will win so that she (Mattie) can swan off to St. Willibald's and she (Maddie) won't have to see her ugly face again.

So that's one down, eleven to go.

We were allowed to wear our own clothes for the show, which didn't really help as my own clothes are marginally less attractive than my school uniform, thanks to the Extreme and Ridiculous Principles of a certain member of my family. Tallulah was practically naked—I mean, that was a hair band she was wearing, not a skirt. Will had dyed his Mohawk blue, and little Rabbit Teeth was wearing one of those terrible bow ties on an elastic string. I suppose his mother must love him, in spite of everything. Serena Dickinson looked perfect of course, and Abi looked divine. Even Miss Moodie was all dolled up like Joan Collins,[*] though the puffball skirt was probably a bit extreme.

When we were ready, we all had to line up on one side of the stage in the auditorium, which had been rigged out with a fancy set and colored lights. On the other side of the stage were the celebrities (Tallulah in ecstasy about being in spitting distance of Seth Dale),

[*]*Big hair, big eyelashes, big bucks.*

and suspended in the middle there was a huge TV screen, showing the highlights of the week's filming. So at least I got to see some of the best bits, like Celia Bunch teaching year 7 to make an amazing meringuey cake concoction in the shape of the Statue of Liberty, and Barbara Beer sending year 12 to sleep in her four-hour lecture on Gender Politics,[*] until Shane Hartson actually rolled off his chair onto the floor and woke up with a broken wrist.

After that, Abi interviewed some of the Celebs, and Sir Harvey Harvey got the biggest cheer from the audience. He is such a babe, honestly. Then Seth Dale sang a song that was Truly Dire, but the audience seemed to lap it up. And all the time Abi kept telling the public to "Vote, Vote, Vote! Don't forget—every penny from the phones goes to How Much Is That Doggie? to help those sick children!"

I felt so sure that I wouldn't get a single vote and would be chucked off straightaway, and I know Tallulah was convinced I would be too, because she had this incredibly smug expression on her horrible face whenever she looked at me. Then I noticed through the

[*]*Translation: "A Woman Needs a Man Like a Fish Needs a Gucci Handbag."*

lights and the noise that Marcus was in the front row of the audience, wearing a T-shirt that said "Go Tallulah!" And I just felt so, so sick and thought, What on earth am I doing here?

And I'm still wondering.

8:40 A.M.

Had some breakfast. Rye porridge with dried apricots. Almost edible.

Anyway, I didn't have time to think about Marcus last night, because just as I spotted him in the crowd, Abi was saying to the camera, "We'll take a break now to count the votes, and we'll be back on air later for the results," when there was an almighty crash and people started screaming, as Kelly Trundle and her lunatic fringe gang actually climbed through the window they had smashed, yelling, "NO ELITES!" and "IT'S A FIX!" and tried to charge the stage. Suddenly all these security men leaped out from nowhere and one of them tried to wrestle Kelly to the ground, but she smacked him in the mouth (she is a Big Girl and not on the hockey team for nothing) and climbed up onto the stage just in front of me. I could see Storm frantically telling the cameraman to carry on filming, as she bellowed, "You shouldn't be on this show, Jennifer James; everyone hates you!" After that I saw the lights over the camera change from green to red, which meant we weren't on air anymore, and the woman with purple hair bundled me and the others out of the auditorium as about ten bouncers dragged Kelly off in the opposite direction.

I'm shaking again just thinking about it. Need to find some chocolate.

10:15 A.M.

The BEST thing has just happened!

I was just about to sneak out on a secret chocolate mission to the corner shop (Jocasta only had raw liquorice wood in the so-called sweets jar) and was wondering how I could smuggle some Smarties back for Jonathan, when the phone rang. I thought it might be Vicki, so I answered it, but it was ABI SPARKES!!! How cool is that?

She said she had called to ask how I was "bearing up" after last night and then talked for ages. She told me not to worry about Kelly bawling at me in front of eleven million people, and that the viewers would probably like me better for it, as the Great British Public love underdogs. I said you couldn't get much more Under than being despised by Kelly Trundle, and she laughed and said that she hadn't been all that popular at school either, because she came in first in every single exam, even general knowledge quizzes at socials.

Then she asked if I hadn't got anything else to wear on the show instead of my old blue shirt (which practically buttons up to my nose) and I sort of hummed and said no, it was a bit difficult, so she said, "You're the one whose mother is Bonkers, aren't you?" I said, "How Right You Are," and she laughed again and said she would see what she could do. THEN she said, "See you next week, Jenny," and was gone.

Can't believe ABI SPARKES rang me and called me Jenny. Must text Vicki and tell her.

Wish I could tell Jocasta, but she just wouldn't get it.

SUNDAY, SEPTEMBER 26
2:40 P.M.
MUST, MUST, MUST do some serious homework.

...

2:55 P.M.

Can't seem to concentrate. Keep wondering what to do when I see Marcus tomorrow. He is blatantly dead keen on Tallulah, what with wearing that T-shirt and all that MATES business.

Unless she bulldozed him into it with her giant gazzongers.

3:05 P.M.

What DOES he see in her????

3:10 P.M.

It's obvious, I suppose. Size D bra, super-slim legs, and cascades of blond hair. Although no one can be that blond naturally, not even Barbie.[*]

Oh, come on Jennifer, get back to business. French. Math. Chemistry.

Reality.

3:25 P.M.

Think ignoring him with Total Dignity would be best.

*Female role model, pushing sixty and still a bimbo.

September 27–October 3: "Fate, Jennifer Dear, Fate . . ."

MONDAY, SEPTEMBER 27
8:55 P.M.

Ignored Marcus all day. The only problem was that he didn't exactly seem to notice.

Got my essay on *Romeo and Juliet* back from Mr. Webster. He looked right into my eyes when he gave it to me and said, "This is very sensitive work, Jennifer," in that brooding Heathcliff[*] kind of voice, and my insides went quite faint. When he got round to Tallulah, he said, "Describing Romeo as a 'boring fart' does not constitute literary criticism, Miss Perkins," and it was a Moment of Triumph.

Kelly going round looking martyred, with a massive great bandage covering invisible "wound" on her forehead, after her Friday-night punch-up. She ate her sandwiches at lunchtime up the tree with the weird guy. Incredible that he is still there. He sleeps roped onto a kind of board that has been wedged between

---

[*]*Passionate hero of Wuthering Heights, obsessed by his dead lover; lies on her grave, digs up her body, starves himself to death, just the usual kind of thing . . .*

two big branches and says he won't come down whilst *Down The Bog* continues to degrade decent schools like London Road.

Actually, London Road seems pretty happy being degraded on prime-time television. The attendance record of every student has practically doubled, and all the teachers are discovering that, amazingly enough, they can give interesting lessons when they are being filmed. Even Mr. Potter has stopped being quite so sarcastic and is showing some enthusiasm for his Chosen Career. But Tree Man doesn't seem to recognize the benefits of competition. He is still protesting, has started to grow a beard, and looks distinctly unwashed.

Jocasta would approve.

HAYDEEZE PRODUCTIONS

TUESDAY, SEPTEMBER 28, 9:00 A.M.
TO: THE STUDENT CONTESTANTS
FROM: STORM YOUNG

So, my little survivors, here we are in Week Two!
You're going to be rewarded for getting through

the first hurdle with the chance to star in your own
sixty seconds of self-promotion. Yes, a whole minute
each of You, You, You! The idea is that every one of
you will be filmed in your favorite class with your
favorite teacher—you know, showing off your best
side. So whether it's blowing up the school in the
chemistry lab, making sweet music, or snogging at
the bus stop (just kidding!) this is YOUR chance to
shine and get your votes cranked up.

Half the items will be shown on Tuesday night
and the rest on Friday. LOOK AT THIS BOARD FOR
THE SCHEDULE.

Love ya!
Storm

TUESDAY, SEPTEMBER 28
5:30 P.M.

Have decided to have my sixty seconds in the library
with Mr. Webster. Hope that will get me one step closer
to St. Willibald's, by letting people see that I am serious
about Fulfilling My Academic Potential and working
hard and all that. It's going to be shown on Friday.

Did wonder about choosing Miss Moodie, because despite the fact that she needs help from Trinny and Susannah* on the clothes front, she is a real Serious Woman with Order, Purpose, Discipline, and all the rest, and I intend to be like that when I am totally grown-up. Only not the clothes. But in the end, it just had to be Orlando.

Wouldn't mind sixty hours in the library with Mr. Orlando Webster, reading poetry, telling him about my secret ambitions to go to Oxford,** looking into his soulful dark eyes, across a crowded desk . . . SO much more mature and interesting than anyone in our year, I mean, Marcus, or anyone like that.

Definitely.

7:05 P.M.

Had the dumbest lesson today with Amanda Knox. It was supposed to be history. Mr. Potter was hanging around "just tidying up these papers" (how convenient), about six cameramen turned up, and all the most revolting examples of Spotty Youth, who usually sit at the back with Tallulah, were practically killing each

*World's bossiest women.
**Classy university with towers and flowers, attended by Chelsea Clinton types.

other to get into the front row. None of them said a word all through the entire lesson, but just stared at Amanda, their little eyes hanging out like dogs' tongues. over on old dish of Yummy Bix.

Pathetic.

Amanda Knox might be big on Page 3 (Jocasta gets all Angry and Radical about newspapers printing photos of topless models like Amanda), but she got very confused on page 87 of our history book. Couldn't tell the difference between the Maginot Line[*] and a Visible Panty Line[**] if it was biting her on the bum. Funny thing is, Tallulah hates Amanda because, apparently, she's getting very, very close to Seth Dale in the Private Parts, so when the lesson mercifully ended, Tallulah said in a very loud voice, "No wonder the goat charged her rear end—it's so big he probably thought it was an invading army," and accidentally on purpose trod on Amanda's surprisingly large feet as she flounced out. And for one tiny, fleeting, fleeing second, I actually felt that I liked Tallulah.

But it didn't last.

...

[*]*Unconquerable defense, conquered in about six seconds.*
[**]*One of the Seven Deadly Sins according to Trinny and Susannah.*

Mega-stressed.

Jocasta had gone out with her All Men Are Pigs chums and Dad had sloped off to his study as usual. I was trying to get on with my French homework and ignore the fact that *Down The Bog* was on in normal households with televisions, and that not being able to watch it was driving me mad, when the phone rang.

"It's on, and you'll never guess who's being shown!" Vicki screamed in my ear.

"I dunno, Kelly up the tree with Weird Guy?" I screamed back.

"No, better than that. It's Marcus!"

Oh. Marcus. The one I'm trying to ignore.

"Ohhermm?"

"Yeah, it's brilliant! He's with Serena Dickinson in her sixty seconds at the drama club. Wow, Mrs. Schuman looks cool. Look, Serena and Marcus are rehearsing a scene; hey, they're good. . . . Oh, rats, it's finished."

"Ohhermm?" I managed again.

"Hate to say it, babes, but I think Serena might be

on her way to St. Willibald's after this. She's actually really talented, isn't she? I mean, not that you're not, of course. . . ."

Of course.

"Wait, hang on. It's Tallulah next; wonder what lesson she's chosen? She's so dumb she probably had to go for doing her mascara at break as her favorite school activity. No, hang on, it's PE of course. Doesn't old Cocky Rocky look pleased with himself? OH, WOW . . ."

"What? Vicki, tell me quickly!"

"It's Marcus again."

"Eerrmmph?"

"Mixed volleyball team . . . Tallulah's warming up with Marcus; she's showing off her moves . . . Now he's giving her a shoulder rub . . ."

Somehow it was worse hearing about it than actually seeing it. I suppose he was wearing his Go-to-Hell-Tallulah T-shirt as well.

"I'm really not that interested, Vicki," I snapped.

"She looks like something out of *Baywatch*,* and so does he. . . ."

*Swimwear parade pretending to be a drama.

"Vicki!"

"What is it, babes?"

"I really need to do my French homework . . ."

"Come on, Jen, don't you want to know what the competition is up to? Then you can blast back at them with your little highbrow chitchat with Mr. Webster on Friday . . . Oh, oh, look, it's the Electric Fish guy, you know, the one with the hair and the guitar . . ."

"You mean Will," I said. And I just knew what was coming next.

"Yeah, right. He's dyed it purple now, and he's talking about the band—hey, I can't believe it: Marcus is on again! Hey, the band is Soooo Gooood, I never realized . . . Jenny? Jennifer, are you still there?"

Yep, I'm still here. Still waiting for my turn. Still boring old Jennifer James. What can I tell people about myself? I can't act, or be on the team, or play in a band. I can't even look good. All I can do is sit in the library with a book and my English teacher. And there'll be no Marcus in the background of my mind-bogglingly boring Minute of Misery. Just row upon row of library books, that no one ever bothers to read.

Going to bed.

THE DAILY RUMOR

TV ROUNDUP

WEDNESDAY, SEPTEMBER 29

An intriguing new twist developed last night on Down The Bog, as the person who really caught the eye of the viewers was student Marcus Wright, filmed along with his classmates on the show. Producer Storm Young said, "This boy is really hot. The switchboard was jammed with calls, from young girls to old grannies, asking if they could vote for him."

Unfortunately, Marcus, who is a talented young actor as well as a singer-songwriter, is not actually taking part in the competition. Shandy P., mother and agent of one of the student contestants, spoke exclusively to the RUMOR after last night's show. "It's no secret that Marcus fancies my Tallulah, know what I mean? But then, all the boys do. It's a shame that girl Jones, or whatever her name is, wormed her way onto the show instead of Marcus. But she won't last long."

Another student and celebrity will be expelled on Friday.

...

5:10 P.M.

Everyone all over Marcus at school today. Tallulah clinging on to him like a bloodsucking leech. Must have been mad to think that he had even noticed that I existed.

This Is It. THE END. No more thinking about him, no more daydreams. From this moment on, Jennifer James is going to be Cool, Rational, and Realistic. Yes. Definitely.

Wish I had never, ever got involved. In the show, I mean. Hope I do get chucked out on Friday. At least then it will be all over and I can go back to being . . . what did Tallulah say? One of life's losers.

DICTIONARY: *Loser*, a person who seems destined to fail . . .

10:35 P.M.

Just wrote a brilliant analysis of photosynthesis for my biology presentation tomorrow. Can't believe I have been so self-pitying and pathetic. So what if Tallulah got Marcus to chuck a stupid ball around with her? I can't do that, so I'm not even going to try. From now on I'm going to be like, "To thine own self be true."[*] That's the important bit.

Okay, I might not be Miss Junior Prom, but I'm doing this for ONE REASON ONLY. Not to show off, or be popular, or get a boyfriend, or anything like that, but to GET TO ST. WILLIBALD'S. I have to keep focused on that. All I have to do is survive this Friday's vote and keep going one step at a time.

"Marchons! Marchons!"[**]

THURSDAY, SEPTEMBER 30
4:40 P.M.

"Marchons" to the nearest bridge and jump off it might be more appropriate. CAN'T BELIEVE Mr. Webster would behave like that! My whole sixty seconds was taken up by him reading from this poem he had written—"The Dead Voices"—and I was just supposed to sit there looking admiring! I could hardly be seen anyway, because he had his endless poem in a huge folder plastered over with his name, which he kept holding up to the camera in front of my face. The

---

[*]*World's best piece of advice.*

[**]*French National Anthem. Translation: Charge ahead and chop off the head of anyone who gets in the way.*

audience will just about see my left eyebrow trying to look intelligent.

Can't believe it, after I have worked so hard hard for him, when half the people in the class were making their copies of his Poem of the Week into paper airplanes. Stormed out of the library afterward and bashed straight into Miss Moodie wearing a revolting electric-blue sweater.

"Jennifer, you seem a trifle disturbed. Has anything occurred to distress you?"

I sort of mumbled that I was a bit disappointed with my filming for the show tomorrow. Was regretting not choosing her after all, despite the awful clothes, when she laughed this really weird, tinkly laugh and said, "Oh, I wouldn't worry about that, Jennifer; it's all in the Higher Hands." I must have looked blank, because she whispered, "Fate, Jennifer dear, Fate . . ."

Think the pressure is getting to her big-time. Oh, Lord, it's certainly getting to me. Got to go through the Abyss of Awfulness AGAIN tomorrow night!

...

EDUCATION
REVIEW WEEKLY

CELEBS STRUGGLE
TO MAKE THE GRADE

FRIDAY, OCTOBER 1

The much-criticized show *Down The Bog*, may in fact be a valuable tool in highlighting the demands of the teaching profession, claimed Mr. Hugo Harbottle of the Boarding Schools' League yesterday.

"Seeing these well-known, successful people struggling in the classroom may bring home to the public what a hard job teaching really is."

He is believed to have been referring to ex-footballer Nazzer McNally, who, although enthusiastic in his approach to the task, finds it difficult to communicate with the students. During his playing career he was notorious for his postmatch comments, which were largely unintelligible, even when subtitled in Standard English.

Asked if he was enjoying his stint at London Road, Nazzer commented, "Like I said, it's a game of two halves, like, and I should have went further, you know, like, in that chemistry, at the end of the day, but the move broke down in the second half, you know, when that test tube blew up, I was sick as a parrot, but it's massive, you know, giving it one hundred and twelve percent. Like."

The other celebrity who seems to be finding life tough at London Road is, surprisingly, Barbara "Barabbas" Beer, the outspoken feminist, who has strong views on education. She is currently refusing to teach any male students on the grounds that they are "natural oppressors," but the girls at the school don't want to be taught by her either.

"She's like a witch," said one year 9 student, who didn't want to be named. "And she said we were all brainwashed morons for wearing lip gloss."

Mr. McNally, Professor Beer, and fraudster Jeremy Lurcher were voted the worst three teachers in a poll in *The Daily Rumor* earlier this week.

Barry Hatter (UTC) continues his "tree protest" against the show, which will be broadcast tonight.

. . .

Midnight

Perhaps Miss Moodie is right; perhaps this is fated, perhaps this is, in actual real reality, the moment when Jennifer James stops losing and starts winning.

The top Abi gave me to wear on the show tonight is gorgeous. I will wear it and wear it until it is worn to pieces like Jonathan's "snuggly" blanket.

Ridiculously happy.

THE DAILY RUMOR

TV ROUNDUP

SATURDAY, OCTOBER 2

Another top Celeb was flushed Down The Bog *last night when lifestyle consultant Carrie Chaplin was given the thumbs-down by the voters. She had made herself unpopular with the other contestants, and the viewers, by complaining bitterly about the décor, food, and the standards of dress at London Road Comprehensive. "What were she expectin' then, like?" commented Nazzer McNally. "It's a school, man, you know, like, not a nobbin' fashion parade, at the end of the day, wotcha."*

In a surprise move, hunky student Marcus Wright was drafted onto last night's show by presenter Abi Sparkes, to read the nation's favorite poem, "How do I love thee . . ." by Elizabeth Barrett Browning, as an example of the school's literary activities. Gorgeous Abi then set the student contestants the challenge of writing their own love poem to be read out on next Friday's show.

Meanwhile, some of the celebrities seem to be coping better than others with school life. TV cook Celia Bunch has reorganized the school's kitchens and is single-handedly serving up gourmet meals to the staff and students every lunchtime, as well as taking on a hectic schedule of classes, and Sir Harvey Harvey has inspired the London Road kids to start a girls' rugby team, a boys' dance group, and a voluntary project to repaint the school buildings.

However, Jeremy Lurcher has been reportedly sneaking out of the campus to meet with friends for champagne dinners, whilst glamor queen Amanda Knox is considering suing her agent for sending her Down The Bog, saying, "If it wasn't for Seth, I'd be out of here quicker than you can say, 'Wazzle Me Happy.' "

3:30 P.M.

Slowly coming down to earth after Friday. Dreamed last night that Storm was taking a class on *Romeo and Juliet*. He made me dance in the ballroom scene* with Paul Johnson, whose hands were sweating so much that he was dripping over me like candle wax. So glad to wake up. Poor Paul, he does get a bit hot and flustered sometimes. Not about math or computers, though. He's brilliant at all that stuff.

Oh dreams, dreams. I thought I was being all Logical and Realistic and not indulging in useless daydreams, but I can't help it. I CAN'T STOP THINKING ABOUT MARCUS.

There, I've said it.

Just seeing him on the stage on Friday night, quietly saying those beautiful words . . . "I love thee to the depth and breadth and height my soul can reach . . . I love thee freely, as men strive for Right . . . I love thee with the breath, smiles, tears, of all my life!" You could have heard a pin drop, a heart beat, a tear fall silently down a lover's face. . . .

It was beautiful. I don't have the words for it. And

Renaissance rave where R and J get it together.

he wasn't like Mr. Webster, who puts on a special "poetry voice," which actually sounds a bit pompous now I come to think of it. He just said the words really simply, as if he meant them.

If Marcus ever said those words to one special girl, she would be the luckiest creature on earth.

4:20 P.M.

Vicki called. Marcus is going out with Tallulah. Paul told her. So That Is That.

I hate Sunday afternoons.

october 4-10:
this Love thing . . .

HAYDEEZE PRODUCTIONS

MONDAY, OCTOBER 4, 8:00 A.M.

TO: THE STUDENT CONTESTANTS

FROM: STORM YOUNG

Well now, that wasn't so bad, was it? And doesn't the public just love you? (Well, not all of you—we've lost two Bog flops already!)

Now, if you want to keep that LURV flowing our way (and all that lovely telephone money!) you know what you've got to do: get writing, scribbling, creating, copying, whatever, until we have some little poetic masterpieces to read out on Friday. Touch the hearts of the Nation and you also touch their wallets—hey, it's for a good cause!

Ciao babes,

Storm

Mattie and Maddie have made it up now that they are both off the show. Which is good. And they have joined Kelly's "JONS" (Jennifer James Out Now Society). Which is bad.

Have finished every scrap of homework as quickly as poss, so that I can start to write my love poem for Abi's "Challenge." This is surely something I can do better than Tallulah. Wonder what Rabbit Teeth is going to write?

The thing is, I have been thinking a lot about love. Yep, the big one. LLUURRVV. I thought that I loved Mr. Webster, but I'm not so sure now. I looked up *love* in the dictionary, and it said, "affection, warmth, fondness, liking, passion, desire, longing, infatuation . . ."

Have a sneaking feeling that my feelings for Mr. Orlando Webster come under the heading "infatuation." It's kind of an ugly word for something that felt beautiful. What Jocasta, in the days when she was Sheila-Mum, would have called a "crush."

But not love at all, really.

I've said loads of times that I "love" Vicki, though that's just "warmth, fondness, liking," and total gratitude that she wanted to be my friend when I arrived at London Road and no one else would be. I suppose she doesn't quite fit with Tallulah's "in crowd" either, with her grungy clothes and her mad mum in Mexico or wherever she is, but the great thing about Vicki, she doesn't seem to care what people think. And I really do love that about her. But deep down, I actually do care. I want to belong somewhere.

Perhaps you only really belong to your family. And when (if?) you get married, that person becomes your family too. But my family seems to be in such a mess at the moment. I mean, there's no one dying or in prison or anything, but it just doesn't feel right. Except Jonathan, of course. He always feels right.

Perhaps I should write the poem about him?

11:10 P.M.

No good. I can't seem to get any further than:

> *My little brother is so sweet,*
> *He has such cute and tickly feet,*
> *He smiles at everyone we meet.*

Which isn't exactly real poetry. Not quite Sylvia

Plath,* as Professor Beer would say, Lord, she is a Seriously Scary Serious Woman. No wonder they call her Barabbas.

Anyway, everyone would pee themselves laughing. "Oh look, here comes Jennifer James, the retard, who's never had a boyfriend, so she has to write about her soppy kid brother! Give it up for Jennifer James, who's never been kissed!"

It would be the super-ultimate Abyss of Awfulness. No Way.

11:45 P.M.

ABSOLUTELY DEADLY SECRET

This love thing.

I know that nothing will ever happen now with Marcus, but it's just that when I see him, I can't help noticing how the color of his eyes seems to change with his moods, and how he pushes his hair away when he's concentrating, and the way his smile starts slowly, then lights up his whole face, and when I think about the time he touched my arm, so, so gently, I do feel something. I do feel "warmth, fondness, liking,"

Brilliant, Doomed, Dead.

and all that, but there's more, a kind of longing. . . .

And I'm just not going to try and put that into words for other people to gawp and whisper and giggle over. Not even for Abi.

No Double Way.

THE MIDCASTER MESSENGER

CELEBS GOOD FOR OUR TOWN, CLAIMS MAYOR

Tuesday, October 5

Concern is growing over the continued presence of a protester, Barry Hatter, who is currently chained up a tree outside London Road Comprehensive as a protest about the filming of a television program at the school.

Reginald Shunter, mayor of Midcaster, claimed, "The arrival of all these telly people is doing wonders for Midcaster's economy. We've had coachloads of folk coming into town hoping to catch a sight of Amanda Knox hanging her washing out. This Hatter is just a nutter. And besides, it's downright unhygienic, under Bylaw 617, Disposal of Waste Water."

Other Midcaster residents are not so convinced that Mr. Hatter is in the wrong. A group of students at the school are keeping a vigil under the tree and ensuring that Mr. Hatter receives supplies of food and water. "He's trying to stick up for all the kids here," said Kelly Trundle, "not just a few pushy types who have wangled their way onto the telly." Local activist Mrs. Sheila "Jocasta" James has also lent her weight to Mr. Hatter's campaign and is organizing a candlelit "Procession of Protest" to coincide with this Friday's live show.

Haydeeze Productions have delivered a large crate of Wazzle Toilet Tissue to Mr. Hatter's tree.

TUESDAY, OCTOBER 5
7:35 P.M.

SHE'S AT IT AGAIN!!!

It would of course be my mother that has to leap to the defense of Weird Guy Tree Man. She is going to drive me literally and completely mad. Soon I will be gibbering and throwing packets of herbs around and drowning myself in the eco-friendly water feature in the garden, like Ophelia.*

Well, not exactly like Ophelia, but anyone who saw Mel Gibson's *Hamlet* in Mr. Webster's English class last year would know what I mean.

I wonder what Dad thinks of Jocasta doing all this? He said to me once that when he met Mum she was the funniest, prettiest girl he had ever seen. And clever, too. Strange to think of them being in love once.

She has gone out again with her Angry Women. No doubt plotting their next step in the Revolution Against Fun.

The only ray of light in the Horror Story of My Life is that Sir Harvey Harvey has started a Latin club at lunchtimes. It is totally brilliant. I thought it would all be *amo, amas, amat,*** and all that, but it isn't; it's about people and history and language and I LOVE it.

Teenage head case who throws herself into a river after singing some rude songs in Shakespeare's Hamlet.

**Translation: I love, you love, he loves.*

Caecilius est pater. Matella est mater.[*] I can actually understand some Latin! So cool.

Marcus was there too. *Amo, amas, amat*, and all that.[**]

Text messages 10/5

20:40: hey Viki wotz on bog sho tonite? Jen

20:42: Nazzer in 2dayz asembli. V x

20:46: o lord

20:49: exactement.[***]

11:05 P.M.

Mum back, all flushed and giggly. She really should lay off the cider.

11:10 P.M.

Wonder if Dad is still in love with her?

WEDNESDAY, OCTOBER 6
8:00 P.M.

Vicki said her dad has joined the Radical Reading Group, or whatever it is that Mum does on Tuesday night with her Witch Friends. Funny, I thought it was

[*]Translation: My father and mother have weird names.
[**]Translation: Can't stop thinking about Marcus.
[***]Translation: "He was a total disaster, wasn't he?"

just women, but they obviously think he is "right-on" enough to let him join. Must be the fact that he still dresses the way he did in 1976. (Vicki has the family photo album to prove it.)

Can't understand why he wants to go to Scary Women's Group. Vicki's theory is that because Hugh Grant* found himself a girlfriend that way, her dad thinks that he might. I pointed out that this only happened to H.G. in a film, not in actual real reality, but Vicki said her dad is so desperate he doesn't really care.

Perhaps some new clothes, a haircut, and a dating agency would be slightly more effective.

9:20 P.M.

Still haven't written my poem. Went to the library for inspiration (didn't find any) and I saw TALLULAH there as well. She looked like a poodle trying to learn to read in a hurry.

Surprised that she even knows that there is a library at London Road, let alone where to find it. There's a camera right over the Serious Literature section, so I

*Only slightly less beautiful than Johnny Depp.

sweetly asked her if she had seen any copies of *Poetry Now!* and she told me to drop dead.

Hope that goes down well with the public.

10:10 P.M.

Vicki just called to say Paul Johnson telephoned her (didn't realize he was in the habit of calling Vicki at ten o'clock at night) and told her that Tallulah has actually asked Mr. Webster if he would help her write her poem AND HE HAS AGREED! Can you get anything you want in this world if you have a large bosom? Are men really that stupid?

I sound like Jocasta. Whoops.

Paul has invited me and Vicki to his party. I think Vicki not-so-secretly likes Paul and wants me to go with her for some moral support. Paul is actually quite human, under the zits, so I will go for her sake. Hope someone will talk to me if they go off together, so that it won't be the usual Jennifer James Party Agony.

I suppose Marcus will be there, with his GIRL-FRIEND. Not that I care. I am never going to speak to him again.

...

Spoke to Marcus. I kind of got stuck next to him as we were lining up before Oggy Ogden came to give us a class. There are no cameras in that part of the corridor, thank goodness, and there was no Tallulah either. She had gone off for Advanced PE or something. Anyway, the class was late starting as Oggy has to use a Zimmer frame when he walks, and he was finding the stairs of G block hard to negotiate. Somehow, Marcus and I started talking.

"So are you an Oggy fan?" Marcus said.

I had to confess that I hadn't really heard of him before Dean Wiggins had gone on about him nonstop for the past three weeks.

"What? You don't know his band, Fallen Angels? They're like the godfathers of rock 'n' roll, you know; retro, but really cool, and Oggy's brilliant."

"But how can he still perform, if he's so, well, old and needing walking sticks and all that?" I asked, hoping it wasn't a totally idiotic question.

Marcus laughed, but in a nice kind of way. "That's the result of years of hard living. But when he's onstage and the adrenalin's going, he's awesome. He can play any instrument—guitar, drums, whatever—but when he sings, he really rocks."

Then Marcus started telling me about The Electric Fish and how he is really ambitious for the band, and their plans and everything, and he said, "You'll have to come and see us play: I'll fix it, if you like." And then he looked straight at me, green-eyed again, and added, "Jenny," very, very softly.

Would I like? Jenny would like very, very much. But I am NOT going to think about it. NOT, NOT, NOT.

Definitely.

That Oggy Ogden really is something else. Man.

FRIDAY, OCTOBER 8
5:45 A.M.

Have woken up in a panic. Still haven't written my poem about love for tonight! Can't believe that of all the things we could have been asked to do, it is my BEST thing—poetry—that hardly anyone else likes, and I CAN'T DO IT.

6:10 A.M.

Have been thinking. About what I said about Vicki

not caring what people thought of her. Have decided to write just what I want to say, without caring what ANYONE ELSE thinks of it. Got an idea for the first line, something like, "You drive me mad, but I love you. . . ."

Well, I'll give it a try. Lord knows what will happen. Actually my dear, I don't give a damn.[*]

THE DAILY RUMOR

TV ROUNDUP

SATURDAY, OCTOBER 9

"You drive me mad, but I love you,
You make me sad, but I love you,
You freak me out, but I love you,
You often shout, but I love you. . . ."

School swot Jennifer James got top marks when her poem, "You Drive Me Mad, But I Love You," brought both a smile and a tear to fifteen million viewers of the must-see show Down The Bog *last*

[*]*Famous last words of gorgeous hunk in your granny's fave film,* Gone with the Wind.

night. "I'd like to dedicate this to my mum," she said, before reading it out. Ironically, Jennifer's mum was outside the school building leading the "Procession of Protest" whilst Jennifer was describing the bitter-sweet mother–daughter relationship so perfectly. The full poem is printed in today's magazine.

Things didn't go so well for Lady Amelia Itchpole, who was wiped out by the Bog viewers. "I'm glad really," she said afterward. "I want to go and see Freddie and cheer him up. And then I've simply got to pop over to Paris to catch some of the fashion shows." Asked if she had enjoyed teaching, Lady Amelia said, "Is that what we were supposed to be doing?"

Oggy Ogden's classes are proving popular, as they consist entirely of him playing recordings of his greatest hits. "This is where it's at, man," he said on last night's show, adding, "Where am I?"

But the runaway favorites for the big title, King or Queen of the Playground, have to be Celia Bunch and Sir Harvey Harvey. The two contestants have formed a strong bond during downtime in the "Private Parts," and they are inspiring the students at London Road to new heights. Their latest project is organizing a concert at the school in aid of the children's charity

How Much Is That Doggie?

"We're calling it Bog Pop, and it's going to be absolutely super," said Celia, who was educated at Ascot Ladies' College. "All these boys and girls are so incredibly keen and talented when you give them a chance. How anyone can call this school 'bog-standard' is completely beyond me."

Viewers can watch all the preparations for Bog Pop on the live streaming, available on Haydeeze Digital.

SATURDAY, OCTOBER 9
10:20 A.M.

Just got back from recording an interview at school for *Happy Mornings with Roger and Julie.* Had to read my poem again, and they asked loads of nice questions about me and wished me luck on the show. And the poem is going to be printed in *Teen Queen* magazine!

The weird thing is that Jocasta doesn't even know, as she went straight from her "protest" thing last night to stay over with her ultra-feminist friend Molly McFadden, so that they could discuss Gender Issues over a bottle of nettle wine. Feel quite nervous about what she'll say. Hope it won't drive her to the Outer

Limits of Wrath, and all that.

I really hope she likes it.

The best bit about last night was that the poem Mr. Webster wrote for Tallulah was so incredibly long and boring that they had to stop her halfway through. And Rabbit Teeth's poem about Amanda Knox's outstanding assets was so rude that they had to stop him after about two lines. Perhaps that was why he was voted off?

But I'm still hanging on in there. Man.

3:15 P.M.

Jocasta hasn't mentioned my poem. Don't suppose she and Molly got round to watching *Happy Mornings* over their bowls of unleavened rice porridge this morning.

Bit disappointed. No—really, really disappointed.

I did try.

8:30 P.M.

I hate the way Storm behaves to Abi. Last night, in between filming, he was sliming his hand all over her gorgeous behind as if he owned it, like a piece of meat, as well as chatting up the production assistants, or girls in the audience, who have come to see Seth Dale actually, not Storm-in-a-tea-cup-and-a-tight-pair-of-jeans. And then he was even trying to smooth-talk Miss Moodie last night! I noticed them all bundled up in a corner together after the show. Miss Moodie was as red as a Bratz doll* with too much blusher on, poor woman. I mean, he's got ABI SPARKES for heaven's sake; he's only exercising his ego on the others. Hope Miss Moodie doesn't get her serious little heart broken by that creepy git.

Tallulah and Marcus were pretty much bundled up together last night as well.

SUNDAY, OCTOBER 10
7:10 A.M.

Had such a HORRIBLE dream! Woke up in total panic. I was in a huge room, about ten times bigger than the auditorium, and there were these big black cameras everywhere and millions of people shouting, "It's a fix! Jennifer James out now!" and all that sort

*Nightmare vision of the future of womankind.

of thing, but the weird thing was that they were all wearing masks to look like Mr. Webster. Then they started to charge at me and I was screaming for help and the only other person there was Marcus, but he was laughing and laughing, and then his face started to change slowly into Miss Moodie's. . . .

It was so, so freaky. Haven't felt as scared by a dream since I was Jonathan's age. Must go and get something to eat, even if it's sesame-seed porridge.

10:40 A.M.

Jocasta says dreams are the work of the SUBCON-SCIOUS MIND and can tell you about stuff that's worrying you, deep down. I can understand dreaming about being chased by cameras, because that's what it feels like at school sometimes, although I am not as self-conscious about them as when it all started. I can't imagine why I would be worried about a whole room-ful of Mr. Websters, though. Unless I really am in love with him after all.

I think the thing that is freaking me out is that, at the back of my mind, I still can't quite understand how I got on the show in the first place. When Kelly was screaming that I shouldn't be on it, I couldn't help kind of agreeing with her. I mean, it seems incredible that I got more votes than anyone in our year except Tallulah. Okay, maybe Dean Wiggins wasn't going to get many, but what about people like Lauren Pike and Nathan Wilson? They're reasonably popular. And what about Marcus? Why didn't he get on?

I don't get it. Perhaps they added up the votes wrong. Perhaps they'll discover the mistake and I'll be kicked off.

HELP!

October 11-17: Humiliation and Possible Death...

MONDAY, OCTOBER 11

4:25 A.M.

MEGA-DOUBLE HELP!

Two major Problems. First, Jocasta has really, really lost it this time. She's up the stupid tree as well now. SO EMBARRASSING, having to walk past her on the way in and out of school, and having to be filmed being embarrassed as well! Okay, making a nuisance of herself in public places for ridiculous causes, that's just her favorite hobby, like other people collect Cabbage Patch Dolls,* hey, I can just about live with it. But what I cannot, CANNOT cope with—are you listening, Lord?—is Problemo Numero Duo.

The thing is, Storm announced the next "Challenge" today. And army assault courses and Jennifer James just do not mix. No Triple Way.

...

*Toys designed specially to frighten little children.

5:10 P.M.

Really cannot do it.

6:05 P.M.

Will have to drop out of the show.

6:35 P.M.

Problem Number Three. If I drop out of the show, it will be a Moment of Victory for Tallulah. As official Queen of PE she can shin up a wall quicker than a snake in the grass and swing on a rope like a performing monkey. But I get dizzy just walking into the gym. I really can't do the assault-course, rope-climbing, wall-jumping, tunnel-crawling kind of thing. I just can't. And she knows it. She was going round all day like a cat with a personal dairy.

But if I do stick it out and have a go (there's a trial run tomorrow and the real thing on Friday afternoon), it will not only be the Abyss of Awfulness, I'll probably break my neck. Is St. Willibald's really worth this?

Have to think about this very, very carefully.

Will consult Vicki.

Vicki says if I walk out now, she'll never speak to me again. So I can either face Humiliation and Possible Death on prime-time television, or the prospect of Utter Loneliness and Misery for the rest of my school career.

Great.

THE MIDCASTER MESSENGER

PROTEST BRANCHES OUT
Tuesday, October 12

The row over Barry Hatter's occupation of a tree outside London Road Comprehensive intensified as his supporters, led by Mrs. "Jocasta" James, unearthed ancient bylaws (Forest Dwelling Land Act, 1792) to prove

that he has the right to reside in the tree. Mrs.
James argued that his "peaceful protest
against the cancer of trashy television" was a
perfectly legitimate activity.

She then spent yesterday in the tree with
Mr. Hatter, burning incense sticks and singing
Bob Dylan* songs.

TUESDAY, OCTOBER 12
8:25 P.M.

Another day of Hell in Bog Land. At breakfast I asked
Jocasta if she would PLEASE not sit in the tree again
with Weird Guy, as it turns my life into a major stress
zone. It's worse than the time she did her Green
Protest outside the nuclear power station and got into
the papers for throwing eggs at Dad. Anyway, she got
all purple and snappy and I got even purpler and snap-
pier, until we were in full-scale battle mode. Had a
really terrible row.

I said I couldn't believe that she would support this
lunatic whose biggest fan is Kelly Trundle—you know,
Mother, the weight-challenged hockey Amazon who is

---

*Certified genius, very deep and meaningful, very old and wrinkly.

organizing a one woman campaign against me? But of course, Jocasta wouldn't even know that, because she never bothers to ask me anything except Have You Done Your Homework AND she refuses to discuss the show.

"Which if you hadn't noticed, Jo-cast-a, is a huge thing in my life right now, and you didn't even bother to read my poem properly, and you know what? You DO drive me mad and I'm not even sure whether I DO love you! In fact, I'm pretty sure that I DON'T!"

Slam the door. Storm off to school. END OF RELATIONSHIP.

Better do my homework. "Describe Romeo's feelings for Juliet." Actually getting a bit hacked-off with *Romeo and Juliet*. It is so not reality. No one thinks I am the sun lighting up their life.

Not even my mother.

9:50 P.M.

Was tempted to write, "He has the hots for Juliet," in the style of T. Perkins, but no, I did my three sides of intelligent analysis out of loyalty to Mr. Webster, though I'm not sure he deserves it anymore.

When I got to school this morning, we had double science and Mrs. Stringer paired me up with Marcus to make a flowchart about Sexual Reproduction in Fish. Was concentrating so much on not looking him in the eye that I wrote on the sheet, "the female lays hundreds of eyes," instead of *eggs*, and Mrs. Stringer read it out afterward to General Ridicule.

After that went straight to Outdoor Pursuits Center of Doom. Decided that death/broken limbs preferable to being Entirely Friendless and Alone in the wasteland of London Road Comp.

Assault course wasn't as bad as I had thought it would be. Just a whole lot worse. Tallulah skipped her way round without getting a hair out of place, but Alice Redknapp didn't look too happy, and Dwight Thingummybob from Will's year was kind of struggling, especially when he got all his gold gangsta bling tangled in the climbing ropes.

But I was The Worst. Simply can't begin to imagine how I was supposed to get over a forty-foot wall, or whatever it was the others were all leaping over.

The only micro-miniscule ray of light is that we have all been assigned a Celeb as a personal trainer to prepare for the real thing on Friday, and mine is Sir Harvey. He is possibly the only person on the planet, apart from David Copperfield,* who could get me through this particular form of torture. Sir H. did some extra training with me in the gym after school and we are meeting again tomorrow.

Asked him how the preparations for Bog Pop are going and he said really well, with all sorts of amazing bands lined up to come! Wow-mega-wow! Then I said, "What if you are voted off before it happens?" (it's not taking place for a few weeks, as there is so much to get ready), and he said that he and Celia Bunch have agreed to stay up in Midcaster and organize the concert even if they aren't on *Down The Bog* by then, just because they think the concert is a good idea for the school, and for HMITD? of course.

They are more than Celebs. They are Stars.

Tallulah thinks the sun is shining out of her (artificially enhanced?) cleavage because her personal trainer is SETH DALE. Perhaps she'll be so wrapped up in mooning over his pretty face that she'll fall off the ropes into the mud. That would be so, so cool.

*World's only genuine living wizard.

Haven't seen Jocasta since this morning, as I went to Vicki's after training and she had already gone out with her Loveless Ladies group when I got home, leaving Dad in charge of Jonathan.

Vicki's dad was going to the Loveless Ladies thingy too. Seemed dead excited about it. Parents really are super-weird.

WEDNESDAY, OCTOBER 13
8:20 P.M.

Jocasta very, very quiet since The Row yesterday, which is probably when she's most dangerous, like a panther. Hasn't been near Weird Guy again though, so that's progress.

Still left with the problem of chucking myself over the assault course like Jonathan's Action Man[*] in front of Tallulah and a few other laughing millions.

Aching all over after training with Sir Harvey. Oh no—have just realized that all my feeble practice efforts will be broadcast! The gym is literally bristling with cameras, which go into overdrive whenever the girls' netball team has a match. It's awful not being able to have any secrets anymore. But at least Sir H.

Me Action Man. Me have big plastic gun and big plastic knickers.

was really helpful and showed me some techniques for climbing and jumping, and loads of cool visualization exercises. I mean, you imagine yourself scaling a ten-foot wall with supreme ease, and your body just follows and does it automatically.

That's the theory anyway.[*]

Sir Harvey said that they want local people and students to audition for a spot in the Bog Pop concert, as well as having professional bands. Decided to hang around the drama studio after training, because I knew that the drama club was on, and that Marcus would be there. I thought I might snaffle Marcus when he came out and ask if The Electric Fish planned to audition. If they did play for Bog Pop, it would sort of make me feel better about him not being chosen for the show in the first place. I just thought I would ask, that's all. Nothing special.

Anyway, when they all piled out, he was there, looking all bright and glowing, like a green-eyed angel. I couldn't help thinking that his hair is just long enough, but not too long, and just blond enough, but not too blond. Then he noticed me and I realized that I had been

[*] *Don't try this at home.*

staring at him with my mouth open. So embarrassing!

He looked kind of surprised, so I turned round to get out of there as quickly as possible. Then he called out my name, but I ignored him and walked off. I could feel the gob-smacked stares of Serena Dickinson and her super-babe drama crowd burning into my back, so I started running, then Marcus was running after me calling, "Jenny, Jenny," and it was getting ridiculous, so I had to stop.

For a moment, we just stood there staring at each other, slightly out of breath, with Serena goggling in the background.

"Um, hi," he said.

"Hi. . . ."

"So, um, how are you?"

"Oh, fine, except for this army-survival thing. Probably won't survive that."

He laughed. Jennifer James actually made him laugh.

"Yeah," he said, "Tallulah told me."

That kind of broke the spell and I turned to go, but he said, "Listen, Jenny, you know about the band—

we're going to this audition for Bog Pop, and you said you'd like to hear us play, so I sort of wondered, would you like to come and see us rehearse? You know, give us a bit of an audience—maybe some feedback?"

"What about Tallulah?" I forced myself to say.

He made a weird face.

"She's not really into our kind of music. I mean, she likes Seth Dale."

"Well," I said hesitantly. "If you're sure . . ."

And he looked straight at me and said, "I'm sure."

Wow mega-wow.

"So, Saturday afternoon at school? Mrs. Schuman is letting us use the drama studio. Okay?"

"Okay."

"Cool."

"Yeah."

Then he just stood there, and I could feel myself actually blushing, until Serena came up and dragged him away.

Okay. Cool. Yeah.

THURSDAY, OCTOBER 14
10:15 P.M.

IN SUCH PAIN! Not only aching in every single bit

of my body, after more training with Sir H. (he sure is tough when he gets going), my ankle is KILLING me where Tallulah whacked it with her hockey stick. I am NOT going to let her get away with this. Who does she think she is with her giant gazzongers and her pea-sized brain?

It was hockey practice and we had gruesome Mr. Rock again, as Sir H. was teaching Latin to year 12. It was raining, of course. I was just thinking that there can't be many things worse than hockey in the rain, and was hanging back in a "defensive position" (so that I could tell Vicki about what Marcus said yesterday) when Tallulah and Chelsea and Kelly came roaring up to me from the other end of the field. They drilled the ball to my feet, then came charging in, smacking into my poor wet legs with their hockey sticks. I was lying on the ground, groaning, and they were like, "Oh sorry, Mr. Rock, we were just going in for a tackle, you know, competitive play. Sorreee, Jennifer," and Mr. Rock didn't tell them off or blow his stupid whistle or anything!

Then Tallulah said in her best sugary voice, "Shall I take Jennifer to the locker rooms, Mr. Rock, and put a cold compress on her leg?" And he said, "That's very thoughtful, Tallulah." (WHAT!) "Yes, off you go." So she DRAGGED me all the way up the playing fields, smiling like a ministering angel every time we passed a camera, until we got into the locker rooms, which is, of course, off-limits to cameras. Then she dropped the smile, pushed me in, slamming the door behind her, and hovered over me with her hockey stick, like some primitive type from the Planet of the Apes.*

"Okay, James," she snarled, "listen up. Keep your scummy little hands off Marcus, do you understand? There's going to be no sneaking off to watch the band behind my back, all right?"

"What do you mean?" I said, trying to look unconcerned.

"What I mean is that you might think you're so clever, but you know what, nerd brain? You're as dumb as they come. Haven't you ever heard of digital streaming? Don't you know there's a camera right outside the drama studio? Me and my mum saw your touching little moment with Marcus and heard every word, so just back off! Or things could get nasty for you, James. Very nasty." Then she jabbed her horrible

*Tallulah's home base.

face right into mine. "You might want to watch your-self on the course tomorrow, because someone just might have got to your ropes and equipment before you. Hope you've practiced your crash-landing technique, Jen-nee, 'cause you'll need it."

And I believe her.

FRIDAY, OCTOBER 15
7:25 A.M.

My ankle has swollen up like one of Tallulah's overinflated assets. Really freaked out by what she said about the ropes for the rock climbing part of the course. She must have been bluffing. Or perhaps I should tell someone? Not Jocasta obviously, as all this is Totally Beneath Her, but perhaps I should tell Dad? Or Sir Harvey?

It's going to sound so dumb, though. "I think Tallulah's out to get me." Sounds like Jonathan and his baby mates in the playground. No one will believe me, and there's no filming in the locker room, so just when I need the evidence of her twisted mind to be caught on camera, it's like, impossible.

Oh, well, if Tallulah doesn't get me, the assault course will. Dear St. Willibald, I hope you appreciate that I am doing this for the sake of your fine educational institution.

And for Sir Harvey.

And for the Honor of Jennifer James.

Here goes.

5:30 P.M.

Honor satisfied. In agony. Off to the hospital.

THE DAILY RUMOR

TV ROUNDUP

SATURDAY, OCTOBER 16

Things are heating up Down The Bog, *as everyone got physical yesterday on a grueling army-style assault course. Each of the Celebs had trained one of the student contestants to tackle a challenging range of strength and agility tests. Blond teen queen Tallulah Perkins completed the course with flying colors and in record time. Her trainer, Seth Dale, said, "I'm very proud of her. We had some really hot* sessions in the gym. She's one to watch."

One to watch could also be young Jennifer James. Spurred on by her coach, Sir Harvey Harvey, she did finally get round successfully, to cheers from the spectators. "I thought she'd just about had it on the rock climbing wall; she seemed rather wobbly," confided Sir Harvey, one of the most popular of the celebrity teachers. "But she stuck to the techniques we had rehearsed and got through on sheer, old-fashioned guts."

According to the bookies, Jennifer's chances of reaching the final have dramatically increased since making her plucky effort whilst carrying an ankle injury. "It's nothing," she said bravely, "just something I picked up in hockey practice." Young Jenny later missed last night's live show as she was taken to hospital to have her ankle x-rayed. The Rumor's message is CHIN UP, JENNY— WE'RE BEHIND YOU!

Nazzer McNally didn't fare quite so well, as his student, Julie Postlethwaite, got stuck in a series of underground tunnels and the fire brigade had to be called in to dig her out. "Like I said, I don't know what went wrong, like, it's just that she's massive,

like, I mean, it's a massive task, we've give it a hun—
dred and twenty percent, but, at the end of the day,
it was a bit of a banana skin and, like I said, I'm as
sick as a parrot. Like."

He and Julie were later booted off the show in
the live vote. Nazzer could only manage to say, "I'm
gutted."

SATURDAY, OCTOBER 16
11:20 A.M.

Lying in bed still. Ankle feeling a bit better. Not actually broken, just badly bruised and strapped up. Jocasta brought me some homemade Witch's Brew drink earlier, but she is still being strangely subdued after last week's little bit of mother-daughter interaction.

Still can't get over yesterday. People actually cheered when I got to the end of the course. I've never felt anything like it, I mean, being a tiny bit popular, even if only for a day. Vicki was there, as we were all allowed to take a friend. She was great, kept encouraging me all the time, and I saw Marcus give me a little thumbs-up sign from Tallulah's corner before I started. As I went on through the course and it got tougher and tougher and my arms were aching and my legs started to shake (especially on the climbing bits) I could actually hear people shouting, "Come on, Jenny," and "You can do it."

It was the Outer Limits of Amazement.

They were all so, so nice to me, and when we got back to school to get ready for the show, Abi made a big fuss of me when she saw the bruises on my leg. She arranged for me to be sent home and for Jocasta to take me to the hospital to have my ankle x-rayed and everything.

Maddie from Year 9 called me this morning to say she was sorry about joining in with all that JONS business and that no one really wants to get me kicked off the show anymore. Except Kelly. Maddie was super-friendly and said she was actually glad she wasn't still on the show, because she would have freaked at the assault course. Funny, I freaked at first, but now I'm glad I did it.

Really mega-glad.

Text messages 10/16
12:50: Hey Jen, howz yr leg? Viki
12:53: Ok how r u babes?
12:58: Cool. in town. bmped in2 paul he

sed Mrcus sed he woz impressd u finishd corse

13:02: really?

13:05: totally

1:15 P.M.

Marcus was impressed.

1:25 P.M.

I am beginning to think that, in actual real reality, he does kind of like me. I know he is going out with Tallulah, which is one of Life's Mysteries, but surely he wouldn't say stuff like that and have come running after me the other day outside the drama studio if he didn't like me a teeny, tiny bit?

But maybe he only feels sorry for me. Maybe it's his beautiful nature just taking pity on Jumping Jennifer. Perhaps I should focus on the color of Dean Wiggins's eyes. Find someone more in my league to get fluttery over.

Because I am fluttery.

I really am.

Think I will get up now and go to the band practice, despite what Tallulah said. It's a free country and Marcus asked me, so he must have wanted me to go.

That's some kind of start, and Tallulah can't actually stop me, can she?

4:10 P.M.

Apparently she can. Got there (Jocasta insisted on me taking Grandpa's old walking stick to lean on) and could hear the music coming from the drama studio, but when I got close, I could also hear the acid tones of Tallulah joining in with the singing. Had to duck down and peep through the window—megaundignified— and there she was in full flight, lolling all over Marcus, stroking his hair, fiddling with his guitar strings and generally Guarding Her Property. And I thought, I don't care, I've as much right to be here as she has, I'll just walk in and say, "Hi, guys; hey there, Marcus, thanks for inviting me over." Easy.

But there was no Sir Harvey there to cheer me on this afternoon.

Gave up, gave in, came home.

8:40 P.M.

Marcus didn't actually look all that keen on being mauled by Tallulah. Interesting.

...

9:10 P.M.

Apparently Weird Guy Hatter is even more bonkers than I thought. Turns out that his childhood dream was to go to St. Willibald's and he's now demanding to be sent there to retake his O levels, or whatever.

Wonder if I will end up swinging in trees and gibbering, if I get chucked off the show, and tragically spend the rest of my life consumed with insane bitterness about St. W.'s . . . ?

Get a grip, Jennifer.

OctoBer 18-24:
That DRess...

HAYDEEZE PRODUCTIONS

MONDAY, OCTOBER 18, 9:00 A.M.

TO: THE STUDENT CONTESTANTS

FROM: STORM YOUNG

Hi-de-hi, my little beauties!

So four of you have gone off to the big black bog that is called Failure (just kidding!) and there are eight of you left, smelling of roses! And what treat has Storm got for you this week, I hear you ask. Well, concentrate, because it's a good one. After the mud, sweat, and tears of last week's Challenge, we thought it was time for a little elegance around this crummy joint! So folks—think fashion, frocks, and fun!

We are going to hold our very own Fashion (Victim?) Show, to be broadcast live this Friday night. Yep, I said LIVE. This is your chance to show how cool, hip, and buzzing you really are. All you have to do is bring in your favorite outfits from home, *rope in your friends to help with hair and makeup, and then strut your stuff. Oh, and you'll get some assistance from the Celebs, who have been assigned different tasks, with our resident style guru Julian Lambrusco-Llewellyn (and St. Willibald's old boy!) in charge as Artistic Director.*

So off you go and prepare for glamor glory!

I'm ready for my close-up . . . [*]

Storm

MONDAY, OCTOBER 18
4:40 P.M.

I actually got some fan mail this morning! Well, two letters, one from a slightly mad-sounding old lady and another from a little girl who says she hates PE at school too, but will try extra hard now that she has seen me complete the assault course. How cool is that?

HOWEVER, back to reality, all that was so last-week. This week's Challenge couldn't be worse. When I say I haven't a thing to wear, I really do mean, I Haven't a Thing to Wear.

---

[*]*Famous last words of mad old Celeb gone way past sell-by date.*

Tried to hover around all day to speak to Marcus and say sorry for not turning up on Saturday, but Tallulah was stuck to his side like a particularly nasty piece of chewing gum.

Now he will think I am some kind of rude, breaking-promises type of girl as well as—well, what exactly? What does Marcus Wright actually think of me?

What?

8:35 P.M.

Have been through my entire wardrobe. Didn't take long. Two pairs sensible shoes, three pairs sensible trousers, four sensible shirts, large quantity sensible knickers, pumpkin outfit I had when I was ten. . . .

Not looking too promising somehow.

9:20 P.M.

Didn't Mary Poppins make clothes out of curtains? Or am I mixing that up with someone else?*

9:40 P.M.

My bedroom curtains are still the ones with the My

*Please see page 5.

Little Pony design that I chose in primary school.

Not looking too promising at all.

TUESDAY, OCTOBER 19
6:40 P.M.

Saw Marcus very briefly after Jeremy Lurcher's so-called class. ("Write four pages on why I would like Jeremy Lurcher to be my MP.") Told him I'd had to look after Jonathan on Saturday afternoon. Couldn't face telling him the truth about creeping around under the window. Didn't think THAT would impress him somehow.

Marcus asked if I had been to the park with Jonathan and I pretended that I had, so now I am blatantly a liar as well as promise breaker, etc., etc.

Went to Vicki's after school and tried on all her clothes. Now, I have to say that Vicki looks great in her grunge gear with her cool Afro hair and everything BUT A) she is taller than me, B) my gazzonger department is considerably less developed than hers, and C) I REALLY don't think black and orange are my colors.

Her dad, Victor, came home in the middle of it and said to me, "Oh, are you planning a costume for

Halloween, Jenny?" as if I was about nine.

Then Vicki explained about the fashion show and he offered to lend me a T-shirt advertising his shop. Then he said he had to change into some "gear" as there was a "lovely lady" at the Radical Reading Group and he wanted her to "dig him."

Poor Vicki. Parents really are the Abyss of Awfulness sometimes, even when you've got only one of them.

11:20 P.M.

Think Jocasta must have been drinking or something. Or on some middle-aged crazed hormone treatment.

She got back from her Serious Night Out about half an hour ago, came into my room and whispered, "Jenny, love, wake up, I've got something here for you."

"Oh?" I said very cautiously in the dark. It sounded like she had forgotten our row, but you can never be sure.

"Something important."

I turned the light on and saw that she was clutching some kind of bundle. She plonked herself on my bed and started to undo it.

"I wore this at the May Ball,[*] when I went with your dad, when we were students." She sighed. "I thought you might like it, darling. Victor told me all about your . . . event."

I just stared at her, totally mind-boggled.

"You know," she said impatiently, pulling out miles of silky cream satin from the bundle, "your fashion show."

She is blatantly drunk, I thought. My mother and the words *Fashion Show* do not happen in the same room. But by now she was prodding me to try the dress on, so I dragged myself out of bed and climbed into this enormous puffy creation, with my pajamas still on.

"Oh Jenny!" she gasped. "You look so wonderful in it."

She pulled me over to the mirror, and it was weird. I looked sort of like those old photos of Princess Di,^{**} all puffed skirts and frilly neckline and shy expression. But I couldn't exactly see myself strutting down the catwalk in it, next to Tallulah dressed like J. Lo^{***} and me done up like the Great White Whale.

*Student party always held in June, don't ask why.
**Princess, Goddess, Angel.
***A totally different kind of Jenny.

"I can't actually wear this, Mum," I said slowly. "It's really nice of you and all that; it's just, like, you know, not fashionable anymore."

But I hated saying it when I saw her face.

And I really wished I hadn't said it when she burst into tears on me, all crumpled and sniveling and sad.

"Oh, Jenny, I thought you could . . ."—sniff— "and your poem . . ."—gulp. "I saw you on *Happy Mornings* at Molly's house and it's been on my mind ever since . . ."—sob—" . . . so beautiful. And then you said, you said"—sob, sob, snort—"you didn't l-l-love me . . . and it's only that I'm trying to have Principles and Express Myself and it makes you"—hiccup— "angry, and your father doesn't even take any notice, not even when I threw eggs at him, but Vict—I mean, some people"—gulp—"think that I'm a unique and special person . . ."

Victor? Victor? Since when has Vicki's dad been my mother's Personal Counselor?

". . . and I thought if you wore the dress it would be a mother-daughter thing . . . to show . . . to show . . . that you didn't . . . ha-ha-hate me," she wailed, "and to remind Eric of when we were"—hiccup—"young and"—blow nose—"happy. . . ."

"Okay, okay, Mum, I'll wear it."

"Really?"—sniff—"Actually on the show? *Down the Toilet*?"

"Bog, Mum; I mean yes, I promise, honestly, just please don't cry anymore. Okay?"

"Okay."

She calmed down at last, folded the dress up, and was about to totter off, when I said, "Mum?"

"What?"

"I do love you."

She turned to look at me, standing by the door, like when I was a kid and she used to come into my room to kiss me good night.

"Really?" she said.

"Totally."

And I meant it.

12:35 A.M.

It's just that now I've got to wear That Dress.

...

12:40 A.M.

Wonder if Marcus likes the 1980s extreme ballgown look.

WEDNESDAY, OCTOBER 20
6:40 A.M.

Terrible night's sleep. Feel exhausted—thank goodness it's half-term next week—BUT had BRILLIANT IDEA that came to me in a flash of inspiration.

Can wear the gorgeous top Abi gave me (why didn't I think of this before?) with my old jeans, which hopefully the cameras won't focus on, and tell Mum that I left her Barbie's Wedding Outfit on the bus. Or that one of the other contestants was sick on it before the show in a fit of nerves. Or that Barry Hatter snatched it in a moment of madness as I walked past his tree. He is deranged enough to do it, as he seems to have forgotten that he is supposed to be sticking up for Kelly and her JONS, and now spends his days chanting weird threats against anybody who has actually been to St. Willibald's.

At this rate, that's how I'll end up. So mega-stressed!

...

WEDNESDAY, OCTOBER 20
FASHION FRIDAY—IMPORTANT NOTICE

Everyone must provide outfits for the following
categories:

1. Beach Party
2. Chilling Out
3. Hot Date
4. Red Carpet

You may not wear ANYTHING you have already worn
on the show, on pain of death. Any event associated
with the Lambrusco-Llewellyn brand has to be
absolutely fabulous.

Bring all your outfits into school on Friday morning
for inspection and rehearsal. Anyone without
suitable clothing will not be allowed to go down the
catwalk, and that will obviously affect your chances
of attracting votes.

"Think Fashion—think Style—
think Lambrusco-Llewellyn."

L-L.

...

So much for my BRILLIANT IDEA. So much for Abi's lovely top. Really don't know what to do. Feel even more mega-stressed. Paul told Vicki that some of the blokes at school are taking bets on which girl is going to look the "hottest."

Wonder if that includes Marcus?

Actually thought about going to see Miss Moodie to complain about this "Challenge." What has wearing trendy clothes and tarting about in a fashion show got to do with deserving a place at the dream destination of St. Willibald's? I bet the students at St. W.'s don't traipse about in leftovers from Top Shop.* No, it's all bottle-green uniforms and school hats down there.

It's okay for people like Serena, who always looks as though she's stepped out of a magazine, and I suppose Tallulah will love exposing herself to public scrutiny, but what about Sophie Simpson in year 7? She's a really nice girl and she has tried really hard, but she's barely out of primary school. How can she "strut her stuff" or look "hot"? Or little Ollie

*Fashion Paradise.

Cotton, who's just happy in jeans and sneakers, kicking a ball around?

Was going to ask Jocasta about how best to Lodge a Complaint, but when I got home she was ironing her beloved Reminder of Youth for me and singing old eighties songs with a soppy smile on her face.

Just when I need Jocasta, I get Sheila.

6:20 P.M.
WHAT AM I GOING TO WEAR???

6:35 P.M.
Perhaps this is the moment when my fairy godmother appears.

9:40 P.M.
No sign of fairy godmother yet.

So far have got:

1. Beach Party—school swimming costume
2. Chilling out—old jeans and blue shirt
3. Hot Date—forget it
4. Red Carpet—the Thing From The Attic that my mother gave me

...

9:50 P.M.

Perhaps I could pretend to be ill on Friday?

Vicki heard that Chelsea and Tallulah are going to bunk off school tomorrow morning and go shopping with Tallulah's mum, who is planning to spend a big chunk of frozen-cabbage cash on a complete new wardrobe for darling little Talloola-woola.

What did Jocasta always say? It's the Inner Woman who counts? Well, my Inner Woman may be very, very beautiful, but my Outer Girl leaves a lot to be desired.

10:15 P.M.

Why, oh, why did I ever get involved with this stupid program? I'm blatantly not going to get through this week's voting looking like the Nerd of the North, so what will it all have been for? I'm no nearer to St. Willibald's than when I started. I wish I could go back to working hard and reading my books (haven't read any Serious Literature in weeks!) and admiring Mr. Webster.

But I can't. Something has changed. Something in me. I'm not prepared to be Jumping Jennifer, the sad geek in the corner, anymore.

I want to win.

And it's not just because of St. Willibald's. I want to prove something—to Marcus, to Tallulah, to Mr. Rock and all the rest of them. But most of all, to myself. And whether I have to dress up or dress down or climb walls or wrestle Tallulah in a tank of mud, I am going to do just that.

"Someday, somehow, somewhere. . . ." *

10:35 P.M.

Dad just got home. He came up to my room, gave me EIGHTY POUNDS (!!!) and said, "You can go shopping after school tomorrow—but don't tell your mum." Said he'd heard about the fashion show at work! Then he patted my head as if I was still Jonathan's age, saying, "Get something pretty, Jenny," and bumbled off again.

Thank you, thank you, thank you!

Darling Dad. I will save all my spare pocket money to get him a Christmas present that isn't socks.

10:50 P.M.

Eighty pounds is totally brilliant, but I guess it won't be enough to get all four outfits. Wonder what I should do?

Song about hope that ends in tears.

10:55 P.M.

Will consult Vicki tomorrow. Must go to sleep now. So tired. Can't wait to have a rest at half-term. Will spend every single day in bed.

Bliss.

HAYDEEZE PRODUCTIONS

THURSDAY, OCTOBER 21, 9:00 A.M.

TO: THE STUDENT CONTESTANTS

FROM: STORM YOUNG

Hi there, you little style stars! Hope you're all getting kitted out for Friday's Fashion Fiesta! Now read this carefully, because today's news is pretty mega and needs a bit of organization, so PAY ATTENTION!

Next week, you lucky, lucky Bog Babes are all going to be taken on a little half-term holiday with Haydeeze and your resident Celebs! Apart from the saddo booted out tomorrow, of course. (Just kidding!)

You didn't think we could leave the Great British Public for a whole week without some Bog activity on their television screens, did you? That

would be no good at all for those little old ratings,
so cancel your half-term study sessions, or plans to
lie in bed all day—we're off to them there hills!

Location: Mudley-on-the-Moors.

Activities: Camping, climbing, canoeing, pothol-
ing, anything muddy, together with cooking (over a
campfire), singing (round the campfire), snogging
(under the blankets). Hey—just kidding!

This is going to be a great-outdoors, crowd-
pleasing vote puller. Wonderful location, wonderful
weather, Amanda Knox in a tent—great TV! And—
don't forget—we're doing it for HMITD? and those
poor little sick kiddies.

Each of you can bring TWO friends to provide
some extras in the crowd scenes. Permission forms,
travel arrangements, and all such matters to be
sorted out with the Mistress of Ceremonies, Miss
Moodie, by Friday at 4:00 P.M. latest.

Okay, izzy-wizzy, let's get busy!

Storm

THURSDAY, OCTOBER 21
5:25 P.M.

So there goes half-term. I do think, as Barry Hatter

might have said, that Storm should be taken out and shot. And whilst I'm at it, Tallulah and Chelsea could join him. What gives them the right to behave like they did today?

Feeling all Angry and Radical.

At lunchtime, Vicki and I were sitting on that little bench outside the food technology room, talking about the Haydeeze Hell Camp next week. She wants me to invite Paul as well as her, as she's getting mega-excited about his party on Saturday, and I think he's getting mega-excited about her, too. Then she had to go off to the Caribbean Cookery Club that Celia Bunch runs (Vicki has promised her granny in Trinidad to learn how to make home-style rice and peas) and I was just quietly planning my shopping trip, when Tallulah and Chelsea emerged from nowhere like a couple of vampires and blocked my escape route.

"So we heard like your Dad coughed up some money for a big makeover for you?" said Chelsea. Everything she says sounds like a question. "So you think you're going to look pretty cool?"

I just ignored her, but Tallulah wasn't leaving it there.

"What was it he gave you? Eighty pence? Oh, yes, eighty pounds, right?" she said, and they both hissed their little hissy laughs like nasty geese. "Well, I've got news for you, James, and your boffin-brain dad: eighty pounds doesn't buy much these days, unless you shop in the charity store, of course. And it sure looks like you do."

More hysterical hissing.

"Oh, and it might interest you to know that my mum has just spent Eight Hundred Pounds on me this morning, and I'm going to blow you off that catwalk. Not that it would be difficult, anyway, James, you're so dumb and ugly, and how you ever imagined Marcus could be interested in a nerd like you . . ."

She went on and on and on. I'm not going to write it down.

The more she said, the more angry and helpless I felt, because if it hadn't been me she was picking on, it would have been someone else. The Tallulahs of this world have to find someone to kick to make them feel better about themselves. I didn't really care what she said about me, but it was what she said about Dad that hurt. It was as if she'd taken his lovely present to me and made it cheap and pathetic. And I just couldn't help it. I know it was the Ultimate Sign of Weakness, but I started to cry.

That seemed to make them pretty happy.

"Save some tears for tomorrow night, loser!" they said as they flounced off.

So there I was on my bench with a red nose and a handkerchief, trying to pull myself together, looking around to see if anyone was staring at me when I noticed something. High on the outside wall of the food tech room, there was one of Haydeeze's little roving cameras. And it was pointing straight at where Tallulah had just been standing.

7:15 P.M.

Yummy-ultra-delicious supper. Jocasta had made an old-fashioned casserole with real MEAT, let me repeat that, MEAT, and a huge chocolate pudding with not a carob bean* in sight. Wonder what's got into her? Is she unwell?

Anyway, Vicki found me after her cooking thing had finished and was such an angel when she saw that I'd been crying.

*World's most disgusting foodstuff—accept no substitutes for chocolate.

"Stuff them," she said. "You can get cool clothes really cheap. Who cares if Tallulah is dolled up like all the Spice Girls[*] rolled into one; she'll still look as ugly as a slapped butt." Vicki is SO good in a stress zone. Then she got a bit of paper out and wrote a list of what I needed to buy, and said, "Voilà!"[**] like a conjurer with a rabbit.

She had written:

1. BEACH PARTY: Sarong made from piece of material Vicki's granny sent over from Trinidad last summer. Artificial flowers in hair (approx £5).

2. CHILLING OUT: Decent new jeans (approx £25) with casual top (approx £15) and bare feet. Hair down.

3. HOT DATE: Same jeans, sparkly top (approx £15), strappy sandals (approx £20 in market). Hair up.

4. RED CARPET: Either Jocasta's retro gown, or Vicki's black dress with a belt to make it fit, with strappy sandals. Flowers in hair again.

Hair and makeup by VICKI, looking stunning by JENNY.

[*]Sporty, Baby, Posh, Ginger, and Scary Girl Power.
[**]Translation: There you go babes.

She made getting all the clothes look so fabulously easy, and it really, really was! Shopping with her was brilliant, and my new clothes are mega-gorgeous. Wish Dad wasn't working late tonight so I could show him.

9:25 P.M.

Funny really that clothes should be so important. This has all been more stressy than the assault course. Ridiculous really.

Jocasta is right. People should judge you for what's on the inside, not the outside. Clothes shouldn't matter at all.

9:35 P.M.

But they do.

FRIDAY, OCTOBER 22
Past midnight. Really Saturday.

Too excited to sleep. Hardly know where to start. Just want to lie here in my dress, hugging the whole day to myself again and again, like a beautiful secret, even though it did all go a bit mad at the end.

The first thing we had to do this morning was take our clothes to the auditorium to show Lambrusco-Llewellyn and have a rehearsal. Only missed geography and biology, but, hey, who's counting?

When I got to the auditorium, Abi came over and said, "I need a word with you, Jenny."

I couldn't imagine what she would need to talk about, and began to worry that maybe they had added up the votes wrong after all, and that this was the moment they were going to tell me. Abi led me right out of the auditorium into the funny little passage where I bumped into Marcus when all this started.

"We're okay now," she said, smiling. "There are no cameras here, it's a Bog-free zone."

"What's the matter?" I asked. Suddenly I felt really nervous.

"Jenny," she said, a bit hesitantly, "I'm only the presenter, and we're not supposed to take sides, but if this was my show, I'd kick that Tallulah off faster than she could press her remote control."

I must have looked amazed, because she explained, "I watched the digital streaming yesterday, as prep for today, and I saw that nasty little episode of her showing off to you about how much money her mum had spent on her clothes. The way I see it, these 'Challenges' are supposed to give everyone a chance to be good at something. It's not about how much money your parents have. Anyway, I thought you might need a bit of a boost after what she said, so I've had a whole lot of clothes sent over from my stylist for you to try on. What do you think?"

For one awful moment I thought I was going to cry again.

"Oh . . . Abi . . . ," I stammered, "thank you so, so much . . . but really, I did buy some nice things with my dad's money . . . and he'd be disappointed. . . ."

"If you don't wear them? Don't worry." She smiled. "We can mix and match."

So I actually went into her private dressing room and tried on all these amazing designer clothes! We decided to keep the sarong made from Vicki's granny's material ("original") and my jeans outfit ("just right"), but for the Hot Date section she picked out a gorgeous skirt and floaty top, with earrings and stuff to go with everything. And THEN, for the "Red Carpet" evening-dress part, she showed me the most eye-bogglingly beautiful dress, quite short and simple, but embroidered all over with the tiniest sparkly beads, so that it sort of shimmered like light on water. It was the most amazing thing I have ever seen and I could see that it would fit me. I wanted to wear it More Than Anything in the World, but something stopped me.

It was remembering the look on Mum's face when she'd said, "You will wear it, won't you, Jenny?"

"I can't wear this, Abi," I said slowly. "I'm sorry."

Then it all poured out about That Dress and Mum and everything, until Abi actually gave me a hug and said, "Good luck to you, Jennifer James. And, hey, if it's any consolation, I won't be the only one who watched Tallulah making you cry." She even gave me a card with her private phone number and said to ring her if I was ever worried about anything on the show!

Storm really does not deserve her. No double way.

Then I dashed back to the auditorium with all her gorgeous things and put them out with the rest of my clothes, just in time for L-L, as we'd been told to call him, to inspect them. Amanda Knox, who was supposed to be his assistant, looked totally bored, but he went mad when he saw Mum's dress.

"How simply, utterly fabulous!" he said. "This is real 1980s authentic vintage wear. This is so now! It will be the highlight of my evening-wear section. All we need now is a partner for you—ah, yes, you with the stunning Mohawk! We'll have you two together, such an interesting juxtaposition, Innocence and Experience . . ."

Hope all the people at St. Willibald's aren't like him.

I could not be a model. It would do my head in. But it was great fun to play at it for a day, and Will kept mucking around and making me laugh when L-L wasn't looking. And the actual show was Mega-Utterly Brilliant, despite what happened at the end, when mad Barry Hatter emerged from the audience and tried to kill L-L with a chunk of his tree.

There's one bit, the very best bit, before it all went totally insane, which I'll remember forever. It was when I saw Marcus looking up at me from the front row of the audience, as I came onto the stage in Mum's dress, with Will holding my arm like a crazy Prince Charming. Marcus had this strange expression on his face, sort of surprised, as if he was seeing me for the very first time. And just behind Marcus, pretending not to be there, was My Mum, with tears in her eyes.

But this time she was smiling.

. . .

THE DAILY RUMOR

BAN REALITY TV, SAYS PSYCHO PROF!

SATURDAY, OCTOBER 23

Reality TV can be bad for you, warns top mental health expert Professor Bruno Finkmann. "These shows encourage unhealthy competition and play on people's insecurities. This is clear in the case of Mr. Barry Hatter, whose erratic behavior can be attributed to his connection with Down The Bog, *despite the fact that he was not even a contestant."*

After trying to attack ex–St. Willibald's student Julian Lambrusco-Llewellyn with a large twig, Mr. Hatter broke down onstage, pleading, "Take me to St. Willi's." He was comforted by the show's presenter, Abi Sparkes, and then taken to a secure hospital by the authorities. All in all it wasn't a good evening for L-L, as he is known, as he was later "expelled" by the public.

The fashion was certainly upstaged by the passion, but some contestants still managed to make a mark. Gorgeous Serena Dickinson looked stunning in a series of outfits that she had run up from an old tablecloth. However, her schoolmate Tallulah Perkins didn't do so well in a collection of expensive but tasteless outfits.

"It was all too short, too loud, too much," said fashion expert Suzy Manky.

Tallulah is struggling to regain her initial popularity on the program, after she was filmed criticizing Jennifer James, another contestant. But Jennifer had shrugged the incident off, and looked radiant modeling a vintage ballgown, complete with a punk prince at her side. "Yeah, that '70s and '80s retro glam is really in," said Suzy. "And didn't Jenny look great?"

SATURDAY, OCTOBER 23
11:40 A.M.

Fell asleep without getting undressed and woke up being strangled by yards of cream satin.

12:10 P.M.

Only just got up. Don't know when I am going to do my homework as it is Paul's party tonight and we leave for the camp tomorrow afternoon.

History and French don't seem to have been so

important to me in the last few weeks, but I HAVE to remember that this is why I did all this in the first place, to get to St. Willibald's, and have the chance to STUDY.

Beginning to wonder what it would really be like at St. W.'s. I didn't think about that at first; I was just desperate to get away from London Road, and home and everything. But actually going to a boarding school, with a whole lot of people I don't know, not seeing Vicki every day, and Maddie and Will and Paul, and Marcus. . . .

It would be weird. I'm even getting kind of used to Tallulah being around as well.

Almost.

She looked pretty gutted last night, when she was SO not as gorgeous as Serena. After Mr. Hatter had been carted off at the end, I saw her march past Marcus and rush straight home with her mum, without speaking to anyone. Tallulah's mum looks exactly like Tallulah, but sort of boiled in Botox.*

Then Marcus came up to me and Will and said, "Nice work, you two," but Will dragged me off to have our photo taken before Marcus could say any more.

Really, really glad Mum was there to hear people

*Poison injected into your face to make your wrinkles disappear, as well as all traces of humanity.

saying "Well done, Jenny," and stuff. And she wasn't even waving a banner. She did go Jocasta-ish again afterward, though.

"You know I don't approve of this kind of thing, Jennifer," she said. "I only came to show some Female Solidarity with you in the ordeal of displaying yourself as a Fashion Object. And don't you dare tell your father that I came."

But she smiled as she was saying it.

1:05 P.M.

Just called Sophie Simpson to see how she was doing. She fell over in a pair of borrowed high heels last night and then got chucked off the show. I thought she might be upset, but she was dead chuffed because she won't have to go camping, which she hates, and her parents are taking her on a trip to Disneyland Europe[*] for half-term instead. And she says she is never, ever going to wear high heels again.

Very Wise.

...

[*]*Just like the real Disneyland, only it rains.*

Parents, honestly!

Mum had gone out to the park with Jonathan and I was trying to make some tea and think about getting ready for the party, when Dad came into the kitchen and said, "Ah," and "Oh," with his hands in his pockets. Then he said, "You can get a lot of nice stuff for eighty pounds then, Jenny?" and looked all pleased with himself, in a secretive kind of way. THEN he suddenly grabbed me and the tea, bustled me into the garage, where all his papers and computers are, and said excitedly, "Look under here." He lifted up a box that looked like a piece of computer equipment, but tucked away inside it was a tiny television!

"I watched you," he was babbling, "on the telly . . . my little girl . . . so pretty . . . my Jenny. . . ."

"Have you had this television all the time?" I demanded. "Since Jocasta's TV ban?"

"Well . . . um . . . yes . . . I suppose so," he muttered. "I wanted to watch the football, that's all, honestly."

All this hiding away in there to "work" and "write up notes," and he's been glued to the sports channel on a four-inch screen!

"Don't tell Sheila," he pleaded. "It'll only cause

trouble. And I want to carry on watching your show. So, it's our secret, Jenny? Please?"

I wondered what he'd say if he knew that she had been there last night, but as I had promised HER I wouldn't tell HIM, I had to promise HIM that I wouldn't tell HER. What a pair.

"You did look nice in that dress at the end, Jenny. Reminded me of something. Can't think what."

"Dad," I said. "You've seen that dress before. On Mum. Remember?"

And I left him in his garage, thinking about it.

11:10 P.M.

Survived the party. Will talked to me most of the time in the kitchen. We were just chatting about the show, then he started telling me about how his three older sisters tease him all the time about his hair and clothes, and about not being the lead singer of The Electric Fish, and not being as good-looking as Marcus and, worst of all, not having a girlfriend.

The things guys will tell you when they've had a couple of beers! I am never going to drink. Well, not beer anyway.

Surprised really, by what he said, because Will

always comes across as loud and noisy and confident. So interesting to find out what people are like underneath. Perhaps Tallulah is as sensitive as a little flower on the inside? Anyway, having Will talk for three hours about himself saved me from the usual PHE (Party Hell Experience).

Had to come home before everyone else as Jocasta insisted on collecting me ridiculously early. Left Vicki very, very involved with Paul. Didn't see Marcus and Tallulah. Think they were in the garden.

Hope she was cold.

Text messages 10/24
9:20: Hi Jen! Good newz—me & Paul r a team!
We got 2getha afta u left
9:23: hey Viki thatz brill!
9:27: p.s. Mrcus & T Perks splt up.

SUNDAY, OCTOBER 24
9:45 A.M.

They split up! THEY SPLIT UP!!! Must be a fairy

godmother out there, after all.

Got to get ready for camp.

11:05 A.M.

Everything packed, including thermal knickers and secret supplies of chocolate.

Asked Mr. Webster to recommend a Serious Book to take with me, to get into training for St. Willibald's, just in case. He gave me a copy of *Silas Marner*[*] by George Eliot. Only she was a girl. George, I mean, not Silas.

Why would anyone call a child Silas? It's almost as bad as Storm. Beginning to wonder what I ever saw in Mr. Webster.

11:20 A.M.

Wonder which of the teachers will get the most votes? Mrs. Woolacott has started to wear hideously revealing low-cut tops in an attempt to get voted out of London Road and into the *Love 2 Teach!* job. It is a truly Horrible Sight.

...

[*]*Cute Victorian tale with slow beginning and fantabulous ending, like a good party.*

11:35 A.M.

Wonder whether Marcus dumped Tallulah (totally understandable), or Tallulah dumped Marcus (totally unbelievable)?

11:40 A.M.

Dad's calling to say it's time to go.

Wonder where Mudley-on-the-Moors actually is?

october 25-31:
Total Mega-Failure...

MONDAY, OCTOBER 25
9:15 P.M.

In the middle of the moors.

Wind. Mud. Rain.

Rain. Mud. Wind.

Paul says Marcus finished with Tallulah, and Chelsea says Tallulah finished with Marcus.

We all went on a long hike this morning to "acclimatize to the conditions." Didn't see anything but rain, mud, wind, etc. Came back with sore feet and every micro-muscle screaming in protest, only to be faced with building a campfire to cook on. Storm threw some logs on the ground and told us to "go for it," then swanned off to the cozy country pub down the road.

Wish he'd go for it. Permanently.

Wonder what Abi sees in him? It really is one of Life's Mysteries. Perhaps all people in television are like that?

Anyway, thank goodness for Sir H. on the firebuilding front and, amazingly, Mr. Potter. He is here as one of the teacher "supervisors" and is a camping genius. If it hadn't been for those two and Celia, we would have starved tonight.

It's strange being away from school. Somehow, we feel much more like a group, all in it together. There are the seven of us who are left in the show: Serena and Alice Redknapp from year 12, Will and Dwight, and Tallulah and Me. Oh, and little Ollie Cotton from year eight, PLUS everyone's guests. I have brought Vicki and Paul (so cute together!), and Tallulah brought Chelsea *naturellement.*[*] At least, it's nice to see Chelsea getting rained on. AND, weirdly, Tallulah invited Dean Wiggins. What as, I ask myself, a bodyguard? Apparently Kelly is furious that Tallulah didn't ask her.

Serena ultra-perfect Dickinson has brought her kid sisters.

As well as Mr. Potter, there's Mrs. Clegg, our ditzy blond geography teacher, and Mrs. Schuman, the head of drama. I've always been a bit scared of her, partly because I am hopeless at drama, which seems cunningly designed with the sole purpose of making you look ridiculous in front of the rest of the class (I can

Translation: She is like SO predictable.

actually manage that without help, thanks very much) and because she is the only female teacher at London Road who could possibly be described as Cool.

The filming is different here. There aren't as many fixed "spy" cameras (nowhere to fix them, apart from the odd tree and tent pole) and there are more actual camera people, who seem really nice. The crew and the production team are staying at the pub, with log fires and hot baths and hearty dinners, whilst we are Camping in the Wild. Except for Jeremy Lurcher, who sent ahead some of his "people" to put up a tent just for him, which is the super-luxury Ultimate of the camping world. It has a king-size bed, a loo, and a cocktail bar, and can probably fly too. Amanda Knox is suddenly being very friendly with him.

Oh, and Will has brought Marcus.

10:25 P.M.

The floor of this tent is very hard.

10:35 P.M.

And cold.

10:40 P.M.

Vicki says will I put that torch out for heaven's sake and go to sleep?

11:55 P.M.

It's not that easy.

12:25 A.M.

Will try and read my Serious Book under my sleeping bag.

TUESDAY, OCTOBER 26
5:20 A.M.

Fell asleep over *Silas Marner* with my torch still on, so batteries are nearly dead. Will have to be careful as only brought one set of spares.

Feel as though Kelly Trundle has been walking all over my back all night long. Can hear the rain outside. And some sheep in the background. And some birds waking up.

Wonder if Marcus is awake yet?

...

7:20 A.M.

TV woman with purple hair (still don't know her name) came round at crack of dawn and took away all supplies of chocolate, sweets, and cash. Said they would be returned later. Tried to hide a jumbo Mars Bar down my welly, but she ferreted it out. This does not look promising.

She told us to assemble outside the pub at 8:00 A.M. to read the day's notices, which will be posted up there, then went off to storm the other tents. No mention of breakfast. Campfire has gone out. I think breakfast will probably be at the pub. Lovely sausages, lovely bacon, lovely fried eggs.

HAYDEEZE PRODUCTIONS

TUESDAY, OCTOBER 26, 8:00 A.M.
TO: THE STUDENT CONTESTANTS
FROM: STORM YOUNG

Good Morning, Campers!

Ah—The Great Outdoors! So folks, this is Survival Time, and in order to survive, you will need your wits about you, so READ, UNDERSTAND, and OBEY!

You may have noticed the lack of breakfast arrangements this morning, my little hungry ones, but don't worry, things can only get worse. You'll each be given a basic set of rations every day, but if you want any hot tasty grub, you'll have to work for it!

All you contestants and your lovely young friends will be split into three teams, known as FEED, ME, and NOW. There'll also be Celebs and a teacher with each team. We have three activities arranged (it's all so perfectly clever, isn't it?) which are A) Climbing B) Potholing and C) Canoeing. For the next three days, starting today, each group will take a turn at each activity. Every day, your mission will be to find your team's FEED ME NOW meal ticket, which will be hidden on the top of the moors, or in an underground cave, or in the middle of that rushing, rocky river. And remember: no Meal Ticket, and you'll be left with cheese sandwiches for your supper. But if you find the Ticket, you find a feast!

Neat, hey?

Oh, and to keep you busy in the long dark evenings, your lovely drama teacher Mrs. Schuman

will be rehearsing an Entertainment for you to per-
form to the Celebs on Friday night, and they'll return
the compliment by performing for you. And for the
Public, of course! Ratings have never been so good!
So get hunting. I'm off for breakfast.

Storm

7:40 P.M.

Am going to memory-erase what we had to do today, as it was All Too Horrible. Thought the countryside was supposed to be beautiful, not a barren waste. By the time we got halfway up the stupid mountain, I could have happily committed murder for a bowl of Jocasta's dandelion soup. Finally, Ollie Cotton found the MEAL TICKET. Ha-ha, so witty hiding it in a pile of sheep droppings. Whoever thought of all this is seriously sick. Oh, and I guess that would be Storm Young. Think someone should launch Operation Find Abi a New Boyfriend.

Was praying that Tallulah would be on a different team, but hey, Isn't It Ironic,[*] we are stuck together on the "ME" team. Should be called the "What About

---

[*]*The world according to Alanis Morrisette.*

181

Me, Me, Me?" team with Tallulah around. I have NEVER heard so much whinging. Still, it serves her right for thinking she can go camping in a denim miniskirt and thigh-high boots.

Thank you, Lord, for all the sensible clothes that Jocasta has thoughtfully provided for me. She is not only Serious, but very Wise. Especially on the thermal underwear front.

I am not on Marcus's team, of course. He is in "FEED," which is Double Ironic, as Dwight dropped their ticket over the side of the canoe on the way back upstream, so they were stuck with sandwiches. Vicki and I tried to sneak a plate of our "hot tasty grub" (looked like standard-issue-all-purpose-camping-stew to me) over to Paul and Marcus's tent, but were stopped by Purple Hair Woman, who really is a bit of a rottweiler.[*]

"NOW" were taken potholing by Mr. Potter. He got them in and out of those caves in record time, and came back to camp with their ticket before the rest of us had hardly started. We had Mrs. Clegg with our team, who was worse than useless. Kept

[*] *World's Scariest Dog.*

going on about geological formations and making us go the long way round to admire them. Also cursed with Barbara Beer, aka The Mad Professor. She now refuses to speak to anyone. Apparently no one in the show is on her Cultural Plane.

Got to go and rehearse for Mrs. Schuman's "Entertainment." Perfect end to a perfect day. Not.

Oh, none of this matters really. The point is that Marcus is Young, Free, and Single, and so am I (surprise, surprise), and What Am I Going to Do About It?

10:35 P.M.

Drama is fantastic! Why did I never realize this before? Perhaps pretending to be an Ancient Briton round a campfire under hundreds of stars is different from double drama in a cold classroom.

Have somehow never been to one of Mrs. Schuman's classes before. When I joined London Road, everyone had already chosen their Creative Unit subject and I went for art, as potentially less embarrassing. But she is brilliant! Feel Totally Inspired. Our entertainment is going to be sort of King Arthur* meets

*Sword-in-the-Stone guy.

Greek tragedy.* Oggy is providing weird background music for it by drumming on the cooking pots. Wicked.

Wonder how he managed in his canoe without his Zimmer frame? Jeremy Lurcher didn't go out on any of the activities. He has hurt his back, apparently, and has to stay inside his tent. Sounds a bit too suspiciously convenient to me.

11:15 P.M.

Have to say Serena Dickinson is a mega-amazing actress. She and Marcus were definitely the best and have been given the leading parts. Had absolutely no chance to get near him. He and Serena were hanging around afterward talking to Mrs. Schuman, and Vicki was admiring the stars or something with Paul behind the stores tent, so I had to go and talk to Will. But eventually it was just too cold to bear, and I staggered back to my tent to get into the so-called warmth of my sleeping bag.

Wonder how Mrs. Schuman manages to look so chic in subzero temperatures? Don't think my Outer

Fate, Horror, Wailing, and Death.

Girl is improved by camping conditions.

Wouldn't surprise me if Marcus and Serena realize they are totally perfect for each other, rehearsing under the starlight and all that. In fact, I would say it was pretty much Inevitable.

Or do I mean Ironic?

12:05 A.M.

The ground just as hard as last night, funnily enough.

12:15 A.M.

Can't sleep. Will have another bash at old *Silas*. Perhaps Tallulah would lend me her *Hey!* magazine tomorrow to read instead? Or then again, perhaps not.

Apparently she is going round saying that Marcus is a "stupid, immature schoolboy" and a "loser with no musical talent." She now spends every spare minute hovering round Seth Dale, hoping that he will notice her.

If there was ever a National Society of Losers With No Musical Talent, then Seth Dale would be voted in as Life President.

5:10 A.M.

Stayed awake until two in the morning reading *Silas Marner*. It is getting fab, especially now poor old Silas has adopted the little girl Eppie. So mega-cute! Weird names though.

Must get some more SLEEP. Don't know how Vicki does it on this lumpy ground, but she is snoring like a baby.

Glad she's here.

7:25 P.M.

I do not like camping.

7:30 P.M.

I do not like canoeing.

7:35 P.M.

I do not like Tallulah Perkins.

She DELIBERATELY paddled her canoe into mine this morning, so that I went out of control and dipped right under the water. Not only did I nearly drown (Minor Detail), I was totally soaking wet and freezing all day after that, AND we didn't even find the ticket.

186

Absolutely mega-starving. Cheese sandwiches some-how not sustaining in Camping Conditions.

Vicki was allowed a phone call home. (Hoping I will get one tomorrow—we weren't allowed to bring cell phones.) She said her dad, Victor, just went on and on and about this "groovy chick" he has met at Jocasta's book group thing. Vicki wondered wasn't he going to ask how she was, and he said he didn't need to—he could watch her 24/7 on the digital. And when was she going to introduce him to her boyfriend?

11:55 P.M.

Think something has happened on the Marcus front!

After rehearsal (I am part of the chorus of wild wailing women surrounding Serena's Tribal Queen) he came over, in that lazy laid-back way of his, to where Vicki and I were chatting with Paul and said, "Hey, I hear you didn't get your meal ticket today."

I had forgotten about that in the excitement of rehearsing, but when he said that I suddenly felt crush-ingly hungry again. He looked around to see if any cameras were near, before whispering, "Come over to our tent in five minutes." Then he and Paul strolled off, all mega-casually, leaving Vicki and me staring at each other. So then we started to wander over to our tent, as if we were going to bed, but carried on and skirted up round the field to get to Marcus and Paul's tent from the back, without anyone else seeing us.

It was a total squash to get four of us into a two-man tent, and even though Paul and Vicki cuddled up together to make more room (I do think Paul is getting better-looking now that he is In Love and Vicki has given him something for his zits), it was still pretty cramped and I couldn't help sort of leaning against Marcus a little bit. He smelled of clean grass and wood smoke and something wild and outdoors-ish.

There was even less room because Marcus had his guitar case out, and I thought he was going to play some music, but when he opened the case, it was crammed full of snacks and sweets and cereal bars and stuff. Old Purple Head hadn't bothered to check there. Vicki and I fell on them like pigs, and we were all laughing and joking and stuffing our faces. But when we'd had enough, Marcus took hold of my hand and pulled me toward the tent flap.

"Come on," he said. "I've something to show you."

We scrambled out of the tent and he slung his guitar on his back and KEPT HOLD OF MY HAND as we walked to the edge of the field. Then we climbed the wall and walked away from the sounds of the camp and the crew and the people still talking round the fire, up toward the lane that leads to the pub. We crossed the lane and followed a little path that went through the edge of some scattered woods. There was no one around at all. From the other side of the trees we could hear the sound of water, and the land kind of sloped away, so that down below we could see the river glinting in the moonlight, and it was so weird, like a picture cut out of old black-and-white film, flickering light, then dark, then silver.

"Cool, hey?" Marcus said. I was really, really conscious of his hand sort of cupping mine, purposeful but gentle, and I couldn't think of ANYTHING to say except, "I think you are totally gorgeous and I'm probably going to faint," which would not have been Wise, so I just sort of murmured, "yeah, cool . . ." in my best village-idiot style. He laughed and unslung his guitar, so of course he had to let go of my hand then.

We sat on a little crop of rocks above the river and Marcus strummed quietly as a cloud went over the moon. We talked about the camp, then somehow got to talking about our families. I knew Marcus lived with his mum, and I thought she was divorced, but Marcus said that his father actually died when he was little. Awful. He worked at the power station in the day and played in a struggling rock band at night. But one night, he was driving back from a gig really late to get home to Marcus and his mum, and he crashed. They think he must have fallen asleep at the wheel.

"That's why music is so important to me," Marcus said, "and why I wanted to be on the show, in case anyone saw the band and liked us."

"Oh Marcus," I said, "I'm sorry—"

"Hey, don't worry about it," he said abruptly, and changed the subject. I hoped I hadn't upset him talking about his dad.

Then Marcus said he didn't know how I could stand having the cameras around all the time, and that even at camp he found them really intrusive and annoying. I suppose I've got used to it.

I said, what if you do become a singer, or an actor, you'd have to be on television and stuff then, and he said it would be different, because that would be for a purpose, to act or sing or do an interview, not just sticking cameras into people's faces and lives. Then he played some more and I just listened, and after a bit, he started to sing very, very softly, and I realized that he was singing something about, "She's not like all the others, she's nice to little brothers, she's one among the many. . . . Oh, Jenny, Jenny . . . "

I didn't know whether he was joking, or sending me up, or what, so I looked at him and he looked back at me, as if he was concentrating really hard, really looking at me, not simply skimming his eyes over me, like most people do. Then he put his guitar down and moved up closer to me, but just at that moment Jeremy Lurcher crashed through the trees in front of us on the way back from the pub and said, "Good Lord, I must have a pee," so I got up and ran like crazy back to my tent. There are some things in life I really don't want to see, and Jeremy Lurcher in Bathroom Mode is definitely one of them.

But what would Marcus have done, if that hadn't happened?

Would he have . . . would he have kissed me?

1:10 A.M.

Cannot get the hang of this sleeping on the ground thing.

. . .

1:15 A.M.

The moon is really high and bright outside. Everything looks sharp and incredibly still.

The countryside really is beautiful, just like they said. Mega-beautiful.

THURSDAY, OCTOBER 28
4:45 A.M.

Will die if I don't get some sleep. Starvingly hungry as well. Even a cheese sandwich would go down well right now.

4:50 A.M.

When I say I don't want to go potholing, I really do mean I Don't Want to Go Potholing.

5:10 A.M.

I mean, look what happened to Julie Postlethwaite on the assault course! Took them three hours to cut her out, and that was only a pretend tunnel. I might get stuck in these caves For Ever, then it will be good-bye, St. Willibald's, and good-bye, Marcus.

And good-bye, Jennifer James.

...

Just had a ME team talk with Mr. Potter about what to expect today. Professor Beer kept interrupting about how she had climbed through much more difficult caves in Australia. Wish she had stayed there. THEN Miss Smug-Bottom Perkins presented Mr. Potter with a signed doctor's note (where did she get it from?), saying that she suffers from claustrophobia and mustn't go anywhere near the blasted caves. Instead, she has now got her wish and been put into FEED, with Seth (and Marcus!) for a nice stroll up and down the mountain.

WHY DIDN'T I THINK OF THAT?

THE DAILY RUMOR

TITTLE-TATTLE TIDBITS

THURSDAY, OCTOBER 28

The RUMOR's *reporter Dick Ratcliff braved wind and rain to catch an interview with the Celebs from* Down The Bog, *as they enjoyed a break from school in the remote countryside of Mudley-in-the-Moors.*

"It's absolutely super," said Celia Bunch. "It takes me back to being a Girl Guide in my Ascot days. And Harvey's old army experience is proving very valuable in a tight spot."

Someone else who also seems to be in a tight spot is Amanda Knox, whose flirtation with Seth Dale has been filling the gossip columns. She now seems to be transferring her affections to suave smooth-talker Jeremy Lurcher. Which way is the blond beauty going to turn? "Seth is what I call gorgeous, but Jeremy's a true gent. He says he will lend me his sleeping bag any time I fancy it."

Asked if she was enjoying the countryside, she said, "It's disgusting, innit? Why can't they cover it up with some shops or something that people really want?"

Oggy fans are concerned about the hazards of outdoor life for their hero, but he is managing to keep up with the students by going up and down the hills strapped to a quad bike. "Man, this is blowing my mind. I've seen the future, and it's raining."

Celia Bunch and Sir Harvey remain neck-and-neck favorites to win, followed closely by Oggy.

...

AM STILL ALIVE! Feel like dancing round the campfire in celebration, like Mrs. Schuman's primitive types, but just had three helpings of stew so better not.

My opinion of Mr. Potter has shot through the roof. He was so cool, and he really helped Professor Beer when she had that panic attack in the final tunnel. I closed my eyes the whole time and held on to the back of Will's waterproofs all the way round.

The NOW team didn't find their ticket and watched us eating every mouthful of hot and tasty, as they miserably munched their sandwiches. Storm made the cameras go right up for close-ups of them looking hacked off. Totally mega-sick. And FEED haven't come back yet.

It's really dark. Hope they are okay. Wouldn't mind losing Seth and Tallulah, but Marcus is in FEED too.

7:20 P.M.

They're not back yet. Probably just Mrs. Clegg being dippy that has delayed them. Better get ready for rehearsal.

8:25 P.M.

Rehearsal canceled. Search party from local Rescue

Center being sent out. Mr. Potter and Sir Harvey going with them. Storm insisted that a camera crew go as well, despite Rescue Person not being happy about it.

"This is a serious matter, sir, not light entertainment," I heard him say. And Storm smiled and said, "Oh, I'm deadly serious. Just keep those cameras rolling."

What did Jocasta say about Scummy Depths?

8:45 P.M.

Have been told to pack our bags and go down to the pub. Think if they don't find the others we will all be taken home. Miss Moodie hurtling over here apparently.

Oh, Lord, this is real now. Please help.

INTERNATIONAL PRESS SERVICE—NEWS FLASH 9:40 P.M. GMT

... Rescue teams searching for the missing school-children. . . . Popular show *Down The Bog* reports absences. . . . Teachers and crew members believed to be with them. . . . Celebrities Amanda Knox and Seth Dale also currently missing . . . Statement expected soon. . . .

...

Can't bear this much longer. Am sitting in the ladies' room at the pub to get away from everyone. Dean Wiggins is driving me mad, trying to sneak into the bar and get served with alcohol. Who cares about a stupid pint of beer at a time like this?

When we got here, Mrs. Schuman took everyone into a couple of private rooms at the back, where we could dump our things. A woman from the pub came in with big plates of baked potatoes and bowls of soup, and huge mugs of tea. So at least the NOW people have cheered up a bit.

Feel sick. Just want to see them all again, even Tallulah.

When Vicki and I were having a cup of tea with Paul just now, he suddenly blu jt, "Marcus finished with Tallulah because of you, Jennifer."

I stared at Paul, totally stunned, and he went on, "He said it was when she was mean to you, about your clothes or something. Marcus hates anything like that. He only went out with her because she kept on asking him." Then Paul clammed up again and went back to looking deathly.

Marcus finished with Tallulah because of me.

And now he's missing.

. . . Missing children found in neighboring village . . . all safe and well. . . . Amanda Knox
refuses to return to camp. . . . Show will go on,
insist producers. . . .

11:20 P.M.

Back in tent.

Might have known Mrs. Clegg had something to
do with it. Will drop geography at soonest possible
opportunity. Apparently she led them the wrong way
and they ended up in the next village, where Seth Dale
bought them all a four-star meal in a local restaurant.
Then he ordered a fleet of taxis to bring them home
and tuck them up in bed at half past ten, but Just
Forgot to Let Anyone Know.

GOING TO BED.

12:20 A.M.

Impossible to sleep. Thank goodness brought
Silas and torch.

Hate camping.

. . .

6:05 A.M.

Last day. Thank you, Lord.

7:35 A.M.

Just been to the so-called shower block with Vicki. (Tent with buckets of freezing water and old bit of soap.) Saw Alice Redknapp from the FEED team. She said that on their expedition yesterday Tallulah ignored Marcus the whole time and Marcus walked with Serena (oh no!) while Tallulah tagged behind Seth all the way, which started to annoy Amanda Knox. She tried to drop a few hints to shake Tallulah off, but Tallulah is hint-proof, which I do kind of admire about her sometimes. So Seth had Amanda AND Tallulah chasing him up and down the mountain like wolves after a lamb. And THEN, in the restaurant where they all went to stuff their faces, whilst the Entire Nation searched for them, Tallulah threw a glass of water in Amanda Knox's face! Amanda stayed the night in the village somewhere and hasn't been seen since.

Apparently Miss Moodie is furious with Tallulah as she is a Disgrace to London Road. Storm is delighted because she is Great Television.

Wonder what family fun is in store for us today?

HAYDEEZE PRODUCTIONS

FRIDAY, OCTOBER 29, 8:00 A.M.
TO: THE STUDENT CONTESTANTS
FROM: STORM YOUNG

Wakey-wakey, rise and shine!

So, this is the last day of Camp Bog, and haven't we had fun! And we're in every single newspaper this morning, thanks to the lovely Mrs. Clegg! Great navigating there, Mrs. C!

Now, we need to keep the pot boiling, so we have a great day planned. It's a Down The Bog Survival Special! Today, instead of looking for your MEAL TICKET, you will be looking for your MEAL. Yes, that's right, tonight you'll be eating whatever you can pick, gather, or catch! So no more cheese sandwiches—prepare for a feast!

Equipment will be available, under the supervision of your teachers, of course. Health and Safety regulations will be carefully monitored. So go grab an ax!

And don't forget, you will be performing your Entertainment live on our special Camp Expulsion Show tonight.

Happy hunting!

> *Catch one for me,*
> *Storm*

8:25 A.M.

Think I'd rather just go hungry than go and find food in the hills. What are we supposed to do, kill little birds and rabbits? Or pick someone to be ritually sacrificed, like Iphigenia?*

Now there's something you could volunteer for, Talloola-woola darling.

8:45 A.M.

Apparently Amanda Knox is back in camp, but has gone straight to Jeremy Lurcher's luxury tent, and they are both refusing to come out. Oh well, nobody will miss them. Wish they would invite Professor

Girl with unpronounceable name in Fate/Death/Horror Greek tragedy—see page 184—who was murdered by her own dad so that he could go traveling. Well, it made sense to him. Then her mum murdered the dad in revenge. Then her brother murdered the mum in revenge. Then—you get the idea.

Beer round there as well.

Have been put in a "hunting pack" with Sir Harvey. Thank you, Lord.

And with Marcus.

6:10 P.M.

Had the most brilliant day. Fishing is Truly Awesome. Okay, it's not very nice that the little fishes Get Done In at the end of the process, BUT at least they are swimming happily around until the Moment of Doom, not like those awful battery egg places where the poor chickens never see daylight and their feet fall off because they are standing on wires. Jocasta gave me a whole lot of newspaper articles about it and it is TRULY DISGUSTING AND WRONG.

No, it's different for fish. There they are, swimming in their beautiful river in the beautiful countryside with the beautiful autumn sun shining on them, until WHAM! they're whipped out and dead before they've had a chance to notice it, and on their way to Celia for cleaning and cooking. At least that's the way with Sir Harvey.

It was just great. The weather was gorgeous after days of rain-mud-and-wind. The sun was shining in a cloudless, pale blue sky, but it was cold and crispy enough to know that you were out on a wild hillside and not stuck in some grotty town (like Midcaster). And there was Marcus, concentrating on his fish and casting his rod like a handsome pioneer type. Wanted to run over to him and say, "Take me away on your wagon, cowboy," but it would not have been Wise.

For once, I felt totally relaxed. There was only one cameraman with our group and he was dead keen on fishing, so he spent the whole time filming Sir H. and the trout or whatever, and left us alone. Vicki and I were chatting with Paul and Marcus, or just being quiet if we felt like being quiet. Marcus kept bringing me worms for my hook and checking my nets for me. Doesn't sound very romantic really, but it was somehow. The whole group seemed mellow and happy, doing something simple outside, and it wasn't about fashion or competing or getting worked up about any of that stuff. It just felt right, being busy with Nature, and whenever I looked up I could see Marcus on the other side of the stream, looking back at me and smiling.

Have the strangest sensation, like a gentle bird fluttering around inside me, that something might happen tonight. And that Marcus feels the same.

Dean Wiggins was with Oggy's group. They got a bit carried away trying to catch a wild rabbit, so Dean has managed to get a hunting knife buried in his foot and has been carted off to the nearest hospital. Storm sent a cameraman with him in the ambulance, *naturellement.**

Then Serena told us that Alice Redknapp, who for some Entirely Incomprehensible Reason likes Dean, got hold of another cameraman and did this whole ranting speech into his live feed about how badly organized the camp has been and how she's had nothing to eat but sandwiches for three days and how there's nothing for supper tonight but raw fish AND that London Road Comprehensive should never have been allowed to be on *Down The Bog* AND that it's nothing to do with our education AND that she's studying for A levels and hasn't been able to concentrate on her work at all AND that the school should be investigated by the Minister of Education. So now Miss Moodie is furious with her as well as Tallulah.

Got to go for supper and the Entertainment. It's

**Translation: What a sicko.*

weird to think the live show will be broadcast tonight and people will be voted off. All that stuff seems so far away, despite having the crew here with us. I'm really sorry anybody has to go. I hope it's not me, but it's funny, I don't actually care that much right now.

I've got my mind on bigger fish.

11:35 P.M.

Kind of disappointed. No, in fact I'm Extremely, Totally, Utterly Disappointed and will probably Never Recover.

But the fish tasted great. Celia showed us how to grill it over the campfire whilst the Mad Professor insisted she was doing it all wrong and that it should be buried in the ground in The True Bush People's Traditional Method, or whatever. The herb-and-mushroom sauce Professor Beer's group had gathered and made was pretty disgusting, but everyone was so hungry that we ate it anyway. Oggy's lot hadn't actually found anything, but said they'd had a wicked time chasing stuff, and Oggy sent for a whole lot of Coca-Cola from the pub for everyone, which was against Storm's rules, but hey, you don't mess with Oggy. And Dean Wiggins had been stitched back together and insisted on coming back to camp, so even Alice was a bit happier.

Mrs. Schuman's Entertainment was fab, really fun to do and so atmospheric, with the starlight and the glow from the fire and Oggy's amazing drumming and occasional howling in the background, which fitted brilliantly with the primitive incantation stuff we had rehearsed. All the other Celebs (except Lurcher and Amanda, who still haven't emerged) and the crew, and a few locals who had sneaked in to watch us, clapped and cheered and it was great.

And as I looked around at everyone smiling and joking and congratulating us on the performance, it didn't feel like the last few weeks had, it didn't feel like winners and losers. I felt part of it, part of the team, surrounded by friends. Vicki of course, number one always, but Paul was there too, and Will, and Serena and little Ollie, and I was in the middle of it all. Belonging, for the first time ever. Even Tallulah wasn't hassling me, as she was hanging on to Seth's every word whilst Amanda was out of the way. It was as if I didn't feel like Jumping Jennifer anymore. I just felt, like, totally myself. Jenny.

And mega-wonderful, on top of everything else, there was Marcus. All through the evening I was aware of him being aware of me, and I kept thinking, It's really going to happen tonight, I know it is.

But it didn't.

Oh poo, my batteries are finally running down.

Can't see to write.

Will have to . . . oh, blast.

THE DAILY RUMOR

AMANDA DUMPED IN BOG!

SATURDAY, OCTOBER 30

In a shock vote last night, Amanda Knox was booted out of the Bog Camp after a display of the sulks. She had been holed up in Jeremy Lurcher's tent, and refused to appear on the Friday-night live show, after a spat with one of the student contestants and an apparent bust-up with her former Bog Buddy, Seth Dale.

Media watchers were surprised by the results, as despite her recent temper tantrums, the up-front girl-about-town is a popular figure. By contrast, Jeremy Lurcher and Barbara "Barabbas" Beer are widely deemed to be the least liked contestants, yet they are still surviving Down The Bog.

School starts again for the remaining celebrity "teachers" on Monday, and everyone will be throwing themselves into preparations for Bog Pop, scheduled to take place in two weeks. Who will still be singing a happy tune by then, we wonder?

Full details in TV Roundup, plus YOUR chance to win FREE tickets to Bog Pop! Turn to page 12 now!

SATURDAY, OCTOBER 30
12:30 P.M.

Utterly mega to have a bed and a bathroom again. Think Jocasta was totally wrong about washing. You can't get enough of it.

2:30 P.M.

Clean at last!

Still feel a bit low about last night. I mean, I'm glad

to be on the show still—poor Alice Redknapp was in floods of tears about being voted off. Vicki's dad said she cried all the way through her postexpulsion interview last night. So at least I haven't had to go through that, and it's great to be home (Jonathan was so cute and happy to see me), but it's just that everything went wrong with Marcus.

After we had done our Entertainment last night, the Celebs had to do theirs for us. Have to say they were pretty dire. Barabbas Beer did Lady Macbeth's* Sleepwalking Scene** in a peculiar accent that she said was authentic Elizabethan (Mrs. Schuman looked totally unimpressed). She nearly walked into the campfire with her eyes closed (authentic being-asleep acting). Even the camera people were trying not to laugh. Then Seth Dale sang the World's Worst Song, which he had written himself *naturellement*.*** It was all about "I'm so fondie of my little blondie. . . ."

Excuse me whilst I puke.

Amanda and The Lurch didn't show up, which was probably a merciful release. Celia and Sir H. dressed up as Justin and Britney and sang together and made

*Mad baby-murderer type with Blood On Her Hands.
**In which she walks around Madly, trying to Wash The Blood Off.
***Translation: So there's no one else to blame.

everyone laugh, bless them. Then Oggy got out his battered old acoustic guitar and played, and it was truly Awesome.

After a while he asked Marcus and Will to join him, so we all sat around the campfire as they played. We sang along and Serena did brilliant little solo bits, but Marcus was looking at me, not her, and I have never felt so happy in all my life.

Eventually Oggy tottered off to his tent with his milk and biscuits, and the camp sort of broke up, but some people said they were going for a walk to see the river in the moonlight. Marcus came over to me and said, "Are you coming, Jenny?"

I nodded and thought my heart was going to burst. I wanted to skip and dance along instead of just walking quietly, and I couldn't stop smiling to myself. I felt as though anyone who saw me would know that I was on the edge of something amazing, as if there was a great light shining out from me and dazzling everyone.

A group of us set off, under the stars, in the direction of the river. I was there and Marcus was there and it was Perfect, except every time I tried to walk next to Marcus, it seemed that one of the camera guys was there. It was the nice one who had been sweet when we were fishing, but boy, did he seem fascinated by me and Marcus walking in the moonlight. Every time Marcus tried to edge closer to me, he just snaked in closer on the other side with his ginormous lens, until I was clamped in between them both like a piece of ham in a sandwich.

We reached the river and everyone drifted off into couples except The Three of Us. Marcus and I stared at the water in silence, whilst I prayed that Dean Wiggins would jump into the river, or that Tallulah would start a fight with Amanda, so that old Stephen Spielberg would take his camera out of my face and go and film someone else instead. Marcus was kind of scowling and turning his back on the camera and I was beginning to feel totally desperate as the minutes wasted away, when Miss Moodie did her popping-up-from-nowhere act. She was waving a flashlight around, blowing on a whistle and jabbering on that it was late and everyone had to go back to camp and she was coming round to do a tour in five minutes and anyone not in their own tents would be in her office first thing on Monday morning. So the Romance of the Night was pretty much trampled on and That Was That.

Total mega-failure.

Even this morning on the bus coming home, Will jumped on and sat next to me on the seat I was secretly saving for Marcus and talked nonstop all the way back. A good thing he did really, as I was too upset to say much. I didn't even get the chance to say good-bye to Marcus, as I was dropped off the bus before him.

I'll NEVER have such a perfect chance to be close to Marcus again. There was music and moonlight and starlight and I was sure that he was going to kiss me, that he really wanted to, but IT DIDN'T HAPPEN and now probably never will. Think perhaps I do hate television after all.

Fed up. Actually feel quite sick.

Better lie down.

3:55 P.M.

Been thinking about the Dismal Failure of last night again (and again and again), and have remembered about something weird that happened, before we did the Entertainment.

Mrs. Schuman had left some of the props in her tent and asked me to run and get them. It was already dark by then, so at first I didn't see Miss Moodie and

Storm talking together near the staff tents, but whilst I was inside Mrs. Schuman's tent looking for the props box (she was sharing with Mrs. Clegg, who seemed to have left the entire contents of her bag tipped all over the place), I heard them arguing outside.

I heard them saying things like, "But it's so good for the ratings." That was Storm of course. Then Miss Moodie said, "I don't care; I want the cameras off her, and as for that other one, she's out the door." Then I couldn't hear, as they seemed to walk off a bit, so I grabbed the box and slipped out of the tent. I tried to get a bit closer without them seeing me (it was really dark), and I heard Storm say, "Okay honey, she can go, but you'll have to stick to the plan and be patient. Anyway, the viewers lap up all that stuff, and you know what happens every time people vote." Then I must have stepped on a twig or something, because Miss Moodie spun round and spotted me. She was really snappy, like, "Don't let me find you in staff quarters again, Jennifer," which was kind of weird, as she's usually nice to me in her own spooky way.

Wonder what they were talking about. Strange that he called her "honey." Though I suppose that he calls every female "darling" and "angel" and "tootsie" and all that. *"Hasta la vista, baby,"** as Dean Wiggins would say.

Oh Lord, I feel so, so sick.

SUNDAY, OCTOBER 31
7:10 A.M.

Think I'm going to die.

Translation: What a mega-plonker.

November 1-7:
What is going on...?

MONDAY, NOVEMBER 1

6:25 P.M.

Think I have died.

THE DAILY RUMOR

BOG STARS STUCK
ON BOG!

TUESDAY, NOVEMBER 2

A mysterious illness has struck down the contestants on
Down The Bog. *Celebs, students, and teachers are
all suffering with tummy troubles after last week's
camping capers. It's thought that rogue "mushrooms"
eaten as part of the Survival Challenge were in fact
poisonous toadstools, causing a gut–busting reaction.
The finger of blame is being pointed at Professor*

Barbara Beer. "I told Barabbas, I mean Barbara, that they wasn't mushrooms, but she never took no notice," Seth Dale is reported to have told the doctors attending the sick Celebs.

Jeremy Lurcher and Amanda Knox are the only ones not to be laid low. "I'm well out of it," said the lovely Amanda. "I wouldn't eat anything that old witch served up. I reckon she's trying to poison the opposition."

Asked about her relationship with Seth Dale, she pouted, "Oh, I've gone right off him. And his new record is a bit of a bummer, innit?"

WEDNESDAY, NOVEMBER 3
1:30 P.M.

Just beginning to feel human again. I will never, never, never eat another mushroom as long as I live, even if it comes with a personal guarantee from Mother Nature.

Will came round to see me this morning on his way to school. Really kind of him and all that, but I couldn't face it. Told Mum I was feeling too grotty to see him.

4:20 P.M.

I seem to have had this worse than some of the others. Vicki called. She went back to school today. So did Ollie Cotton, Dwight, and Serena. Dean Wiggins only threw up once on Sunday morning, then sat down and ate his Sunday lunch as normal. He must have insides made of iron, like Robocop.* I am feeling slightly better though.

Wonder how Marcus is? Vicki said he was still off school. Wish I had let Will come up now, to find out if he had any news of him.

4:35 P.M.

Wonder if I should call Marcus? Would he think I was being pushy? We were getting on so well at the camp, surely he wouldn't mind? Haven't got his phone number, but could get it from Paul. Or Will. But then they would know I was calling him. Blast.

4:40 P.M.

Wonder why he hasn't called me?

...

*Improbable metal policeman, half man, half can.

THE DAILY RUMOR

TV ROUNDUP

THURSDAY, NOVEMBER 4

Down The Bog *is in danger of going down the pan, as the majority of the Celebs and students are stuck in bed, only getting up to go to the toilet. There has been very little live action this week, as Jeremy Lurcher was the only Celeb able to report for teaching duties.*

It now seems unlikely that there will be an expulsion vote this week. Storm Young, the show's producer, said, "Don't worry, though, folks, stay tuned, as we've got some great Bog News being announced on Friday's live show. See you then, Bog Babes!"

However, Storm Young might be in for a stormy time himself, as the Minister for Education, Deidre De'Ath, has stuck her oar into the murky waters. "This show is a disgrace. Children lost, knife wounds, food poisoning—it's all exactly why this government is planning to ban school outings. Who was in charge of Health and Safety Risk Assessment?

*What's going on at London Road? Where's the head
teacher? We need immediate answers and we need
them now."*

*In spite of this bad publicity, the troubled show's
sponsor, Wazzle Toilet Tissue is making the best of the
situation. The company is planning a new advertising campaign featuring the Celebs' current problems.
The slogan will be "When you gotta go, you gotta go
Wazzle!"*

THURSDAY, NOVEMBER 4
2:50 P.M.

Spent all day in bed reading *Silas Marner*. Eppie is
grown-up now and in love with Aaron and it is dead
sweet and simple.

Why can't Life be like Books?

5:10 P.M.

Vicki came round. That "lovely lady" her dad met at
the Wild Wailing Wimmin's group is Jocasta.

Beginning to get very worried about my mother.
One minute she's protest-marching, the next she's
chatting up my best friend's dad! What Is Going On?

Oh, Lord, I feel sick again.

7:25 P.M.

Dad just came up to say there was a phone call from Purple Head to say ALL contestants MUST go in to school for the live show tomorrow night, however bad we are feeling. Apparently Storm thinks that being ill is a crime against ratings, and we have to do something to keep the audience interested. Must suggest synchronized vomiting to him. Though he has probably dreamed that one up already.

Felt so bad when I saw Dad. Wonder if he knows that Victor has got the hots for Mum? Wonder if Mum knows? She did go on about him that night she gave me her dress. I really hope Vicki is wrong about this one.

8:10 P.M.

It's Bonfire Night tomorrow and Jonathan has been begging for sparklers and firecrackers. Think it's awful really, celebrating poor old Guy Fawkes being hung, drawn, and quartered,* but don't suppose that part has sunk in with Jonathan yet.

Feeling a bit better on the chucking-up front. Actually looking forward to going to school tomor-

*Very horrible history, sad but true.

row and seeing everyone. As in, seeing everyone including Marcus Wright.

FRIDAY, NOVEMBER 5
Bonfire Night 11 P.M.

Might have known Storm would come up with another form of TORTURE. I can't carry on doing this. Army assault courses, potholes, mountains, fashion shows, toadstool dinners, and now, The Ultimate Horror.

Singing.

THE DAILY RUMOR

TV ROUNDUP

SATURDAY, NOVEMBER 6

Haydeeze Productions pulled out all the stops last night to transform their damp-squib show Down The Bog *into a firecracker, after the usual Friday-night expulsion had to be postponed. Whilst the Celebs struggled back onto their feet after a week of heavy Wazzle usage, luscious Abi*

Sparkes announced a tempting lineup for Bog Pop, the musical extravaganza planned by Celia Bunch and her soul mate Sir Harvey Harvey as a Down The Bog *fundraiser for How Much Is That Doggie? Major stars are due to jet into London Road for next Friday's live event, and Seth Dale is also keen to perform.*

Oggy Ogden will make a rare live appearance, and it is partly thanks to his contacts that the eager-beaver pair have been able to attract such a glittering cast. Sir Harvey's charitable work over the years has also earned him friends in high places, and it is rumored that there will be a Royal presence at the show.

Local bands, choirs, and youth music groups have also been invited to participate, and Abi revealed that all the student contestants will have to sing a song during the concert. Will the presence of international stars be an inspiration or an unbearable pressure to the young hopefuls?

The next live vote will be held at the end of the concert. So book your seats in front of the telly for Friday night!

...

SATURDAY, NOVEMBER 6

10:20 A.M.

Just woke up and remembered. Oh, help!

10:25 A.M.

Cannot sing. Cannot sing. Cannot sing.

10:30 A.M.

Am not going to think about it. Going back to bed.

10:35 A.M.

Permanently.

2:20 P.M.

Suppose I'd better get up. Jocasta is yelling from downstairs that I have to get out of bed.

It was so weird, the show last night. There was no vote, so it all felt a bit flat. Celia wasn't there, as she is still feeling really poorly. Probably Barabbas gave her a double dose of Death By Toadstools on purpose. But Sir H. was there, looking a bit thinner, and Tallulah looked really rough. Apparently she was sick six times in a row, all over her mother. Will was there, joking and messing around as usual, but Marcus wasn't in the audience. He wasn't in school yesterday either. Paul says he's been mega-ill. Hope he is okay.

Perhaps I could send him a get well card?

Or I could go round to his house and say, "Please don't die Marcus, you are the Light of My Life."

Perhaps not.

Anyway, to jolly things up, Storm had arranged a huge fireworks party in the school grounds, and the fireworks were brilliant, totally spectacular. There was mulled wine for the celebs and fruit cup and sausages and stuff for us. That was fine, only Storm took it too far, as usual, because there was also a massive bonfire (don't think Mr. Rock will be too happy with the state of the football field on Monday morning) and Storm had arranged for all these dummies to be dressed up as the people who had been chucked off the show so far. We were then supposed to chuck the dummies into the bonfire and look really happy that we were Survivors and they were Losers. No one seemed very enthusiastic though, except Tallulah and the Lurch, so darling Sir H. came to the rescue and said, "Look here, chaps, I vote we save these lovely . . . er . . . models of our gallant comrades and . . . um . . . raffle them off as part of our fund-raising efforts, and . . . er . . . let's drink a toast to Absent Friends, shall we?"

So we did. And I silently thought of Marcus.

Then we all trooped back to the auditorium clutching a dummy each. The huge TV screen was suspended over the stage as usual, but there was nothing much to show from this week, so Abi announced that the best highlights so far of the Celebs' "teaching careers" at London Road would be shown instead. But the weird thing was that the clips were all of Seth and Barabbas and the Lurch, and hardly anything of Celia and Sir H., though everyone knows they are miles better than the others. And someone had edited the footage to show things that didn't really happen. I mean, there would be a shot of, say, Jeremy Lurcher, then a shot showing rows of happy little faces in class. Well, there was never a single happy student within a mile of his lectures on the Joys of Being Lurcher, so that was all a sham.

Wonder why they did that? Perhaps even Haydeeze are ashamed of their Three Stooges.[*]

[*]*Dumb, Dumber and Dumbest.*

Anyway, Abi looked a bit embarrassed and said at the end of the piece, "And don't forget, you can also vote for our lovely Celia, Harvey, and Oggy, who've done such great things at London Road." And we all cheered. Except Tallulah of course.

Arrrrrrgh! Just remembered again about the Do-Re-Mi* thing.

Going back to bed.

Text messages 11/6

19:01: hey Jenny itz Marcus r u betta?

19:03: yeah loads now thnx! wot about u?

19:08: ok. do u & Viki want to come 2 bnd rehersal tmoro? we r in bog pop

19:12: gr8! wot time?

19:15: 3 P.M. @ skool

19:18: ok c u then

19:19: ok

7:25 P.M.

Marcus has invited me to the band practice!!! Yes, yes, YES!!!

How to Sing by the divine Julie Andrews, aka singing nun, magical nanny, and the mother of all Grand Dowagers.

7:30 P.M.

This time, I am NOT going to skulk around under the window.

SUNDAY, NOVEMBER 7
6:10 P.M.

Why, why, why is my life So Complicated? It's like what they say about buses, you wait and wait and wait and then TWO come along.

Got there and Marcus came bounding over to me, all smiling and golden like Jonathan, and then Will came bounding over too, all dark and noisy and pushy like a big tactless puppy.

They both fussed over me and got me coffee, and then Vicki and Paul and Gonzo arrived, and Brad who plays drums. Doesn't say much, but makes a lot of noise when he gets going. Paul had brought his laptop with him. Apparently he has all their music, schedules, everything on computer, and even the keyboards that Gonzo (he's really called Gareth) plays are computerized, and Paul looks after all that side of things.

The band is really, really good. When Marcus sings,

it's as if he's in a world of his own, just him and the music. I was thinking, "I wish I could do that," when they finished the set and Marcus asked, "Have you decided what to sing in the concert, Jenny?" and my stomach fell down to Australia and began to go into Toadstool Rejection Mode again.

I had to confess that I hadn't even started to think about it, and that I still have nightmares about the time I had to sing a solo line in "The Wheels on the Bus" in kindergarten. Vicki and everyone started to suggest songs, things I'd never even heard of, but Marcus said, "Wait up, guys, give her a chance." Then he tried to persuade me to sing notes after him, just to get an idea of my range he said, but I felt really shy, so he pulled me over to the keyboards and asked Gonzo to play the notes. He kept hold of my hand the whole time and I actually sang a teeny-tiny bit, which was kind of agony, but it didn't matter, because I would have gone on forever, wobbling up and down the scales, just to keep holding his hand.

But THEN Will pushed in and said that what I really needed was "breathing technique," so he got hold of me and put his hands on my ribs and went on about my diaphragm and intercostal muscles until I didn't know whether I was supposed to be breathing in or blowing out. Then Vicki started to fall about laughing, which didn't come across as Very Sympathetic, but she told me later that Marcus and Will looked like two dogs fighting over a bone.

Only the bone was Me.

I never got to talk afterward with Marcus because Will walked with us all the way back to my house and Mum beckoned me in to do some homework as soon as we got there.

Can Vicki really be right that Marcus and Will both like me, at the same time and together? Seems too *incroyable* for words.

9:10 P.M.

When we were leaving school after the rehearsal this evening, we saw Tallulah hurrying across the back courtyard. She ignored us, or didn't see us. Wonder what she was doing there? Blatantly not extra math.

And not watching the band this time, Tallulah baby.

November 8-14:
So That Was the
Good Bit...

MONDAY, NOVEMBER 8
6:55 P.M.

Tallulah going round looking dead smug today. She must be up to something. The funny thing is that Miss Moodie is going round looking dead smug too. She's super-friendly with Storm and is always rushing over to his office waving her little clipboard. I'm surprised she is so keen on a program like *Down The Bog*. Would have thought boring documentaries would be much more her thing.

I keep wondering what Storm meant that time he was talking to her at the camp, when he was saying, "Okay, she's out," or something like that, and then went on about people calling in to vote. It's bothering me somehow. If he was talking about the votes, it's not up to him to keep people in, or get them out, so why was he saying that? Strange.

Perhaps I heard wrong.

Don't think anyone at London Road is doing any

work anymore. Everyone is just thinking about Bog Pop. The whole school is involved in some way, whether it's helping with tickets, publicity, or refreshments, or setting up the huge outdoor stage and heaters and lights on the football field for the concert. (The stage is just over the burnt patch from Storm's bonfire.)

And some of us are singing in it, including a certain Jennifer James.

Marcus has found me a song that I like and has promised to coach me. Will is going to accompany me on acoustic guitar. Think Marcus would have accompanied me if Will hadn't been there. Think Will would have done the coaching if Marcus hadn't been there.

This is Seriously Weird.

7:25 P.M.

Wonder what Tallulah is going to sing? Perhaps she's looking smug because she has discovered a way of cheating her way through this one.

7:35 P.M.

Marcus held my hands again in our coaching sessions at lunchtime and after school. Said it was to balance my posture.

The strangest thing is that I am terrified of singing in front of people, but when I hold Marcus's hands to sing the scales and stuff, I don't feel frightened, just sort of floaty.

Wish the concert was in three months' time and we had to practice every day until then.

HAYDEEZE PRODUCTIONS

TUESDAY, NOVEMBER 9, 8:00 A.M.
TO: THE STUDENT CONTESTANTS
FROM: STORM YOUNG

So, my precious bundles of bog-standard stardom! Have we all wiped our bottoms? Have we all choked off the chuck-up instinct? Okay then, let's move on from our unfortunate little camping crash to the glorious heights of BOG POP! Don't let Celia Munch and old Lord Ha-Ha (just kidding!) tell you it was their idea—I saw this coming all along.

You know what you have to do: every one of you has to perform a song during the concert on Friday night (televised live to millions and trillions, we hope!), and this will help to bring in those Votes, Votes, Votes and that Money, Money, Money! For

those dear little poorly kiddies, of course. All you
have to do is look gorgeous, sound great, and the
world is your chicken teriyaki!

Now, because we didn't lose anyone last week,
due to the fact that all you little bog babes were
losing half your guts, it is my sad duty to inform you
that TWO celebs and TWO students are in for the
big chop this Friday. So it's twice as exciting!

Yours till the votes are counted,

Storm

TUESDAY, NOVEMBER 9
5:55 P.M.

Had the Lurch for English. Dean Wiggins threw a desk at him. Nice one, Dean.

Went to see Mr. Webster afterward, to return his copy of *Silas Marner*. He started giving me an impassioned lecture on the nineteenth-century novel and its influence on his own Artistic Development, whilst running his fingers through his luscious locks. I soon realized that he wasn't talking to me, but to the little overhead camera in the library corridor. He must be dead keen to win the teachers' competition and leave London Road. As far as I'm concerned he can go to

"Love 2 Teach" and good riddance.

The thing is, I am dead keen to win the student competition, but do I want to leave London Road?

Interesting Question.

6:10 P.M.

Definitely don't want to go anywhere right now, except to singing lessons with Marcus. We have practiced every spare minute, and it's like "If music be the food of love, play on. . . ."*

I could play on with Marcus forever.

6:15 P.M.

I do kind of wish Will wasn't there ALL THE TIME, like Big Brother.** If Marcus doesn't want to get romantic in front of the cameras, he's not going to want to in front of Will, is he? Isn't Will ever going to leave me and Marcus alone together? Just for five minutes?

6:25 P.M.

Marcus says I need more confidence and presentation.

*Quotation: Twelfth Night *by Shakespeare (naturally), girl dresses up as boy, everyone falls for the wrong person, and love is all around . . .*

**The Ultimate Nosy Neighbor.

In actual real reality I need to be magically trans-
formed into someone who can sing. All very lovely
holding hands and going la, la, la, mee, mee, mee,
maw, maw, maw, but I have to actually SING a SONG
in front of millions (and assorted super-ultimate Rock
Stars) in approximately seventy-two hours.

He took me off to see Mrs. Schuman at lunchtime,
and she was mega-fab. Showed me relaxation and
breathing techniques (SO much easier to understand
than when Will was panting down my neck) and how
to think about interpreting the actual words of the song.

Wonder if all this coaching is actually going to save
me from the Abyss of Musical Humiliation that will be
Friday night? Oh well, at least Tallulah will be happy
if I screw this one up. Always look on the bright side,
and all that.

7:45 P.M.

What is GOING ON in the James household?

Just now, My Mother—is she Mum, Sheila, or
Jocasta, for heaven's sake, or some new creature I have
never seen before?—came into my bedroom wearing

the most outrageous low-cut red top, sparkly earrings, a tight skirt, boots, and LIPSTICK (!!!) and said, "Do I look all right in this, Jenny?"

All right? All right? All right if you want to look like Julia Roberts* at the beginning of *Pretty Woman*** BEFORE she gives up streetwalking, only about twenty years older with a bit of a tummy! So no, actually, Mum, not all right, not all right at all.

"Um . . . yeah . . . fine," I lied. "Why are you all . . . um . . . dressed up?"

"It's Tuesday. My book group night. Just wanted to make a bit more of an effort, that's all."

"But Mum," I said, "what about being a Serious Woman and Lipstick Is An Abomination? And that top—I mean, isn't it a bit, you know . . . Flaunting Your Body and all that?"

"I WANT to flaunt my body!" she suddenly said. "I'm sick of wearing sacks and no makeup and eating brown rice and protesting about things when Eri— nobody . . . nobody . . ." (oh no, she's going to cry again, I thought) "nobody takes any notice of anything I say or do."

*World's most beautiful woman.
**World's best-ever fairy tale.

Then she pulled herself together and said, "But Vict—I mean, some people do notice me. And think I am special. And that's what I want to be. Not Serious, or Radical, or Angry. Special."

Then she looked up at me, all brave and defiant and sad at the same time and said, "I just want to be happy, Jenny."

She looked so much as if she hadn't been happy in a long, long time, that I just said helplessly, "I want you to be happy too, Mum. And I think you look, um, lovely."

"Really?" she said, perking up.

"Mmm, yeah, totally."

"Okay, then," she said, hitching her skirt up. "I'll go for it." And she toddled off, all happy and hopeful.

But the awful thing is, I think she really might go for it. With Victor.

Oh, Lord.

Oh, Dad.

Oh, help.

Seventy-one hours to go.

...

8:25 P.M.

Seventy hours to go.

9:30 P.M.

Sixty-nine.

WEDNESDAY, NOVEMBER 10
8:15 P.M.

Forty-seven hours to go.

8:20 P.M.

Approximately.

8:35 P.M.

If Mum and Dad got divorced and Mum married Victor, Vicki and I would be sisters. Sort of.

That would be the only tiny ray of light in this Nightmare Scenario of Horror.

8:40 P.M.

Oh, Lord, it really would be a nightmare. Have GOT to do something to stop Mum and Dad messing up big-time. I know they really do love each other. But perhaps they've just forgotten that?

Have launched Operation Eric-and-Sheila-4-Ever.

Went and sat in Dad's study (it's freezing in there) with him. He was pretending to work whilst watching *Down The Bog* on digital. Celia was cooking for everyone, whilst Oggy lay on a sofa knitting, and Jeremy Lurcher was caught on camera scratching himself in the Private Parts.

Gave Dad a long lecture about neglecting Mum. Finally persuaded him to turn the TV off and go into the house and make her a coffee and talk to her.

"Do you really think she wants me to?" he asked finally, looking all hopeless and hesitant.

"Of course she does," I said.

"But I just make her angry and then she starts chucking things."

"Well, chuck some flowers at her when you come home from work tomorrow and see what happens."

"Do you think that's a good idea?" he said.

"Yeah, Dad, I do."

"Really?"

"Totally."

Parents, honestly.

THE TRIBUNE

Prince Told to Get Off Bog

THURSDAY, NOVEMBER 11

Prince Charles's press secretary confirmed yesterday that the prince plans to attend the charity concert Bog Pop tomorrow night, organized as part of the television program *Down The Bog.*

"It is for a splendid cause, giving hope to sick children through How Much Is That Doggie? The Prince is also delighted to encourage the efforts of all the young people at London Road Comprehensive who are working so hard to make the occasion a success."

However, Professor Barbara Beer, whose anti-monarchist views are well known, has criticized the Prince's decision to attend. "His presence will send out the wrong message. It will be interpreted as encouraging reality television and the dumbing down of broadcasting standards." When questioned as to whether her own presence on *Down The Bog* also contributed to this process, the controversial academic snapped, "That's entirely different. I've got my career to think about."

Professor Beer is widely tipped to be voted off the show this weekend.

THURSDAY, NOVEMBER 11
5:35 P.M.

Okay, this is getting out of hand.

Tallulah got hold of me in the loos this morning, where she was smoking and chewing gum and painting her nails all at the same time. She pushed me into a cubicle, locked the door behind us, and said, "Enjoy your last show, James, because you're in for a surprise on Friday night."

"Why?" I said. "Are you going to look pretty, or say something intelligent?"

It took her a couple of moments to work this one out, but when she did, she slammed my head against the cubicle wall and jabbed her cigarette around as if she was going to stub it out on my eyebrow and said, "Don't get smart with me, dog-face, because I've just about had enough of Jenny this and Jenny that. You think you've been so clever, don't you, with your poor-little-me act? Oooh, I'm so brave climbing up this little rope in my secondhand dress, reciting my sloppy poems! Well, enough is enough, James. It's over. Get it?"

I tried to push her off me (she is majorly strong) and said, "Leave me alone, Tallulah; I've as much right to try for St. Willibald's as you have."

She let go of me in astonishment and cackled. "St. Willibald's? St. Willibald's? I don't give a toss about old St. Bollockbald's, Jennee, but I do care about winning—very, very much. And when you see my little secret weapon on Friday, you'll know that there's only one winner round here. And it's not you, babes."

She unlocked the cubicle and sauntered out to where Chelsea was on guard.

"So you've really been told now, James?" Chelsea sniggered. "So, like, you're finished?"

They were going off giggling together, when Tallulah turned back and said, "Oh, and James, if you think Marcus and Will actually like your sad little personality and your disgusting appearance, the whole school—except you—knows that the only reason they force themselves to go near you is to get onto the show to promote their band. It's The Electric Fish they're interested in, not you, turd features. Sorry to disappoint you and all that."

And they were gone.

For the first time since this all began, I want to give

up. For real, this time. I want to crawl into bed and never, never come out again. Because I know that she must be right. It's like suddenly seeing The Truth written in huge letters like the Hollywood sign. Marcus had even said, that night at the camp, how he wanted to be on the show because of the band. And now I can see that I've been kidding myself all this time. Girls like me don't get guys like Marcus. LIFE IS NOT LIKE BOOKS.

It just isn't.

Text message 11/11
18:15: hey Jenny y u not @ rehersal 4 song? M

6:20 P.M.

Turned my phone off. Going to do my homework.

10:35 P.M.

Will go and see Miss Moodie tomorrow and tell her I am quitting the show.

It's time I got back to reality.

...

FRIDAY, NOVEMBER 12

6:10 A.M.

Awful night. Lay awake most of it.

6:15 A.M.

Hope Vicki will understand.

6:20 A.M.

Don't know how to tell Mum and Dad. Especially Dad. He tried the flowers-after-work stuff with Mum yesterday, and has asked her to go with him to the concert tonight. Apparently they were dead keen on Oggy in their student days, and Mum has been getting all excited about what she's going to wear.

6:25 A.M.

Think I'll still go and watch in the audience. Feel I owe that to Sir H. And I would like to see The Electric Fish do well. I really would.

6:30 A.M.

Even though they have broken my heart.

...

THE DAILY RUMOR

BOG POP
COMES TO TOWN!

FRIDAY, NOVEMBER 12

The excitement is mounting over the musical event of the year, Bog Pop. The stars are streaming into Midcaster for the final preparations for tonight's show. Security is tight for the A-list collection of royalty and celebrities who are gathering to raise funds for the popular charity How Much Is That Doggie? Straight after the concert, the result of the Down The Bog vote will be announced, although media insiders are saying that the voting is all a bit too predictable.

"The concert will be great; it has generated a lot of interest," commented Zane Muck-Williams, popular presenter of rival show Child Swap. "But it's obvious that Celia and Harvey are headed for the final, so that's taken a bit of heat out of the competition. Oggy's very popular too, but Seth's probably got the young girls and grannies on his

side, so it's a closer-run thing for third place. And the sooner those two unmentionable prats go, the better. But I'll definitely be tuning in to watch Oggy give it some welly."

The show's producers are hoping that many others will be doing the same, and they are predicting a record audience of nearly twenty million.

Late. Past Midnight.

Don't know what time it is. Don't know what to say.

Later

Totally, utterly, mega-ly gob-smacked.

SATURDAY, NOVEMBER 13
5:50 A.M.

So restless. Can't believe any of it. Dwight will be okay, but poor, poor Will.

6:10 A.M.

I am so, so upset about Sir H. and Celia. I know they will get over it and they have their lives to go back to and all that, but it just seems so unfair. Unreal. And they put on such an awesome show last night.

I've never actually been to a rock concert before. Not surprising given Jocasta's ban on radios, CD players, TV, and anything that might introduce the Curse of Popular Culture into the James household. But Jocasta doesn't seem to be around much these days.

We all started to get ready to go out last night, and Molly McFadden came round to look after Jonathan. Poor child. Eventually Mum came down, all dolled up again in tight jeans (Molly looked green with shock), and then Dad came down looking sheepish. He was wearing an old T-shirt from about 1983 with OGGY— KING OF ROCK printed on it, but the words had to stretch out a bit over his front where he's gone a bit cuddly.

Mum didn't seem to notice that, but just said, "Oh, Eric, you remembered," in her soppy Sheila voice, then they jabbered on in the car about concerts they'd been to a hundred years ago. I'd not seem them look so bright and awake-looking for ages, but I was simply churning in the back, wondering what they'd say when they saw that I wasn't in the show. Miss Moodie had been weirdly furious when I'd gone to see her in the afternoon to explain, and had made me promise not to tell anyone in case I changed my mind at the last minute. But I didn't see that happening, somehow.

"Don't you have to go backstage?" they said when we got there, and I just mumbled something about it being a "surprise" and we managed to get seats down toward the front.

The concert was utterly mind-blowing. There were lights and cameras everywhere, and the whole place was going crazy to get a glimpse of Prince William. He was in a special seating area with his dad, the mayor of Midcaster, the chairwoman of HMITD?, and Mr. Mephistopholousos (boss of Haydeeze Productions), and even Miss Moodie and Storm. But no one took any notice of the VIPs when the music started.

It was so mega-brilliant that I forgot everything but the noise and the rhythm and the crowd singing along in ecstasy, and then after all the big stars had played, Oggy roared out, "And introducing . . . THE ELECTRIC FISH!"

And then Marcus was there, rocking round the stage like Apollo[*] with a guitar, and I tried to hate him for using me like Tallulah had said, but I just couldn't.

I couldn't.

Anyway, the crowd went wild, and after that there

*Extremely fit Greek god.

was a local gospel choir and some kids playing steel drums and it was all so great, until Oggy said, "Man, we've got some cool kids here doing their thing tonight, so let's hear it for the Bog Babes, yeah, let's rock!" Then Will and Tallulah and Ollie and Dwight and Serena came onstage, and whilst everyone was clapping, Dad gave me a funny look, as if to say, "Why aren't you up there?" and for a moment, I wished that I was.

Serena was brilliant. Oh, Lord, can she sing.

Ollie and Will did a mad punk number together and made everyone laugh and stomp along with them. They were fab. And Dwight did this wicked "London Road Rap" that he'd written himself.

Then there was Tallulah.

What can I say?

8:25 A.M.

Mum just brought me breakfast in bed (bacon and eggs with WHITE BREAD). She kissed me, said, "You must be exhausted, darling; stay there as long as you want," and went off humming to herself. She and Dad are going up into the attic now to rescue the stereo system and Dad's old collection of rock music.

Oh, Tallulah, Tallulah. So that was your secret weapon. That's why you were sneaking round London Road on a Sunday afternoon.

Seth Dale.

They were wearing matching outfits and they sang that well-known classic, "I'm So Fondie of My Little Blondie."*

They looked pretty fond of each other, too. Seth will have to be careful, as I don't think well-known TV personalities (you can't exactly call him a star) are supposed to do that kind of dancing with a schoolgirl.

The one thing you have to say about Tallulah is that she gives it everything she's got, and probably everything she hasn't got as well. Like talent.

But she looked happy, up there with Seth. I can't understand why, I mean, the guy has the personality of a poached egg, but hey, what do I know? It seemed to be a night for everyone to be happy, somehow. Until it all came crashing down round Celia and Sir Harvey.

...

*The world's worst song.

THE SUNDAY RUMOR

BOG VOTE SHOCK!
CELIA AND SIR H.
FLUSHED OUT!

SUNDAY, NOVEMBER 14

Sensational scenes scorched across our screens on Friday as Down The Bog *bounced back as the hottest show of the year with its Bog Pop concert, attended by Prince Charles and his son Prince William.* * *Tickets sales raised thousands for HMITD?, but the event's organizers, Celia Bunch and Sir Harvey Harvey, were unaccountably squeezed out of* Down The Bog *when the result of the vote was announced. The surprise results threaten to overshadow the huge success of the actual concert.*

After an amazing parade of star performers, the final part of Bog Pop was given over to the student contestants. Highlights included Serena Dickinson, who blew the audience away with her singing voice,

*Stunningly handsome, fantastically famous, amazingly nice.

and Tallulah Perkins certainly made an impact with her raunchy duet with Celeb contestant Seth Dale.

When everything seemed to be over, Oggy Ogden, master of ceremonies for the night, came back onstage and said, "Slow down, man . . . where's that nice little kid who wrote the poem? She hasn't done a song yet; where is she?"

The show's presenter, Abi Sparkes, followed this up by asking, "Where's Jenny?" and the audience roared out their approval, shouting "Where is Jenny?" Finally, reluctant young Jennifer James bravely took the stage for a fitting finale to a memorable evening. All in all, the RUMOR's *message to its readers is VOTE FOR JENNY!*

A charity recording of BOG POP is available for only £9.99; call 0700 13 13 13 now!

SUNDAY, NOVEMBER 14
2:30 P.M.

The phone hasn't stopped ringing all weekend, what with people calling from school and Roger and Julie trying to get me to do an interview for their show and all sorts of newspaper people calling me—including the *Daily Rumor*! Mum didn't even bat an eyelash, just said, "It's the *Rumor* on the phone for you, Jenny darling!" and passed it over to me. It's weird—I half sort of miss Mum being Jocasta. At least you knew where you were with her then. I DEFINITELY don't know what's going on anymore. She and Dad have had Oggy's greatest hits blasting out on the stereo since breakfast, and Jonathan is rushing around pretending to play the guitar and eating chocolate biscuits and thinking he's gone to heaven.

And for a while, it was like a little bit of heaven on Friday night. I want to remember that bit forever, so that even if nothing nice ever happens to me again, I'll always have it, like a secret rainbow tucked away in a place no one can touch it.

After Tallulah and Seth had finished singing, Mum and Dad were looking at me as if to say, "Go on, Jenny, do your stuff," and I was just going to explain to them how I had been to see Miss Moodie earlier in the day to tell her that I was pulling out of the show, when Oggy started saying something about, "that funny kid who wrote the poem . . . the one that made me cry. . . . Where is she, man?" And suddenly the whole place seemed to be saying, "Where is she, where's Jenny?" Then Abi came onto the stage and took it up, saying, "Does anyone know where Jenny is?" until the whole audience was stamping and clapping and calling "Jen-ny, Jen-ny, We Want Jen-ny."

Dad went sort of boiled pink, ripped off his Oggy T-shirt and waved it around madly, shouting, "She's over here!" A huge spotlight swooshed blindingly in our direction and shone down on me, then from nowhere (how does she do it?) Miss Moodie was at my elbow, squeaking, "Get up on that stage NOW, Jennifer, and don't you dare say no!"

So somehow, I scrambled up onto the stage and Abi said, "Here she is, Jennifer James, and she's going to sing for us!"

Then everyone quieted down, and there was a strange hush. I looked out at a massive sea of faces and it reminded me of that very first time in the auditorium, when we had to do those awful speeches, but this time, instead of feeling that everyone was waiting for me to fail, I felt that they were waiting for something good to happen. And when I looked at the huge crowd who had come specially to London Road, and saw our little year 7 kids having the time of their lives, and Mrs. Schuman and Mr. Potter looking dead excited, and all the amazing people in the VIP section, and even the goat pricking its ears up way in the background, I thought to myself, This is my school.

And I felt so, so proud.

Then I remembered that I had to sing, and everything seemed to go into slow motion. Will came onstage with his guitar and started to play the chords of the song's introduction that we had rehearsed, but when I heard the music it was like a dream. I didn't seem to be able to make my mouth move or breathe or anything, and it was as terrifying as I had always known it would be. I looked desperately into the wings to see if I could escape, but instead I saw Marcus.

He was watching me and his eyes were shining green and true, and I knew then that Tallulah was wrong, and I'd been wrong to believe her. But I still couldn't start singing, until Marcus walked onto the stage and held my hands like he had when he was coaching me. And I sang for him. I know I haven't a great voice like Serena, but I sang from my heart. For Marcus, for Mum and Dad, and Vicki and Paul, and Oggy and Celia and Harvey and Abi, and all the people I love who were there. Then Marcus joined in, and so did Will and Serena and the gospel choir and everyone in the audience, until it seemed that the whole world was singing

"Amazing Grace" with one voice. And then Oggy took it on and, oh Lord, did we rock that place.

So that was the good bit. But when Abi got ready to announce the vote, I could see by her face that something had happened. I really cannot understand why those two nutters, Jeremy Lurcher and Barbara Beer, are still on the show (Seth isn't my cup of tea, but I know lots of little kids and ancient grannies like him), and yet Celia and Harvey have gone! Perhaps people didn't bother to vote for them because they thought they were miles ahead and safe? At least Oggy is still here. Hope he wins now.

OH, LORD, IF BARABBAS BEER WINS, I PROMISE I WILL LEAD THE DESK THROWING MYSELF.

After the results were announced, the program finished and went off air. But people in the audience were shouting "No!" and "Not fair!" and refusing to go home. It was awful. We all wandered dismally off the stage except for Tallulah, who was practically doing cartwheels because she and her beloved Seth had got through. Then Mum and Dad found me and they were hugging and kissing me (and hugging and kissing each other even more), before having to rush home and rescue Jonathan from Molly McFadden. I said I would stay around a bit at school. I wanted to go and say good-bye to Sir H. and Celia before they went.

And I wanted to go and find Marcus. Not only to say thank you for helping me with the song, but to get things sorted out once and for all. I felt I couldn't keep playing this "will he, won't he" game any longer. Holding hands and mooning over his eyes and wondering whether anything would ever happen between us wasn't enough anymore. I needed to know. But as I was making my way over to the backstage area, I found someone else instead.

Will.

He was sitting on a huge upturned amp with his back to me, crying his eyes out. Because he had been voted off, as well as Celia and Sir H. And I thought, This is really and truly the Abyss of Awfulness, seeing someone else being that upset. It was much worse than being chucked off myself, or not having the right clothes, or paddling around in a canoe, or any of the stuff that I've been stressing about all this time.

I sat with him for ages and listened quietly, whilst

he went on about how his family would think he was a failure and his sisters would give him a hard time. I said I was sure they wouldn't, but he said, "They will, they will," like Jonathan when he's inconsolable. So I put my arm round him, as if he really was my brother. He put his head on my shoulder (his Mohawk was very tickly) and began to calm down a bit and said, "Thanks Jennifer. You're really nice, even if people did think you were a nerdy weirdo to start with. You know, I really like you." Then he gave me a great big bear hug, so I said, "I really like you too, Will," and hugged him back. And that's when Marcus came round the corner and saw us.

Moment of doom.

November 15-21:
It's All Getting Too
Horribly Complicated...

THE DAILY RUMOR

HOW DID IT HAPPEN?

Monday, November 15

The public is still puzzling over the fate of Bog favorites Sir Harvey Harvey and Celia Bunch. We sent our roving reporter Dick Ratcliff up to Midcaster to discover local reactions.

"She was ever so lovely," said Winnie Herring, 83, a long-standing Midcaster resident. "And her recipe for chocolate muffins turns out a treat." Gerald Tucker, 43, commented over a pint in the Pig and Ferret pub, "That Sir Harvey, he's an old-school gent and not frightened of getting his hands dirty. I voted for him." And young Ishmael Khan at London Road Primary School said, "The pop concert was wicked. They shouldn't have got rid of them two what did that. My big brother says it's a fix, innit?"

Oggy Ogden has also been upset by the results.

"It's really heavy, man. Sir H., he was like my brother. I've gotta get my head round this."

Haydeeze Productions refuses to disclose the voting figures, but released a statement saying that the counting of the votes was independently audited. The RUMOR*'s message to its readers is this: if you voted for Celia and Sir Harvey, text BOG RUMOR 999 to show your support.*

It's the least we can do for the gallant couple, who are now heading to the Isle of Wight* for a well-deserved break.

MONDAY, NOVEMBER 15
8:25 P.M.

Really did get proper fan mail this morning—loads of cards and letters from people saying how much they enjoyed Bog Pop! Have been trying to answer some of them. Think Serena will be pretty busy, as Alice Redknapp told me that extra post office vans were needed to deliver all the mega-sackfuls of Serena's letters this morning.

This should all be really exciting, but everyone is

Sun-drenched paradise. Not.

still too stunned over the voting results (not to mention Tallulah's Performance). With Will and Dwight out of it, there's Serena, Tallulah (why, oh why?), Ollie, and me left. So I reckon it must be blatantly obvious that Serena will win now, what with all that fan mail, and the Natural Talent and everything. But no one seems that interested in who's going to win anymore; everyone is just going on and on about Celia and Sir H.

Dean Wiggins said we should go on strike in protest, and some joker said there weren't enough trees for all of us to sit in. Especially since Kelly tried to hack down Barry Hatter's tree with her dad's chainsaw. After his attack on L-L, she finally realized he was a lunatic ego-head, not some kind of knight in shining armor. That's the trouble with hero-worshipping people—when they let you down, they let you down big-time.

Oh Lord, I know Marcus thinks I have let him down. Saw him in Seth's pathetic attempt at a chemistry lesson (getting so sick of classrooms with cameras) and tried to talk to him afterward, but he just gave me this really distant, buttoned-up little smile and went off with Paul and some of the lads.

Vicki says I should just tell him what happened, but it doesn't seem as easy as that somehow. "Oh Marcus, you know how you were going to ask me out the other night? Then you saw me locked in an embrace with one of your best mates? Well, that was only me being friendly, so can you please carry on wanting to ask me out? Please?"

Maybe Vicki could manage to say that with Charm and Poise,* but I know I couldn't.

Must place it all in the Higher Hands, like Miss Moodie said. Think Miss Moodie was actually a bit tipsy on the VIP champagne on Friday night. She was hanging on to Storm's every word AND to his arm after the show. Abi seemed to notice too, as she said, "Storm, sweetheart, are we going back to the hotel? It's getting late." But Storm said he had some details to work out with Miss Moodie about the schedule for this week, so Abi went off alone.

Wonder what the "schedule" is going to be? What on earth can he come up with next? Only TWO MORE WEEKS to go, whatever happens, and then I

*Feminine skills lost to all except The Queen.

can get back to normal. Except that nothing will ever be normal again.

Because this time, I really am in love.

Came home and found Mum sitting at the kitchen table, drinking hot chocolate topped with marshmallows and reading a newspaper.

"Mum," I said, "since when did you start reading the *Rumor*?"

"It's got some very good articles," she said quickly. "I mean, it's fascinating from the socio-economic-cultural viewpoint"—great slurp of hot chocolate—"and I love the fashion section."

I tried again.

"Mum," I said, in my Let's Be Serious voice, "why aren't you at work? You don't usually get back from the café and picking up Jonathan from the after-school Advanced Learners Program until much later than this."

"Oh that," she said airily. "I decided to give up

263

work. Got a bit tired of making whole-wheat milk-shakes. And I thought all that ALP stuff was wearing Jonathan out. I got the feeling he'd be happier relaxing at home."

She looked a bit self-conscious, though, as if something was going on. So I went into the living room to look for Jonathan, and there was my little brother WATCHING TELEVISION in a cloud of ecstasy. And not just that old telly we had before, but a huge plasma-digital-silver-shining-thing like a ginormous space rocket.

"MUM!"

"It's a surprise. For Eric. To tell him I love him."

*Amo, amas, amat** and all that.

"But, Mum," I said, "what about not being taken any notice of and everything you said . . . and, you know . . . Victor?"

She actually blushed when I said Victor's name, then Laughed Girlishly (mega-scary) and said, "Oh that! That was all a misunderstanding. Victor has been great, and I told him I'd always be grateful to him for talking to me and paying attention. I think he's actually

Love actually is all around.

quite keen on Molly McFadden, so he'll be okay. But Eric is the only man for me. And when we went to the concert, it was just like old times. He told me he was so frightened to realize that he had almost lost me. Oh, and we're going out tonight salsa dancing; you don't mind staying with Jonathan do you, Jenny?"

"No Mum, of course not." Just let me go and lie down in a darkened room and recover from the shock. "But what about the women's group? Aren't you going there tonight?"

"Not tonight, not next week, not ever," she said recklessly. "And Jenny, it's all because of you, darling. Eric said it was when he saw you on television in my old dress, he remembered how things used to be, and then after that wonderful night at the concert, we didn't go straight home; we stopped for a bit by the old slag heaps." She giggled and blushed, and I thought I might Die of Embarrassment at the idea of what they were getting up to in the back of the family car.

Then she calmed down and looked serious and gave me a hug.

"So thank you, thank you, thank you, darling. I'm

sure you're going to win now, Jenny, and you were right and I was wrong all along. This is a great chance for you, and St. Willibald's is a great school. I'll miss you dreadfully, but you'll have a marvelous time when you go there."

When I go to St. Willibald's? *When?* What happened to *If?*

HAYDEEZE PRODUCTIONS

WEDNESDAY, NOVEMBER 17, 8:00 A.M.
TO: THE STUDENT CONTESTANTS
FROM: STORM YOUNG

So we're nearly there, home and dry, at the finish line—almost!

There's just one more step to take before we reach the Grand Finale and it's a big one. I hope you haven't forgotten that there is actually a prize at the end of this particular rainbow—sorry, it's not a highly paid television contract; that's for the grown-ups! No, for you little school slaves the prize is that instant transfer to the premier league of academic experiences—St. Willibald's College!

We're all off to have a look round the old Coll

on Friday. So best foot forward, brush up your
Shakespeare, calculators at the ready, and all that—
oh, and don't forget to prepare a touching two-
minute speech telling your public why YOU deserve
the privileges of Old Saint Willi and why YOUR
RIVALS should stay behind in the murky swamps of
London Road.

Reach for the stars, Bog Babes!

Storm

WEDNESDAY, NOVEMBER 17
4:45 P.M.

Oggy has dropped out.

5:15 P.M.

Serena has dropped out.

5:55 P.M.

Will dropped in to ask me out.

. . .

THE DAILY RUMOR

OGGY WALKS!
ROCKER SAYS "BOG OFF"
TO "BOG"!

THURSDAY, NOVEMBER 18

It's the end of an era—Oggy Ogden has ended his highly entertaining "teaching" career in a storm of controversy. He walked out of London Road last night, claiming that the remaining contestants were "doing his head in."

More disturbingly, he seemed to add fuel to the growing belief that the voting system on Down The Bog has not been totally accurate. "I dunno what's goin' on, but there's a bad vibe round here, man; something sucks. I gotta go. And anyway, I'm missing my dogs."

More than one million RUMOR Readers have so far texted to show their support for expelled favorites, Celia Bunch and Sir Harvey. The popular pair seem to be happy consoling each other, however, and have been spotted walking romantically in the *rain, at their Isle of Wight hideaway.*

The show has also lost a student contestant, the highly talented Serena Dickinson. "I've been offered contracts for modeling, singing, and acting, so I'm flying out to Hollywood tomorrow to consider all my options. I'd like to thank my parents, teachers, and fellow contestants for their support. And I'll be donating half of whatever I earn to How Much Is That Doggie?"

Haydeeze Productions have confirmed that the Friday-night expulsion will go ahead as usual this week, whittling the contestants down to only two students and two Celebs for the Grand Finale, rather than the planned three. However, pressure is growing for Haydeeze to publish the voting statistics, a move that will be strongly resisted by owner Luciani Mephistopholousos, a notoriously secretive figure.

THURSDAY, NOVEMBER 18
12:20 A.M.

Can't face going to school. It's all getting too Horribly Complicated with Will and Marcus. And school isn't the same without Oggy and Celia and Sir Harvey.

There's a weird atmosphere, as if someone has died. Mum fell for the dreadful stomachache line and has been bombarding me with TLC all morning. Finally persuaded her that I will survive without her Lady of the Lamp* act.

Have been lying in bed reading *Romeo and Juliet* again, for Mr. Webster's end-of-term tests. It's great and all that, and I know Juliet had her little problems, but she didn't have to cope with Marcus being all brooding and sensitive AND Will being all brooding and sensitive at the same time.

Will is still feeling Low (I thought it was only girls who did that?), so I couldn't just turn him down flat *comme ça*,** when he asked me if I would go out with him, so I tried to be tactful and said I would think about it. So he told Dwight (Dwight isn't going all menopausal about being voted off) who told Dean who told Paul, who told Marcus that I am dead keen on Will but just need to concentrate on the show at the moment.

Aaaaaargh!

Can't believe the show is nearly all over (like my love life). And it's a total mega-stunner that Serena is

*Florence Nightingale—famous mopper of fevered brows.
**Translation: Like a deflated Wonderbra.

off to America. I was sure she was going to win. Well, she blatantly won't now.

So there's still hope.

Text messages 11/18
13:15: Jen I need 2 tlk 2 u, Viki
13:18: wots up? iz it Mrcus?
13:20: no somthin odd cal me afta skool
13:24: ok babes, Jen x

4:35 P.M.

Vicki's right. Something odd is going on.

She was going up to the French classroom when Miss Moodie nobbled her and told her to go across to the little Haydeeze production office in the science block, with a letter from the High Master of St. Willibald's—something about the arrangements for our visit tomorrow—and give it to Storm, who was working there.

Anyway, when Vicki got there she heard angry voices, so, Vicki being Vicki, she had a bit of a listen-in at the door and heard Storm and Barbara Beer arguing.

She was saying something about, "You know how much I need to stay in, Storm. The people from *Culture Vulture* say the job is mine if I make it to the Grand Finale. But I simply haven't got what you want just now."

"Sorry, baby," Storm said. "You know the deal. No pay, no play. I've got votes pouring in for Seth now the others have gone, so if you want to hang in there, you've got to come up with something tasty."

"But what about Jeremy?"

"Oh, Jeremy's all sorted, thank you very much."

Then a whole lot of year 8 kids came trooping past, so Vicki had to knock on the door and hand the letter in. She said Professor Beer looked like the Wicked Queen* in Snow White** at the moment she turns into the old hag, all green round the edges.

It sounded spookily like old Barabbas was trying to BRIBE Storm to let her stay on the show! And from what he said about "Jeremy," it looks as though the Lurch is in it too! It all ties in with what I heard that time at the camp, yet seems too *incroyable* for words.

Perhaps we should try to find out what's going on?

*Unnaturally Nasty Person.
**Unnaturally Nice Person.

5:10 P.M.

Problemo Numero Uno. We've no proof. No one is going to believe Vicki if she just turns up on Haydeeze's doorstep and says she thinks she heard Storm talking about fiddling with the voting figures, are they? Anyway, it could all have been about something else. It is odd though.

5:15 P.M.

We would need someone who knows Storm really well, who could watch him for a bit and get some hard evidence. Someone that he wouldn't suspect, but who knows his true character.

5:20 P.M.

Have just thought of someone: Abi.

5:25 P.M.

Utterly, totally Impossible. Forget it.

...

EDUCATION
REVIEW WEEKLY

COLLEGE OPENS DOOR
TO A DREAM

FRIDAY, NOVEMBER 19

St. Willibald's College is preparing to welcome the young hopefuls from *Down The Bog* today, despite the cloud of controversy currently enveloping the show. Three students from London Road Comprehensive will visit the college's historic premises, prior to tonight's vote deciding who will go through to the final of the show. Founded by Henry VIII,[*] St. Willibald's occupies a site of national historical and architectural interest. The winner of the competition will soon be taking up an all-expenses-paid place at the exclusive school.

A spokesman for St. Willibald's said, "Our students are offered the finest facilities and an individual educational program designed to suit their exact needs and interests. We're very pleased to be able

Liked chopping bits off his wives, usually their heads.

to open our doors to the winner of the show. I
can promise whomever it may be that coming to
St. Willibald's will be a dream come true."

FRIDAY, NOVEMBER 19
11:10 P.M.

I just got back from the show. Little Ollie voted off.
Feel very Low. Very, very Low.

So it's me and Tallulah in the "Grand Finale."
Ta-ra, hooray, Moment Of Triumph and all that.

Not.

11:20 P.M.

When I started all this, getting to the final really would
have been My Dream Come True, but it somehow
doesn't seem that important anymore. It's that old
things-never-turn-out-how-you-think-they-will thing
again. On the other hand, it is deeply and desperately
important, because there's only one more round of
voting separating me from St. Willibald's now. And that
is kind of scary.

When Tallulah and Ollie and I arrived at the college

this morning, it was everything their Web site had said, and anymore. Tallulah looked totally bored, of course, and spent the whole time texting Seth, but Ollie was really up for it and went off to try out the Olympic-size pool.

The buildings and grounds are a sort of Educational Fairyland. They have a real miniature farm, stocked entirely with Rare and Endangered breeds. Would have thought our goat was pretty endangered when people chuck their empty cola cans at it on the way out of school. But it was more than just the buildings. There was an air of ease and calm and space and confidence about the whole place. The students were friendly, in a polite kind of way, the teachers are practically all world-famous experts in their subjects, and the library—that was something else, man, as Oggy would say. I could see I would learn so much, not just Latin, but Greek, Arabic, Japanese, Sanskrit, little-green-men-from-Mars language, whatever.

But when I tried to imagine myself as a pupil there, really, really imagine it, it wasn't the thought of missing home and Vicki, or the extremely remote possibility of Marcus Wright being something more in my life than a beautiful disaster—it wasn't any of that which made it feel wrong. It was when I looked around at the perfectly ordered classrooms and rows of bright eager faces, I thought, Something's missing from this school. I couldn't think what it was, until I realized.

Dean Wiggins.

There was no one like him, or Kelly Trundle, or Lauren Pike, or mad Gary Mitchell who tried to burn down the music block last year. And instead of thinking, Hallelujah Baby, I kind of missed them. What did Miss Moodie say about our school? Vibrant and individualistic? Yeah, well I reckon that Dean Wiggins must be the King of Vibrant and Individualistic, and I'm just not sure anymore that I want to go to a school where there's no place for someone like him, however impressive the exams results are.

So, finally, after all this time of slogging away to get to St. W.'s, I now know The Truth. I was blind, but now I see.[*]

I DON'T WANT TO GO.

*Check out "Amazing Grace."

Midnight

The trouble is, I Know that I Know, but no one else Knows that I Know. Everyone was there earlier tonight for the expulsion show, all being madly excited. Except me.

Afterward, Mum and Dad were practically bursting with pride about me getting through to the final. I had to persuade Mum not to rush out and order the St. Willibald's school uniform first thing tomorrow morning. Even Jonathan seems to think I'm going and keeps asking, "Will you sleep in the classrooms at Saint Willibob's, Jen-Jen?" Vicki and Paul are willing me on to beat Tallulah in the final, and have made up this ridiculous song, "Go Jenny," which they were singing raucously whenever she was in earshot.

Don't know what Marcus thinks. He was being all distant-and-cool-and-just-friendly, like the students at St. W.'s. Will was being not-at-all-distant-and-more-than-friendly and kept saying soppily, "I'm going to miss you so much when you go to St. Willibald's, Jennifer," like a big sloppy labrador* eyeing up a pack of Yummy Bix.

But the WORST thing is that the guy from the

Slobbery dog with big brown eyes.

Rumor, Dick Ratcliff, was there after the show, asking everyone nosy questions. He looks as though he would kill his puppy for a good story. Apparently he's been up in Midcaster all week, snooping around, and is going to be here until the final next week. According to him, the paper is going to run a campaign with a picture of me grinning out of the front page and the headline VOTE FOR JENNY, because their readers have seen Tallulah mouthing off on camera once too often and they don't approve of the Seth thing. And I just wanted to beg him, "Please tell them NOT to vote for me. Please."

I know I should be grateful for everyone's support but I feel that I'm on a merry-go-round and it's getting faster and faster and faster, and I just want to get off.

2:15 A.M.

Can't sleep. Again.

2:25 A.M.

Feel that something is wrong.

...

Have just realized what it is.

MOMENT OF REVELATION.

I have been wallowing in worry about St. Willibald's, and about Will getting too close and Marcus getting too distant, and generally being entirely self-obsessed and TOTALLY IGNORING THE REAL PROBLEM. Which is, of course, all that stuff about Storm and Professor Beer and the votes and everything! Old Barbara Boot-Face did get kicked off last night, and perhaps that was because she didn't come up with whatever Storm was asking for? I mean, there could be some CHEATING going on here, in actual real reality. It's been at the back of my mind all day, nagging away like a zit that's going to erupt.

I don't care a crumb about Barbara Beer, but I do care about Sir Harvey and Celia, and even more about the other students who have been on the show. The thing is, it's all very well, me lying here worrying about NOT wanting to go to St. W.'s, when there could be one of the others lying awake tonight, wishing with all their heart that they COULD go. And if Storm really is tinkering around with the celebrity vote, what's to say he hasn't done the same with the student vote?

Maybe Sophie Simpson should really have been in the final, or that little boy with the teeth right at the beginning. Or Maddie, or Mattie, or Ollie, who was pretty gutted about being kicked off last night. Maybe one of their lives would have been totally changed by going to boarding school and getting five hundred A levels or whatever, and maybe they've had the chance snatched away from them by that prat in a poncho, Storm Young. Perhaps it should have been any of them getting the chance, instead of me and motor mouth Perkins. Well, I am NOT going to let that happen!

It's a Matter Of Principle, as Jocasta used to say. I've got to find out what is really going on.

Operation Reality has begun.

THE DAILY RUMOR

TV ROUNDUP
SATURDAY, NOVEMBER 20
The lineup for the Grand Finale of Down The Bog *was announced after the last of the expulsion shows yesterday. Though some popular faces are*

missing, after some questionable voting results, the contest between Seth Dale and Jeremy Lurcher will be intriguing. Can the caddish ex-MP do the impossible and become the King of the Playground, after being consistently derided as the worst teacher at London Road Comprehensive?

In the student competition, the public is now offered a clear choice between hardworking, have-a-go Jennifer James (the Rumor's Choice!) and her less than sporting rival Tallulah Perkins. When Jenny was asked what she thought of the grand prize, she said simply, "I think I have learned more in the last few weeks at London Road than I ever could at St. Willibald's." In contrast, Tallulah made it clear that she feels destined for better things. "I can't wait to get out of Midcaster. The whole town can go down the bog as far as I'm concerned."

The vote for the most popular real teacher will also be announced on this week's Finale. Mr. Orlando Webster, the enigmatic poet and English teacher, seems to have caught the eye of the public, along with colleagues Mr. Potter, Mrs. Clegg, and Mrs.

Woolacott, whose dress code has become more and more daring as the competition has progressed. Flamboyant head of drama, Mrs. Mandy Schuman, is also thought to be a favorite.

SATURDAY, NOVEMBER 20
12:35 P.M.

Utterly Exhausted.

Had to do an interview at school for Roger and Julie this morning. Tried to get out of it, but Miss Moodie called at the crack of dawn and told Mum it was good publicity for London Road and she was counting on me to be up at the school to record the interview at 7:45 A.M. sharp. Julie is really very nice and seemed to know loads about me, which was weird. I forget that so much of what we do at school is filmed. She even asked me about Marcus and whether I planned to sing with him again. Black Hole of Embarrassment.

Anyway, that's all totally irrelevant. There's less than ONE WEEK left to stop the prizes being grabbed by the wrong people. That's ALL I'm going to think about from now on. Definitely.

Going to call Vicki and get her to come round and decide what to do. This is bigger than anything. It's like Truth, Dare, Kiss.*

Truth comes first.

THE SUNDAY TRIBUNE

De'ath Keeps Eye on Bog

NOVEMBER 21

Concerns have been expressed at the apparently blossoming relationship between Miss Tallulah Perkins, one of the schoolgirl contestants on the lowbrow TV show *Down The Bog*, and aspiring singer Seth Dale, 26. They appear to have struck up a close friendship since the departure of his former amour,** Amanda Knox.

The Minister for Education was questioned about the situation last night as she attended a launch of the government campaign, More Rules for Schools. Mrs.

*World's best game.
**Translation: Arm candy.

De'Ath reacted angrily, commenting, "Why isn't that child wearing proper school uniform and taking an interest in her studies, as laid down in government policy, instead of hanging around with these so-called celebrities nearly twice her age? What are her parents thinking about? What's going on? I'm ordering an immediate review of the management of London Road."

Asked when the review would take place, the minister admitted that it would be six months before a review committee could be convened. "But don't think I'm not watching proceedings at London Road closely," she added, "because I am. Every Friday at 8:00 P.M."

Also in the spotlight yesterday was Professor Barbara Beer, a former contestant. She was forcibly ejected from the opening of the new Tunnel Vision art gallery last night, after allegedly approaching the head of BBC Arts Programs and begging for a job as a presenter on the late-night show *Culture Vulture*. The position, however, has been promised to rival academic Dr. Bonnie Bargepole.

"It should have been me!" Professor Beer screamed as she was dragged away. Her outburst has raised further questions as to the long-term psychological effects of appearing on reality television shows.

4:35 P.M.

Vicki came round. She brought Paul. Paul brought Marcus. We have decided what to do and sworn each other to Total Secrecy. We now have A GRAND PLAN and it's only FIVE DAYS to go now until the Moment of Ultimate Doom.

Just hope we can pull it off.

4:45 P.M.

Wish I could decide what to do about Marcus. Should I tell him straight out that I don't fancy Will? Perhaps he's not bothered anymore. Perhaps his green eyes are looking elsewhere now.

4:50 P.M.

It was majorly embarrassing when he turned up in my bedroom with Paul, and he looked a bit uptight too. But after the first few minutes of explaining everything that Vicki and I had come up with, it was fine, and soon we were all jabbering away, planning the Plan.

Afterward, we went down to the kitchen to get some hot chocolate. Mum and Jonathan were making biscuits, and Marcus helped Jonathan decorate his with great dollops of icing. Then he and Paul kicked a ball around outside with Jonathan, and when they had all gone, Mum said in her new Perfect Mother Mode, "Who is that very nice young man, Jennifer?" and I thought, Just don't ask Mum; don't ask.

November 22-28: Moment of ultimate Doom...

HADEEZE PRODUCTIONS

MONDAY, NOVEMBER 22, 8:00 A.M.

TO: THE STUDENT CONTESTANTS

FROM: STORM YOUNG

So, Tallulah Perkins and Jennifer James, This Is Your Chance!

And haven't you done well to make it this far, by triumphing over your fellow students and generally doing in the opposition? (Hey—you know me—just kidding!)

All you have to do now is sit tight and look pretty until our big fat Friday Finale sends one little star into orbit and the other little loser straight DOWN THE BOG! Whoa, hasn't this been fun?

Make it a good one, babes,

Storm

Got paired up with Kelly in Seth's French class. *Quelle blague!*[*] Kelly was actually quite nice, and in between role play of buying a cow in French (didn't know that was in the syllabus, Seth) she whispered would I forget the JONS stuff, and that she had written to Barry Hatter to say she would never trust any man again after her campaigning hero turned out to be a wimpy, self-obsessed jelly, and if she turned out to be a Man Hater it would all be his fault. She was kind of leaning over me whilst she was whispering, and I have to say she really is Very, Very Big. Really glad she has stopped trying to punch me in the teeth.

And I'm glad that we seem to be friends.

The bad thing about Seth and Lurch being the only Celebs left is that we get stuck with them "teaching" us far more often. Seth is okay—we can get on with our own thing whilst he burbles away to Tallulah—but the Lurch is positively poisonous. Mr. Potter and some of the other teachers like Mrs. Schuman and Mr. Barker are now refusing to let him

---

Translation: What a joke.

into their classrooms, praise the Lord.

FOUR DAYS to go. From what Paul and Marcus reported at lunchtime today, things are looking very, very hopeful on the Grand Plan front.

THE DAILY RUMOR

VOTE FOR JENNY!
SEND HER TO ST. WILLI'S!
TUESDAY, NOVEMBER 23

The RUMOR *is urging its readers to send "Bog Babe" Jennifer James on her path to academic glory at that fine English institution, St. Willibald's College. The* RUMOR's *message is, WE'RE BEHIND YOU, JENNIFER JAMES!*

Turn to page 21 for full color pictures of Jennifer's "Bogtastic Bogventures!"

TUESDAY, NOVEMBER 23
5:10 P.M.

Never thought I would see what I saw today. Don't

know if I will ever recover from the Shock. Perhaps I will be permanently damaged by it, like Kelly with Barry Hatter. It's like a nightmare version of that soppy song "I Saw Mommy Kissing the Easter Bunny" or whatever. Only I saw MISS MOODIE kissing STORM in the STAFF TOILETS! I'd sneaked in there because I was bursting on the way to Seth's history class, but I'll never break another school rule again as long as I live.

It wasn't just a friendly let's-pretend-we're-actors-who-kiss-a-lot kind of kiss. It was a real, mega-stonking, lip-smacking, tongue-lashing kind of kiss.

The utter, mega-utter Abyss of Grossness.

I backed out of there without them seeing me faster than you could say, "Pass me the Wazzle."

Oh Lord, it is all becoming Horribly Clear. They are IN LOVE. Well, in lust at least. Storm! With MISS MOODIE!!! With her dreadful hair and clothes and mad-chicken behavior! You can't even say he must have been attracted to her by her Serious Mind, because Abi is practically a certified genius as well as a Halle Berry[*] look-alike. How can he two-time ABI with MISS MOODIE??? And there I was worrying

Gorgeous Oscar winner who cries beautifully.

about Miss Moodie getting her heart broken by the slime-faced slug! There are no words for my utter, total, mega-astonishment.

The only consolation is that if Storm and Abi split up, it will surely be a merciful release for her, in actual real reality. Definitely.

I think it might be time to use that phone number Abi gave me.

6:15 P.M.

"I have done the deed."[*] Abi's going to meet me and that reporter Dick Ratcliff tomorrow after school at the whole-food café. We should be safe, as no one from school ever goes there. In fact no one ever goes there, period.

Text messages 11/23

21:16: hi Jen! Paul & Mrcus got the stuff! Viki

21:18: everything?

21:22: yeah totally

21:24: mega-fab! meet me afta skool tmoro at mud caff—URGENT

[*]*Quotation: What Lady Macbeth's husband said after he had done in his boss.*

22:22: ok

22:24: & bring the boyz

10:30 P.M.

I really do feel like Macbeth now, with everything getting ready for the Final Unstoppable Tragic Act. Or like the *Titanic*[*] heading for that little old iceberg.

ONLY THREE DAYS TO GO!!!

Just hope, hope, mega-triple hope, that we're doing the right thing.

WEDNESDAY, NOVEMBER 24

7:35 P.M.

Just got back from the whole-food café. Told Abi and the others everything. Abi didn't seem all that surprised about Storm and Miss Moodie. She just shrugged and said, "That's showbiz," and that she thought her heart would survive. Must be a bit hurtful though. Hope she finds someone gorgeous next time. Not Dick Ratcliff though—he is so, so bald.

Anyway, she actually thinks our Grand Plan is

*Unsinkable ship that . . . well, you know what happened.

brilliant! She is a true star, and we are all set for Friday. Only TWO more days, and Thunderbirds Are Go.

THE DAILY RUMOR

TITTLE-TATTLE TIDBITS

Thursday, November 25

The RUMOR's *top man, Dick Ratcliff, has been unearthing a few secrets up in Midcaster, home of fave show* Down The Bog. *Things aren't quite as they seem in the quiet little town, with passion and drama going on behind closed doors. "RUMOR RATCLIFF" can reveal EXCLUSIVELY that the flame of romance is burning between strait-laced deputy head, Miss Maybelline Moodie (43) and the show's producer, Storm Young (44). The two not-so-young lovebirds were students together at the University of Bognor back in the money-hungry eighties.*

"They were always all over each other in those days," said mother of four, Tracey Hartle, also a former fellow student, "but then Storm went off to try to get into television. Funny them still having the

hots for each other, isn't it?"

It may indeed seem strange when Storm's official lovely lady is top beauty Abi Sparkes. So will SPARKES fly this Friday night?

Another bite-sized Bog Bit to come to light is that hunky English teacher Mr. Orlando Webster started off life as Reginald Pratt, and regularly enters ballroom dancing competitions under his real name.

THURSDAY, NOVEMBER 25
4:15 P.M.

Managed to avoid Will most of the day. Still haven't told him that I can never, never go out with him. I must, I must, I must tell him!

Why is everything about LURV so DIFFICULT? I mean, I really don't want to hurt Will. And although I'm glad Marcus seems to have decided to be friendly, whilst we have all been getting the stuff ready for tomorrow, I am aching for more than friendliness. Friendship isn't enough. It sort of hurts all the time when I see him, like not being able to breathe properly. Love is so, so painful. Wonder if all this gets easier as you get older?

Though Miss Moodie is practically ancient (43!) and she's making a complete mess of things. Not that she deserves any sympathy. Kissing someone else's boyfriend in a bathroom is definitely Not Allowed. She was in the foulest mood today (so was Mr. Webster—sorry!—Mr. PRATT), no doubt something to do with Dick Ratcliff's little scoop in the *Rumor* this morning, and the fact that the entire school is discussing her love life with Storm in disgustingly intimate detail. Don't worry, Maybelline, because Things Can Only Get Worse.

And believe me, they will.

11:25 P.M.

So worried about tomorrow. The utter megahugeness of our Moment of Ultimate Doom Plan has just hit me.

The thing is, it's far too late to back out now. This time tomorrow the show will be all over, and we'll either be heroes or in big, big trouble. So big it will make Kelly look dainty.

But whatever happens, I'm glad I've done this.

Glad I've seen the stars over the moors, and learned how to climb without looking down. Glad that I've worn a dress my mother felt beautiful in when she was young. And most of all, I'm glad that I held hands and sang with Marcus Wright.

Oh, Lord, I sound like Pollyanna.[*]

11:45 P.M.

Wonder what Tallulah is thinking about right now? She doesn't seem to think about anything but Seth these days, and even said hello to me yesterday in a sort of haze of Love Bliss.

11:55 P.M.

Perhaps she didn't realize it was me.

Midnight

It's practically tomorrow. So it is finally here at last, in actual real reality.

The Day of Reckoning.

...

Vile child who was glad all the time. Very poor substitute for all-time heroine, Anne of Green Gables.

THE DAILY RUMOR

CELIA TO BE BOG BRIDE!

Friday, November 26

Celia Bunch and Sir Harvey Harvey have announced their engagement on the eve of the Down The Bog *finale. "We owe everything to meeting on the show," said Sir Harvey, who tragically lost his first wife in a lawn mower accident ten years ago, "so we'd like to share our joy with the viewers." Blushing bride-to-be Celia added, "And with all those super students, of course. We're going to invite the whole school to the wedding."*

Celia has never married before and is already planning her wedding cake, which will be a scale model of London Road Comprehensive, with sugar figures of the bride and groom sitting on top of the Private Parts.

The only celebrities currently occupying that notorious hot spot are Seth Dale and Jeremy Lurcher. Tonight's show will decide which one of them will walk away with the title King of the Playground. The fabulous prizes on offer to the students and staff at

London Road are also up for grabs.

Asked about tonight's show, Abi Sparkes said tantalizingly, "It's going to be a must-see event. I can promise that there'll be a real sting in the tail."

As well as Sir Harvey and Celia, many famous names from the world of showbiz are going to be in the audience, along with the regular students and locals who have been following the progress of young hopefuls Tallulah Perkins and Jennifer James. The reclusive multimillionaire and owner of Haydeeze Productions, Luciani Mephistopholousos, is also rumored to be planning to attend. So don't forget: park your behind on your favorite stool in front of the TV tonight, for the BIG BOG SHOWDOWN!

FRIDAY, NOVEMBER 26
2:15 A.M. (So actually it's Saturday)

It's all over. We've done it. The police have finally allowed us to go home. Nothing will ever be the same.

Must get some sleep. Then tomorrow, I suppose I'll get on with the rest of my life. Funny; there'll be no show, no cameras, no voting, no competition, no more prizes.

But there'll be one hell of a bunch of headlines.

THE DAILY RUMOR

THE "BOG" HITS THE FAN!
IT'S A FIX, CLAIM STUDENTS!
SATURDAY, NOVEMBER 27

THE TRIBUNE

Bog TV Scrapes the Bottom of Broadcasting Barrel

SATURDAY, NOVEMBER 27

THE PEOPLE'S PRESS
SATURDAY, NOVEMBER 27

WHERE'S SETH?
I SAW HIM ABDUCTED BY ALIENS, CLAIMS FAN!

Everyone has been asking questions, questions, questions, until Mum finally said a firm "no" and that I had to rest. But I can't rest in my head! It's all whirling round and round in there like when Alice in Wonderland* was falling down the rabbit hole.

When I went to get ready for the show last night, it was really weird, because it was just me and Tallulah stuck together on our own in the little waiting room near the auditorium. I could hear a whole lot of the teachers talking in the next room as they got ready as well, and presumably Seth and the Lurch were fixed up with some kind of luxury dressing room somewhere. Wonder what they had to say to each other?

Conversation was clearly not on Tallulah's mind. She was fiddling with her nails and makeup and hair and totally ignoring me, so I thought, I'm not even going to make the effort to try to speak to her. But once she had tarted herself up to her satisfaction, she turned round from the mirror in a sort of "aren't I gorgeous" trance and looked at me with a faintly

---

The Incredible Shrinking Girl.

surprised expression, as if she had only just noticed my revolting existence.

"Oh, James, it's you. . . . You're still here then?"

"Obviously," I retorted. Funny, I'm not scared of her anymore. I'm really not.

"Well, there's something going on round here that might not be Quite So Obvious, you poor little dumbhead. You think you've done oh-so-well, getting to the final and all that, but you know what? There's only one prize I'm interested in now."

"What's that?" I couldn't help asking.

"Wouldn't you like to know!" she hissed hysterically. "I'll give you a clue, though."

And she actually came and whispered in my ear, in a horrible smog of perfume and cigarettes and hot Tallulah breath, "Just don't expect to see me in school on Monday, that's all." Then she slung her bag over her shoulder, made for the door on her killer heels, and purred, "Bye-bye, Jen-nee, nice knowing you. Not."

At that moment Purple-Headed Woman appeared and said, "Come along, Jennifer; you don't want to be late," so I followed them both into the auditorium.

There was the usual setup on the stage, with the big screen overhead, but this time all the people who had been chucked off in previous weeks had been invited back. The Celebs were together on one side of the stage. Well, all except Freddie. Perhaps he'd got lost again. Oh, and poor old Weird Guy Hatter wasn't there, as he's still recovering in the hospital. But it was great to see Oggy again, and Sir Harvey and Celia standing hand in hand, looking so happy.

On the other side of the stage were the "expelled" students—Will and Maddie and Mattie and Alice and everyone—and when I looked at them, I couldn't believe it. Every single one of them was wearing a huge badge with JENNIFER JAMES on it. And in the audience, there were banners—banners for me! I could see Mum right at the front, next to Dad and Jonathan, waving her banner, and it wasn't anything about battery hens or power stations, it just said, WE LOVE JENNY.

And I thought, Oh Lord, I hope I'm not going to cry, or turn bright red or do anything majorly embarrassing. I had to stay focused, so I looked up at the balcony at the far end of the auditorium, and in the shadows I could just make out Vicki and Paul and Marcus giving me the thumbs-up sign.

Then Abi came onstage to huge cheers and was

checked for sound and mikes and everything before we went on air. As she passed me, she whispered, "Ready?"

And I whispered back, "Totally."

There was a sort of tier of seats in the middle of the stage, like in a theater or a football stadium. The six teachers who had got the most votes since the beginning of the whole show were all sitting there. Mrs. Schuman was looking fab and really relaxed, chatting away to Mr. Potter, and Mrs. Woolacott was wearing a dress that seemed to be made entirely of gold string. Even Tallulah would have had difficulty with it. Mr. Webster-Pratt (or is it Pratt-Webster?) was wearing a purple velvet jacket, a long black cloak, and an idiotic expression. The others were Mr. Barker, and—absolutely mega-stunning—Mrs. Stringer! Well, at least it wasn't Mr. Rock.

In front of them were four high stools for me, Tallulah, Seth, and the Lurch. And over all of us was the massive screen, flashing out, "FOR ALL YOUR BOG NEEDS—CHOOSE WAZZLE!"

Nice.

It's weird, but I can't really remember everything. It's all become jumbled up, like a big bag of mixed biscuits. There was the usual fanfare of Abi whipping up the audience with "Tonight's the Big One!" and "Keep those Votes coming!" and interviewing famous people in the crowd about their favorites on the show. She even went right up to Mr. Mephistopholousos and said, "So here's the man who made it all possible! Give it up for the big guy!" and he smiled and waved around to the audience like a great fat pantomime dame.

Then there was a tacky kind of drumroll as Abi said, "It's the magic moment—the voting lines are now closed! So whilst all those votes are counted, let's see some of the highlights of the past ten weeks. Here we go: all the Best Bog Bitz are coming up now!"

This was when things really started to get going. The lights went down and the big screen flickered into life, showing a clip of the day the Celebs arrived at London Road, with Amanda's frilly knickers being charged by the goat. The audience was just laughing comfortably when the screen went black. A few seconds later it flashed back on, but instead of rolling out more footage of the Celebs, which was what people expected, it now displayed great long lists with the REAL voting figures from the night of Bog Pop, showing that Celia and Sir Harvey had been MILES ahead of everyone else, and PROVING that they should never have been booted off.

It was just some of the mounds of Incriminating Evidence that Paul had found when he and Marcus hacked into Storm's computer system last week, just the tip of that particular iceberg. They had shown everything to Abi, who had persuaded a couple of the technicians on the show to look at the stuff and believe our story. Then Abi had got them to rig the control desk last night, so that the voting figures would be shown instead of Storm's let's-pretend-everything's-totally-aboveboard highlights package.

As the audience took in what they were seeing, a collective gasp of shock rolled round the auditorium. The screen flicked to huge blowups of e-mails from Storm to Miss Moodie, with a voice-over done by Abi and her techno-mates. A voice rang out, saying, "My darling Maybelline, when we've got these suckers voting for our stooges, the money will be rolling home to you and me and Luciani like a river of gold. Every time those little phone lines ring, more than half the money will divert itself into our lovely, lovely off-shore bank account, and when it's all safely in there we'll be rolling in honey—"

At that point Storm leaped into action over by the control desk. There were shouts and scuffles as he tried to push Abi's technicians out of the way. Then the screen went blank again, and all the lights went out except for the spotlight Abi had been standing in. Storm came whirling onto the stage and snatched the microphone, whilst a very angry Mephistopholousos lumbered up and tried to drag Abi away. But Kelly and Dean and their gang (we'd asked them to be standing by as bodyguards) were onto Mr. M. in a flash. They shoved him into a corner and surrounded him whilst Kelly sat on his head. She really is a Really Big Girl, bless her.

Storm was still sweating to hold things together, standing in that lonely spotlight and saying, "Ladies and gentlemen, folks, don't listen to all that crap! This show has been hijacked by liars and extremists, but stay calm! Security has been alerted! This is Storm Young here, and everything is under control! So let's get this little baby skinned and tossed into the frying pan!"

He rambled on desperately, trying to get the audience back on track, but everyone was muttering and talking and he had to shout out, "So, here we are, folks, for the Grand Finale of your favorite show, *Down The Bog*! And the winners are . . ."

And I knew what was coming.

"SETH DALE AND TALLULAH PERKINS!"

There was a halfhearted cheer from the audience, and one by one a few lights flickered back into life on the stage. But there was no sign of either Seth or Tallulah.

They had vanished.

10:35 P.M.

Vicki came round to gloat about last night. Mum fed us pepperoni pizza and chocolate doughnuts. Jonathan still in state of excitement every mealtime after spending his early years thinking that all food tasted like soy cutlets.

There's still no word about where Tallulah and Seth are exactly, and Mrs. Perkins has been cautioned by the police. Apparently trying to pull off the head of one of Her Majesty's Ministers is not a good thing to do.

Whilst Storm was frantically looking around the stage for his so-called winners last night, like a magician who can't find a rabbit in his hat, Chelsea totally lost it. She screeched out from the audience, "So you'll never find them? Like, they've run away?" Poor old Chelsea, she was probably exploding with Suppressed Jealousy and the Great Burden of being Tallulah's best friend. More horrified-but-delighted gasps from the audience, who by this time seemed to have decided to sit back and enjoy the show.

Then, an untidy-looking woman in a shapeless kind of suit leaped up onto the stage, grabbed the mike from Storm, and said, "I insist on knowing what is happening in this school! Has this poor child been abducted by Mr. Dale? Call the police immediately and search the building for this evil monster!"

I was just beginning to take in that the lunatic in the suit was in fact the Minister for Education, when up popped Mrs. Perkins and socked her one on the chin, and all hell broke loose everywhere. It made the night Barry Hatter tried to attack L-L look like a church tea party. Jeremy Lurcher was screaming, "Seth's not here! He's backed out! That means I win! I WIN!!!" By now, Storm was absolutely green and I could see Miss Moodie in the wings, madly telling him to get off the stage and cut the transmission.

It was at this point that a vaguely familiar man

wandered onto the stage, looking as though he'd just reached the Outer Limits of Astonishment, and as the police charged in on cue (Abi had arranged for them to be called at exactly the right moment), he said faintly, "Can anybody tell me what's going on in my school?"

And I realized who he was: Mr. Smedley, Our Headmaster.

Abi helped him to sit down on one of the stools and she just had time to say, "So, ladies and gentlemen, this is Abi Sparkes reporting from the set of *Down The Bog,* and we'll be handing over now to the police . . ." when Storm bellowed "CUT!" and That Was That.

But it was Great Television while it lasted.

THE SUNDAY RUMOR

"IT'S ALL POO!"
SAYS STORM

NOVEMBER 28

In the TV sensation of the year, Abi Sparkes went live on Friday night, not to announce the results of Down The Bog *as expected, but to claim that students had*

discovered that the entire show was a scam, master-
minded by the show's producer, Storm Young.

Working in league with Haydeeze boss, Luciani
Mephistopholousos, and London Road's deputy head,
Maybelline Moodie, Young allegedly rigged votes and
accepted bribes from some of the celebrities to keep
them on the show. But the most serious allegations
revolve around what has happened to the money from
the phone-in voting lines. Sparkes claimed that the
money, intended for a children's charity, has in fact
gone to line the pockets of Young and his fellow con-
spirators.

Storm Young strongly denies all the allegations,
claiming that they are just the jealous ramblings of his
ex-girlfriend Sparkes, who broke up with him when
she found out about his affair with Moodie (43).

The police have seized all computer and other
records from the show and are conducting a full inves-
tigation. Also under urgent police scrutiny is the where-
abouts of Seth Dale and a young contestant, Tallulah
Perkins, who both disappeared on Friday night.

. . .

4:20 P.M.

Feel so flat. It has all finally hit me and sunk in. Everyone's arguing about who is telling the truth, but when the police and the TV-regulator people check it all out, they'll see what is actually real.

Such as, that Celia and Harvey should never have been chucked off. That Barbara Beer and Jeremy Lurcher would have never got past the first two weeks, if they hadn't paid Storm such whacking bribes to stay on the show, in their desperation to win and start new careers presenting ballroom dancing programs, or whatever. And that a certain Jennifer James actually won the student prize in the end, not Tallulah Perkins.

Except Jennifer James should never have been on the show in the first place.

Paul didn't tell me that when they first got access to the records last week. But when we got to the police station on Friday night, it all had to spill out . . .

How Miss Moodie's journals showed that Marcus and Tallulah had actually been voted onto the show by the rest of the class, way back in September, just like I'd always imagined they would be.

How dear darling Maybelline had thought that I would show the public a better side of her precious school than a guy in a rock band, so she switched the results. Swapped Marcus for me. Good, studious, nerdy Jennifer—what a great ad for London Road Comprehensive!

And how she had always intended to fiddle the figures for Tallulah to win, so that she would get Tallulah (and her mother) out of her life—and school—forever. Miss Moodie was apparently convinced that she would soon be the head of London Road and that life there would be so much sweeter without Miss Perkins to deal with.

So all that stuff I've been thinking, about people getting to know me, and even like me a bit, all those students wearing badges to support me on Friday, that fantastic feeling that finally, finally, I actually belonged in London Road at last—that was all built on a lie. And I fell for it. Jennifer James: Number One Sucker.

And though I technically "won"—got more votes than Tallulah in the last week—there's not going to be a scholarship to St. Willibald's, after all. It would be too impossible now to untangle who should really have got through to the end of the competition. Turns out that the little rabbit-tooth boy AND Alice Redknapp weren't voted off by the viewers, but by Miss Moodie, because she didn't like what they were saying. And Tallulah should have gone the week of the fashion show. Apparently her being caught on camera slagging off my dad didn't do her any good with the Great British Public.

That is my ONLY consolation. I shouldn't have been in the Grand Finale, but then, neither should she.

6:35 P.M.

Every time I think about it, it seems worse. I know I said I didn't want to go to St. Willibald's, but oh Lord, now I wish that I could go there, anywhere, and curl up and die. Perhaps I could transfer to Battly End School on the other side of town? I can't face anyone at London Road, ever again.

Especially Marcus. What on earth will he think of me? Well, I can guess. I persuade him to risk big trouble (hacking into people's computers is not exactly seen as a Childish Prank these days) to expose fraudulent goings on, and it turns out that I am the biggest fraud of all.

I TOOK HIS PLACE ON THE SHOW.

It should have been Marcus, not me. All those dreams he had of letting people hear his music through the show, of making something of his big chance—all ruined because of me and that unspeakable woman, Maybelline Moodie. What on earth was she thinking of, playing around with people's lives like that? And I actually liked her! Well, apart from the clothes. But I trusted her—and Marcus trusted me.

But that's all over now. Any chance of getting from Just Friends to More Than Friends (even if he doesn't still think that I fancy Will!) has got to be a big fat mega-zero. That dream really is over. *Finito la commedia.**

The only thing Miss Moodie didn't rig was that Mrs. Schuman won the teacher vote, in actual real reality. That gave Moodie the perfect chance to get rid of a teacher who's a million times more talented and popular and better-looking than she is. But Mrs. Schuman has turned down the prize anyway. She says she wants

*Translation: End of story.

to teach, not talk about teaching on some fifth-rate TV show. So it looks as though *Love 2 Teach!* will have to find another presenter, and London Road can carry on having great drama lessons.

Yeah, it all worked out great. MYSTERY SOLVED! FRAUDSTERS CAUGHT BY STUDENT SLEUTHS! I can just see the *Rumor* going mad with it in the next few days, before people are bored and it's all forgotten. But it didn't work out for me. No St. Willibald's, no prize, no Marcus.

No happy ending.

THE DAILY RUMOR

SETH FOUND WITH RUNAWAY BRIDE!

MONDAY, NOVEMBER 29

Amidst rumors of child kidnapping and sordid entanglements, Seth Dale has emerged from the manure smelling like roses. His dramatic exit from Down The Bog last week, apparently in the company of underage schoolgirl Tallulah Perkins, had shocked even his most ardent fans. However, the RUMOR can reveal exclusively that the pair headed straight for Gretna Green in true romantic fashion, and they were married at the traditional lovers' tryst on Saturday morning.

Concerns for Miss Perkins's welfare were dispelled when her mother revealed that the "Bog Bombshell" is in fact eighteen, having secretly repeated several academic years at a previous school before joining London Road Comprehensive.

*"She's not thick or nothing," confided her mum,
Shandy. "It's just that we traveled around so much
building up our frozen-cabbage business that she had
missed a lot of school. Anyway, she's not missing out
on nothing now, I can tell you. She's well set up. Oh,
and she's really in love with Seth, and all that. Yeah."*

*The radiant young couple are going to release a
single, "I'm So Fondie of My Little Blondie," to celebrate their marriage. They have also been invited to
appear on a celebrity version of the popular quiz
show* What Color Are My Knickers?

MONDAY, NOVEMBER 29
10:45 A.M.

Looks as though Tallulah got her happy ending at least.
Though being stuck with Seth Dale for the rest of your
life isn't exactly my idea of Il Paradiso.[*] Mum picked
up the *Rumor* from the shop after walking Jonathan to
school and brought it home to show me.

So weird that Tallulah is eighteen. Thought it was
just the cigarettes and the late nights that made her

Total mega-utter bliss.

look older. But not wiser. Don't know what I feel about her really. Part of me feels so miserable that I resent anyone who isn't as unhappy as I am. But I have to admit, she knew what she wanted and she went for it. Go Tallulah, and all that. Yeah. It was Il Inferno* knowing you, but way to go, Tallulah baby, way to go.

Mum has been brilliant. It is so sweet the way she and Dad are falling in love all over again, and she is now so amazingly good-tempered and understanding that it's like having Snow White** for a mum instead of the Wicked Queen.*** No sign of Jocasta anywhere. I am so pleased for them, I really am. Just wish they wouldn't kiss quite so passionately in public.

Anyway, she agreed that I was overexhausted and didn't have to go to school this morning. I should think it will be chaos there today anyway, what with Mr. Smedley trying to catch up with everything that has been going on and Miss Moodie in total headless-chicken mode after Friday.

All the cameras will have gone now, and the production team and everyone. Abi did promise that she would keep in touch, but it's as though she has gone back to

*Total mega-utter hell.
**See page 272.
***See page 272.

another planet, almost as if none of this ever happened. And like Tallulah said, now I go back to being a nobody.

Can't wait for this term to end. Not long to go now. I know I can't stay here forever, hiding under my quilt, but I'm just not ready.

Not today.

WEDNESDAY, DECEMBER 1
5:55 P.M.

A new month. Christmas to look forward to. Jonathan bursting with joy because Mum has bought him one of those Advent calendars with little chocolates behind the doors. Last year he got twenty-four reindeer-shaped rice cakes.

Wish I had something to look forward to. Oh, come on, Jenny, stop being so disgustingly self-pitying. At least you're not facing a possible lengthy prison sentence like Miss Moodie and Storm-who-loves-ya-baby.

Vicki came round and told me that the police swooped down on the school today and took away loads more paperwork from Miss Moodie's office. And then they took her away too, kicking and screaming and protesting her innocence. Poor old Moodie-Cow. She did get her heart broken by Storm after all.

Mr. Smedley has disappeared again, so apparently no one's in charge now, except a bunch of suits sent in by the education ministry. Poor old London Road, really. For a while it actually seemed like a good school. Wonder what is lower than bog-standard? Bog-substandard?

Vicki didn't say anything about Marcus. It's like a forbidden subject, especially as she is so completely wrapped up in Paul and he is being treated like a hero for knowing all the cool stuff about computers that brought Storm down. She did ask when I was going back to school, though. She said lots of people had been asking.

Strange. Wonder why?

THE DAILY RUMOR

POLICE SWOOP ON BOG PLOTTERS

THURSDAY, DECEMBER 2

The media tycoon Luciani Mephistopholousos, his producer Storm Young, and Maybelline Moodie (43) were all arrested yesterday and charged with fraud. Moodie screamed as she was taken from

London Road School, *"I did it for love!"* which is, coincidentally, the title of Seth Dale's forthcoming CD.* The police issued a statement saying that the trio will not be granted bail. Professor Barbara Beer and Jeremy Lurcher are also being questioned.

It remains to be seen whether, if found guilty and convicted, the scheming threesome will be allowed to serve their sentences on the reality TV show Punishment Island.

Zack Clifford the publicity guru rumored to be representing them, issued a statement saying, *"If you have to do time, do it on prime time."*

THURSDAY, DECEMBER 2
5:25 P.M.

Suppose I'd better go into school tomorrow.

5:40 P.M.

Get it over and done with.

5:45 P.M.

Will text Vicki and tell her.

...

Warning: Do not buy this record.

EDUCATION REVIEW WEEKLY

BELEAGUERED BOARD REPLACED BY HAPPY HARVEYS

FRIDAY, DECEMBER 3

The entire board of governors at London Road Comprehensive has resigned over the *Down The Bog* fiasco, but the news that Sir Harvey Harvey and Celia Bunch, (soon to be Lady Harvey) have agreed to act as co-chairs of the new board was widely welcomed.

"This is a wonderful school, and we are going to dedicate ourselves to making the rest of the country realize it," said the happy pair.

The role of the absentee head, Mr. Bill Smedley, is under personal investigation by the Minister, Mrs. De'Ath. "It's an absolute disgrace that he was allowed to be away from his school for so long. No wonder things went wrong. I intend to uncover the truth about this cesspit of incompetence."

She is due to publish her findings tomorrow.

...

FRIDAY, DECEMBER 3

5:20 A.M.

So brilliant about Celia and Harvey! And so, so brilliant to be back at school!

Mum's calling me to help with supper.

7:10 P.M.

Steak and chips and treacle pudding. Outer Limit of Bliss. And it was bliss to be back at London Road. Can't believe it, but it was.

Vicki had been a complete star. She must have told everyone I was coming in, because when I got to our classroom, there was one of the banners from the final, a bit torn but still readable, pinned up over the blackboard. And it said, "Jennifer James—Our Choice."

That's all. Absolutely gob-smackingly, totally, utterly *incroyable.**

It wasn't just that, though; it was the little things. Like Dean Wiggins giving me a high five (nearly broke my hand), and Kelly asking to sit next to me in biology and copying all my notes, and Lauren Pike chatting to

---

Translation: A bit of a surprise.

me in the lunch line. Just the ordinary little things that make the day feel comfortable, like you're at home. I thought people would laugh at me for being on the show when I shouldn't have been, or hate and despise me, but they don't. They really don't.

Marcus wasn't there. No one seemed to know whether he was ill or what. Not going to think about it. Concentrate on the good stuff. Like talking to Will. Had a really BRILLIANT conversation with him. Thank you, Lord.

I hadn't seen Will properly for ages, as I had been avoiding him like mad since he asked me out, but when I was lining up for lunch he pushed in front of Lauren to stand next to me. He looked sort of odd, as if he was trying a bit too hard to be laid-back, and I thought, Oh, no, he's going to ask me out again. But he went rabbiting on about last Friday and how amazing it all was, and how he and the other "expelled" students had gone back to his house whilst we had gone off to the police station, and how it had turned into a bit of a party, and that he and Maddie had "just clicked." By the time we reached the sad little row of yogurts they call dessert, I realized he was telling me that he fancied her to pieces and was practically asking my permission to ask her out!

"You don't mind, do you Jennifer? I mean, I think you're great and all that, but this is like, Maddie, I mean, I know what I said about you and me, but I never realized about Maddie, you know. . . ."

"I think it's great, Will," I said. "In fact, I think it's brilliant."

"Oh, yeah, cool," he said, looking desperately relieved. "So we're like, cool, you know. . . ."

"Yes, Will," I said, suddenly smiling all over like Jonathan when he wakes up in the morning, "we're cool." And I gave him a great big hug, right there in front of everyone, and was instantly grabbed by Mrs. Woolacott and marched off to lunchtime detention for "unseemly behavior." She was in the foulest mood and has gone back to wearing hideous slacks and polyester polo necks. She says I have to go to detention EVERY LUNCHTIME next week too. After all that Flaunting Her Body in front of MILLIONS, I get a week's detention for one measly little hug!

It is really good about Will, though. All I need now is for Marcus to A) come back from wherever he is, B) forgive me Utterly and Totally, and C) realize that I am Jennifer James—His Choice.

That's all.

8:10 P.M.

Wonder how Will decided between Maddie and Mattie?

9:45 P.M.

Mr. Webster has been offered the job as presenter on *Love 2 Teach!* It was announced in Assembly that he is leaving London Road at the end of term. So only a few more days of his brooding cloak swirling to put up with. He is practically bursting with joy, doing the cha-cha-cha down the corridors, and he told us in English that he has started writing an epic poem* to celebrate.

Can't wait to read it. Not.

9:50 P.M.

It's kind of spooky to think that London Road is now

Eye-bogglingly long, long poem.

officially a Tallulah-free zone. Chelsea going round as if she's had a Traumatic Experience. Can't decide whether that's due to losing Tallulah, or the shock of liberation.

THE DAILY RUMOR

DE'ATH BITES THE DUST

SATURDAY, DECEMBER 4

Deidre De'Ath, the Minister of Education, resigned late last night amidst a flurry of recriminations. News had leaked that her report (due to be published this morning) on the role of London Road's head teacher, Bill Smedley, showed that not only was he absent from the school on official ministry business, but that Mrs. De'Ath had personally authorized his absence many months ago.

"Oh yes," said a flustered De'Ath on the doorstep of her home in Clacton-on-Sea, "Him. I'd sort of forgotten." She later issued a statement saying that she hadn't actually forgotten but had suffered from temporary Memory Fatigue Syndrome due to overwork.

The persistent rumors that Mr. Smedley was suffering from a nervous breakdown have turned out to be completely false. He had in fact been commissioned by Mrs. De'Ath to undertake a top–secret study into how to make it impossible for anyone to fail their GCSE examinations, and is now in line for a knighthood.

Text message Sunday 12/5
16:15: Jenny itz Marcus. Can I c u tmoro?

SUNDAY, DECEMBER 5
4:20 P.M.

Oh Lord, oh Lord, oh Lord! What shall I text back? What does he want? Stop, breathe, THINK. Think. If he is furiously angry with me and wants to have a complete go at me, then it blatantly doesn't matter what I put in the text. And if he's not angry . . . well, perhaps then it doesn't matter either. Think, think, think!

No, don't think. Just do it.

16:23: hi Marcus ok what time?
16:25: lunch?
16:27: ok
16:28: ok

. . .

Help, help, mega-triple help!

Just remembered I've got stupid detention tomorrow lunchtime. Wonder if I should text Marcus again and tell him?

No—will look totally uncool.

What if I don't get out of detention quick enough to see him?

Perhaps he meant actually at lunch lunch, in the cafeteria?

Why do I feel so Totally and Utterly Hysterical?

Because I am still totally, utterly, and hysterically in love with Marcus Wright.

December 6–11:
"How Do I Love Thee...?"

MONDAY, DECEMBER 6
7:35 P.M.

Really do think there might be a tiny-teeny glimmer of hope! Please, please, please let it happen this time.

Marcus didn't really look at me all morning—just a quick half nod at the beginning of class—and he wasn't in the cafeteria at lunch. I hung around after lunch as long as I dared, hoping he might turn up, but finally had to drag myself off to report to Mrs. Woolacott for detention. When she finally, finally let me out, I stuffed my books into my bag and raced out to try and find Marcus, but as I was charging out of the classroom into the corridor, I slapped straight into him. It reminded me of the day I met him in the "Bog-free zone" corridor, all those weeks ago, but he wasn't smiling today. I backed off, and he followed me into the empty classroom.

"So," he said. "Detention."

"Yeah," I said.

"For hugging Will," he said. "I heard."

"Yeah," I said again, wishing he hadn't heard.

"So"—he hesitated—"I thought you might be upset." He was looking anywhere except at me. "You know . . . about Will and Maddie."

Then Marcus did look at me, in a funny, questioning kind of way, as if he wanted to know what I was thinking. Suddenly everything seemed to jump into my mind all at once, all the times I had been too shy to speak to him and had been left just hoping and wondering, with nothing ever happening, and it crossed my mind that maybe he was shy too. Just because he's male and good-looking and can perform onstage doesn't mean he always knows exactly what to say. Not when it really matters.

I just knew that if I didn't do something drastic, this might turn out to be another of those times, just another might-have-been, and for some weird, weird reason I thought of Tallulah. How she grabbed whatever it was that she wanted, even if things stood in her way. A tiny little voice in my head seemed to say, "Go Jenny," from about a hundred miles and a hundred years away.

So I did.

"Marcus," I said, all in a rush, "I really like Will and all that, but, he isn't . . . I mean, I don't . . . Well, I'm glad he's going out with Maddie, that's all."

"Really?" Marcus said, looking right at me now, his eyes burning into me like little bits of green fire that seemed to go right down to the pit of my stomach. "Really?"

"Actual real reality," I said.

"But I thought you were, you two . . ."

"NO," I said. "No way; definitely not."

Then Marcus smiled his gorgeous golden smile and said, "So it wasn't the depth and breadth and height and all that?"

I must have looked really amazed that he was quoting from Elizabeth Barrett Browning, because he laughed and said, "I learned the poem for Abi that night on the show, remember? And besides," he added teasingly, "I can read, you know."

At that precise moment the bell rang, and Mrs. Woolacott came bursting into the classroom like an irate buffalo.

"What are you doing here, Jennifer James?" she shrieked. "Off you go, or you'll be late for afternoon attendance and in my detention after school as well as at lunchtime! And you too, Marcus Wright!"

So we hoofed it back to our own classroom, caught up in the usual mad scramble of a thousand people trying to use the same corridors to go in opposite directions. But there was something else I was determined to say to Marcus before we went into class.

"Marcus," I said, panting slightly as we were hustled along, "I want you to know that I am so sorry about what Miss Moodie did at the beginning, you know, switching us around. I would give anything for it to have been you, I really would. You've got to believe me. Please."

I must have sounded a bit desperate, because he stopped bang in the corridor, with all these millions of people trampling past.

"Hey, Jenny," he said, "of course I believe you. She was just bonkers. It doesn't matter."

"But what about your music and being on the show so that people could see you and all that . . . ?" I asked.

He grinned. "I reckon enough of the right people saw me anyway. You know on Friday when I wasn't in school? I was down in London, seeing Oggy. He asked me to go and have a talk with him about things for the future, for the band. I've been talking it over with all the others this weekend."

"Oh, Marcus, that's brilliant!"

"Yeah . . . and I reckon my dad would have been pleased."

He looked all happy and modest and excited, and about a hundred times more beautiful than ever.

"I'm so glad," I said. "So it all worked out?"

"Well," he said. "There's still one thing not quite worked out. . . ."

"What's that?" I managed to say, as my heart seemed to kind of stop.

"Um . . . well . . . are you doing anything on Friday?"

"No," I breathed, thinking that I'd happily see him every Friday for the rest of my life, but I just said, "Why?" and tried to look calm.

"Oh"—he shrugged—"it's just that when I saw Oggy, he asked if the band could play at a special gig this weekend. I thought you might like to come." He smiled again. "Perhaps do a guest spot of your famous vocals?"

"Not on your life," I said. "But I'd love to see the band."

"Cool. I'll fix it up then." We were outside our

classroom by now, and Marcus seemed to be concentrating on pulling books out of his bag.

"So, see you around then, Jenny."

"Yeah, see you around."

And then it was back to math and French and history for the rest of the day, but all the time my heart was floating and floating, as if it was going to burst out singing.

THE TRIBUNE

Police Investigate "Doggie" Donations

TUESDAY, DECEMBER 7

More disturbing allegations have been made in the so-called Bog Bribes case. A spokesperson for How Much Is That Doggie? has confirmed that no money has yet been received from Haydeeze Productions by the children's charity.

However, members of the public had been encouraged to call in and vote on the basis that children were being helped by donations from the *Down*

The Bog phone-in lines. The police are investigating the situation.

Meanwhile, Oggy Ogden announced on his Web site, www.oggyoggyoggy.com, that he is to give an undisclosed sum to HMITD? to make sure that the children will not lose out.

"I just love kids, man," said the evergreen rocker. "And doggies."

TUESDAY, DECEMBER 7

7:55 P.M.

The BEST thing happened today. Celia and Sir Harvey are back at London Road and they took Assembly. I have never seen so many people actually listening at nine o'clock in the morning.

Everyone was cheering like mad when they read out the reports in the papers about Oggy coming up with the money for the kids. And Celia's got loads of brilliant ideas for (genuine) fund-raising for HMITD?, like baking the world's longest line of biscuits. But the best news is that a new Head is going to be appointed after Christmas, one who actually cares about London Road and wants to be here. Well, Celia didn't exactly say that bit, because she wouldn't be rude about Mr. Smedley (sorry, SIR Smedley*), but you could tell that was what she meant. Dean Wiggins is already taking bets on it being Mrs. Schuman, with Mr. Potter for deputy.

Then darling Sir H. said that the whole school would be invited to their wedding on New Year's Day. They are going to get married quietly in a local church, then come to the school for a special reception with all of us, and the goat as mascot of honor. Everyone was going totally bonkers, whistling and clapping, when Sir Harvey called for quiet and said, "There's just one more thing. . . . You've all been such jolly decent chaps, and everyone's put such a lot of effort into carrying on and working hard in these difficult days, and it is nearly Christmas, so Celia and I, um . . . that is, the board of governors thought that you should have a smashing big party here in the auditorium. This Friday night at eight oclock! And our very own Electric Fish will be providing the music!"

So that was the special gig Marcus was telling me about. Friday night at eight.

Seventy-two hours to go.

...

*Hasta la vista, baby.

9:05 P.M.

Seventy-one.

10:30 P.M.

Sixty-nine and a half.

THE DAILY RUMOR

HAYDEEZE SET TO CRASH

WEDNESDAY, DECEMBER 8

Investigations into the business empire of Luciani Mephistopholousos, which includes Haydeeze Productions, indicate that the media tycoon is in serious financial difficulties, as well as facing a hefty prison sentence. Speculation is rife that this may have been his motive for allegedly grabbing the cash that was meant for How Much Is That Doggie? and stuffing it into his own pocket. Several planned Haydeeze shows have been cancelled, including Love 2 Teach!

Mr. Mephistopholousos is reportedly very

unhappy with the food being served in the prison where he is being held to await his trial, and is spending his days watching repeats of Down The Bog *and losing weight. Storm Young is apparently being advised by Jeremy Lurcher on how to write a best-selling prison diary, and Maybelline Moodie (44) celebrated her birthday last week by dancing topless and singing "I Will Survive" to her fellow inmates. She is being referred to a counselor for psychological support.*

WEDNESDAY, DECEMBER 8
7:15 P.M.

Mr. Webster going round looking like something out of one of Mrs. Schuman's Greek Tragedies[*] now that his TV career has been snatched away from him. Oh, and he doesn't have a teaching job anymore. Bye-bye, Orlando Reginald Webster Pratt. Thanks for the memories.

10:10 P.M.

Forty-five hours and fifty minutes to go.

...

*Doomed, Devastated, Dead.

9:35 P.M.

Mum sent me a text after school (she has actually discovered how to work her new cell phone) saying that a parcel had arrived for me from London. I had been planning to go into town with Vicki and look in the shops to see if I could find something to wear tomorrow night. (Mum is giving me a regular clothes allowance now. *Incroyable* and all that.) But when I got the text, we decided to go back to my house first and open the parcel, then go on to the shops. They are open late on Thursday anyway.

As we were walking along back to my house, Vicki and I got really giggly over nothing, like we do sometimes, and I felt ridiculously excited, like a kid looking forward to Christmas. Then we started running like crazy and laughing as we ran, and we got back home totally out of breath to find Jonathan and Mum sitting at the kitchen table poking the parcel and trying to guess what it was. Jonathan was just as excited as me, so although I was dying to rip the paper off, I said he could open it. He took ages, as it was really well taped up. It had "Express Courier Service" written on it and a London address that I didn't recognize. By the time Jonathan managed to get the wrappings off, I was practically hopping up and down with impatience. But when it was all finally opened up, I just stopped and stared.

Inside a nest of fragile tissue paper was the dress Abi had offered to lend me the night of the fashion show, when I'd worn Mum's old dress instead. In the warm muddle of our kitchen it looked a thousand times more delicate and shimmering and precious than I remembered it. As I carefully lifted it out, I saw there was a little card pinned to the shoulder strap.

It just said, "Go, Jenny."

FRIDAY, DECEMBER 10
5:55 A.M.

Fourteen hours left. Can't sleep. Wonder how many hours' sleep I have lost this term?

What if I have built this whole thing up out of nothing? Okay, Marcus asked if I wanted to see the band tonight, but about a thousand other people are going as well. What's so special? Perhaps he really doesn't fancy me. Perhaps he's just kind, or a bit flirty, or absentminded, or I don't know. I just don't know.

What if I turn up in my gorgeous dress and it's all just, "Hi Jenny . . . nice to see you . . . cool," and nothing else?

I can't go on like this. If it doesn't happen tonight, then I am going to put Marcus Wright out of my mind forever. Take up jogging or sewing, or start writing an epic poem on the Meaning of Life. Perhaps I could try to get to know Dwight; he seemed quite nice when we went camping. Or perhaps Paul has a computer-geek cousin he could introduce me to.

Or perhaps I could spend the rest of my life nursing a broken heart.

8:00 A.M.

Twelve hours. That's all. Then I'll know.

Oh, Lord, I'll be late for school if I don't get going.

Midnight

Tomorrow really is the first day of the rest of my life. But there'll be no headlines this time, no newspaper reports, no audience. Just Life going on, one step at a time.

But I'll never forget this day. Never.

. . .

Mum is singing downstairs (now I know where I get my Lack of Musical Talent), Jonathan is joining in, and Dad is calling out, "Have you seen my football boots, Sheila-love? I said I'd take Jon to the park for a kick-about this afternoon." There's the sound of pots and pans being clattered about in the kitchen and the smell of bacon frying for brunch, because I missed breakfast.

Mum has just brought me a cup of hot chocolate in bed. "Did you have a nice time last night, love?" she asked.

I said, "Mmmm," and buried my face in my cup, and she went off saying, "Good, good," and warbling away happily like a nightingale with hiccups.

Did I have a nice time last night? Oh, yes, a mega-nice time, in so, so many different ways.

"Let me count the ways . . ."

There was Vicki, my dearest, best friend ever, who came over early to help me get ready before she went off to dance all night at the party with Paul. He is what you might call an eccentric dancer and she is mega-amazing, but they were happy. That's what matters. Happiness.

There was the school, all done up by the sixth form with Christmas decorations and a massive tree in the auditorium, and a whole crowd of faces—pretty, plain, spotty, radiant, people I didn't know, people I did know, Will, Maddie (and Mattie), Dean, Lauren, Alice, Dwight, everyone, all wanting to have fun at the school party—and I wasn't frightened or threatened or cold-shouldered by any of them. My school, my party, my mates.

There was Celia with her beloved Harvey, holding hands and gently swaying to the music in a retro kind of way, and Mrs. Schuman and Mr. Barker and Mr. Potter and all the rest of them, even Mr. Rock, looking forward to the holidays no doubt, but glad to be there, smiling indulgently and wearing silly party hats.

There was the stage, and the lights and the music, and the band.

And there was Marcus. He and the band were totally inspired last night. They got the whole place dancing and buzzing and singing along. I was right at the front with Vicki and Paul. It just felt good to be there, in my beautiful dress, caught up in the music. Marcus's music. Then, at the end of the set, when they seemed to have finished and Mr. Potter was getting ready to play some CDs, Marcus stepped forward and said, "We're going to quiet things down now with one last song. You know, sometimes you can say things in music that you can't normally say. So, this song is for someone special—I'd like to dedicate it to her."

My heart was yammering away as the names flashed through my mind of a million girls Marcus might have written it for, but he looked straight at me as he started to play. Then he closed his eyes and sang:

> *"How do I love thee, Jenny. . . .*
> *Let me count the ways . . .*
> *I love thee, Jenny . . .*
> *To the depth and breadth and height*
> *My soul can reach . . . oh, Jenny . . ."*

There he was, Number One Cool Dude, singing Elizabeth Barrett Browning for me, in front of the whole of London Road Comprehensive. It was as if time didn't exist; there was only the music, going on forever. . . .

But eventually the song ended. Marcus handed his guitar to Will, got down from the stage, and came straight over to where I was standing. It was just him and me, and no cameras. He looked at me, smiled, and touched my arm gently. And then he kissed me.

My first kiss. With someone special.

I can't describe it. It was soft and warm and tender and exciting, but I don't have the words for it. Yeah, I could say, "It was the Outer Limit of Wonderfulness" or whatever, but that wouldn't do it justice. No way.

It was perfect.

Then he held my face in his hands and said, "Hello, Jennifer James." My insides seemed to be melting and burning at the same time, and I felt so, so happy, and weirdly safe at last, as if I had reached dry land after being lost out on the ocean. He took hold of my hand, and it wasn't, "Oh, Lord, what does this mean?" anymore. I knew what it meant, that he wanted to be with me just as much as I wanted to be with him. Bingo.

He pulled me gently to follow him out of the auditorium. As we pushed through the crowds dancing to the music, I could see Vicki grinning all over her face at us like a lunatic and I suppose I grinned back, but I can't really remember; I seemed to be just drifting along next to Marcus without actually making my legs work, floating in a warm pink glow of bliss.

Outside it was cold and my dress was thin, so he

took off his jacket and wrapped it round me, then wrapped his arms round me, as we watched the moon struggling to come out from behind a cloud. It reminded me of being at the camp, and I said to Marcus, "Do you remember . . . ?" and he must have known exactly what I was talking about, because he spluttered, "Yeah, and do you remember the Lurch bursting in like that?"

It suddenly seemed the funniest thing in the world and we were laughing and laughing, which I don't suppose was exactly the most romantic thing in the world, but it didn't matter, it was so good to let go and laugh and not care about anything anymore. Just then, some people spilled out of the auditorium to get some fresh air, and they were all saying, "Hi, Jenny. . . . Hey there, Marcus," and looking at us differently. Like we were a couple.

Then we decided to leave all the people and the noise and the party, and walked down to the playing fields. We saw where the concert had been and the bonfire, and the posts where the little swiveling cameras used to be, and talked about all the weird things we had done this term, until I shivered with the cold, despite the jacket.

So Marcus held me closer than anyone has ever held me before, and kissed me again, and again, and again, until all the fuzzy orange lights of Midcaster seemed almost beautiful, as if they were shining specially for us, two tiny people under the stars.

5:00 P.M.

Better get ready. Marcus is coming round later. Mum dying of curiosity to "have a good look at this young man of yours, Jenny." Why is it that even the dearest and nicest of parents can't stop themselves from being the Absolute Abyss of Awfulness? Is it genetically programmed—Me Parent, Me Embarrassing?

She wanted to hear all about last night in minute detail, but I couldn't get further than, "You know . . . he's nice. . . . We're going out . . . that's all." It's as if I don't really want to say too much and talk it all away.

I used to think there were words for everything, in poems and books and plays that famous people had written, but there aren't. Words can help you to remember what it feels like to do things, but it's doing the things in the first place that counts. I don't just want Words, Words, Words anymore, I want Life,

Life, Life—actual real reality.

In fact, I'm going to stop writing this diary. My pre–New Year Resolution is to stop thinking and start living. Anyway, I'm going to be too busy for a diary, what with Latin Club, and fundraising for HMITD?, and having a boyfriend. . . .

HAVING A BOYFRIEND!!!

More than just any old boyfriend. My green-eyed, shy, brilliant, beautiful Marcus.

So This Is It. *Le fin. Das Ende. Final feliz.*
THE END.

5:35 *P.M.*

Oh, and another thing. I am never, ever, ever going to appear on television again.

NO   MEGA-TOTALLY   UTTERLY   WAY. Definitely.[*]

Famous last words of Jennifer James.

Jennifer's Poem
"YOU DRIVE ME MAD,
BUT I LOVE YOU"

TO MY MUM

You drive me mad, but I love you,
You make me sad, but I love you,
You freak me out, but I love you,
You often shout, but I love you.

You think you're right, you make
    the rules,
You fuss about my grades at school,
Short skirts are in, you buy me long,
You say my hair is just all wrong.

But though we don't see eye to eye,
I think I know the reason why—
It's hard for mothers to let go
Of little girls and watch them grow.

Don't worry, chill, I'll be ok!
I will take note of what you say,
And when my growing up is done,
You'll always be my number one.

So, Mother, Mummy, Mutter, Mom,
Mamma Mia, Mère or Mum,
These words I say are simply true,
You are the best, and I love you.

J. J.

Elizabeth Barrett Browning's Poem

Sonnet 43

How do I love thee? Let me count
  the ways.
I love thee to the depth and breadth
  and height
My soul can reach, when feeling out
  of sight
For the ends of Being and ideal
  Grace.
I love thee to the level of everyday's
Most quiet need, by sun and candle-
  light.
I love thee freely, as men strive for
  Right;
I love thee purely, as they turn from
  Praise.
I love thee with the passion put to
  use

In my old griefs, and with my child-
  hood's faith.
I love thee with a love I seemed to
  lose
With my lost saints,—I love thee with
  the breath,
Smiles, tears, of all my life!—and, if
  God choose,
I shall but love thee better after
  death.

E. B. B.

Glossary of Britspeak

A levels—Advanced Level school exams taken at eighteen to gain entry to University; a bit like SATs.

Alco-pops—Cute little bottles of lemonade dosed with vodka. To be avoided.

BBC—British Broadcasting Corporation, set up to Inform, Entertain, and Educate the British people.

Bin—Trash can.

Biscuits—Ultradelicious cookies.

Boffin/Swot—Geeky clever type.

Bog—Lavatory, toilet. As in "I'm on the bog," i.e., using the bathroom. But don't say this if you happen to be introduced to the Queen. Also, if your life goes "down the bog," you are seriously up to your ears in doggy doo.

Bog-standard—Theoretically means ordinary, but actually means really, really awful.

Bog-standard comprehensive—"Ordinary" neighborhood public high school, aka a really terrible school.

Bonfire Night—Right, this is a good one. About four hundred years ago, this guy called (literally) Guy Fawkes tried (and failed) to blow up the English king and we still haven't forgiven him, so every year we commemorate the joyful fact that poor old Guy was caught and put to a gruesome death, by burning a model of him and setting off fireworks. And you thought England was such a cute little country?

Christmas cracker—Okay, get this, it's a tube of cardboard, like the middle of a toilet roll wrapped up in colored paper. On Christmas Day you hold one end and your embarrassing granny holds the other. Then you both pull like mad, the cracker goes bang, granny falls over, and out pops an entirely useless plastic toy and ridiculous paper hat that your family forces you to wear all through Christmas dinner. It really is as strange as it sounds.

Chuffed—Majorly pleased.

En-suite—Smart private bathroom attached to your bedroom.

Footballer—Soccer player. A breed known for quickness of feet rather than quickness of mind.

Gazzongers—That part of the female anatomy for which brassieres were designed.

GCSE exams—General Certificate of Secondary Education, school exams taken at sixteen.

Gob-smacked—When you are so utterly and majorly astonished that your mouth can't work and you are, like, totally speechless.

Grammar school—Academically selective high school.

Grotty—Dull, miserable, yukky.

Headmaster/head—Not the thing on top of your neck, but a school principal. And the deputy head is the vice-principal, natch.

Innit?—Doesn't really mean anything, but sounds good, know what I mean, innit?

Knickers—Panties.

Lav—Super-common word for the bathroom.

Loos—Bathrooms.

Mate—Friend.

MP—Member of Parliament, model citizen trying to help people. In theory.

Naff—Tacky, lame, totally uncool.

Netball—Tame version of basketball played by British girls. But you can still get kicked around playing it.

O levels—Ordinary Level school exams, old name for GCSEs; different name, same pain.

Page 3 Girl—Topless glamor model whose photo is printed on page three of a tacky newspaper.

Pantomime—A gender-confused fairy-tale show for kids. It's the rule that the handsome prince has to be played by a girl and the fat old mother/washerwoman/cook has to be played by a man. One of Life's Mysteries.

Pantomime dame—Fat old mother/washerwoman/cook, etc.

Plonker—You cannot get dumber than this.

Posh—Seriously upmarket.

Potholing—Climbing through nasty, wet, narrow caves in the remote countryside. Some people do this for fun.

Prats—Jerks.

Row—Fight.

Sink School—Mega-hopeless school, as in everything sinks to the bottom—get it?

Sixth form—Senior year in high school. Top of the pile. Also confusingly called Year 13, but don't let it worry you . . .

Sixth former—Someone belonging to this exalted level.

Snogging—Kissing.

Spots/spotty—Zits, covered in zits.

Sprog—Cute little kid.

Toff—Aristocratic, upper-crust superior type with a butler and a ginormous country house.

Torch—Flashlight.

Treacle pudding—You have to taste it to appreciate it.

Trinny and Susannah—Awesomely well-dressed style gurus on British television who tell people What Not To Wear.

Welly—Very unattractive rubber boot, very useful in the countryside. ALSO

Welly—as in "Give it some welly." Don't ask why, but it kind of means "Go for it." Yep, that's really odd.

Whinging—Complaining, moaning, bitching.

Wotcha—Unintelligible but friendly greeting, as in "Wotcha, mate!"

Year 7 through year 13—School grades, starting at eleven years old and going up to eighteen.

Yob—The kind of boy your mother doesn't want you to bring home.

Zimmer frame—Wraparound walking stick needed by seriously burned out seniors.

Gillian Shields

was born and raised in Yorkshire, England. Her two passions, books and theater, led her to study English at St. Catharine's College, Cambridge, then acting in London. She has worked in a drama school, becoming vice principal, and has also authored several picture books. She lives with her husband and family in England. This is her first novel.